DOCTOR WHO

THE GALLIFREY CHRONICLES

LANCE PARKIN

BBC
BOOKS

DOCTOR WHO: THE GALLIFREY CHRONICLES

3 5 7 9 10 8 6 4 2

Reprinted in 2007 by BBC Books, an imprint of Ebury Publishing.
A Random House Group Company

First published 2005
Copyright © Lance Parkin 2005

Lance Parkin has asserted his right to be identified as the author of this Work in
accordance with the Copyright, Designs and Patents Act 1988

Original series broadcast on BBC Television. Format © BBC 1963
Doctor Who and TARDIS are trademarks of the BBC

The Random House Group Limited Reg. No. 954009

Addresses for companies within the Random House Group can be found at
www.randomhouse.co.uk

A CIP catalogue record for this book is available from the British Library.

ISBN 978 0563486244

MIX
Paper | Supporting
responsible forestry
FSC® C018179

Printed and bound in Great Britain by Clays Ltd, St Ives PLC

Certain dialogue and events within 'Interlude: The Last Gallifrey' are reproduced
from The Ancestor Cell by Peter Anghelides and Stephen Cole (Originally
published by BBC Worldwide Ltd, 2000).
Copyright © 2000 Peter Anghelides and Stephen Cole.
Quoted by permission of the authors.

Commissioning Editors: Shirley Patton and Stuart Cooper
Editor and Creative Consultant: Justin Richards
Project Editor: Christopher Tinker
Cover imaging by Black Sheep © BBC 2005

The Random House Group Limited supports The Forest Stewardship
Council (FSC®), the leading international forest certification organisation.
Our books carrying the FSC label are printed on FSC® certified paper.
FSC is the only forest certification scheme endorsed by the leading
environmental organisations, including Greenpeace. Our
paper procurement policy can be found at
www.randomhouse.co.uk/environment

To Brie Lewis

Thanks to Allan Bednar, Simon Bucher-Jones, Jon Blum,
Mark Clapham, Mark Jones, Brie Lewis, Mark Michalowski,
Jonathan Morris, Kate Orman, Philip Purser-Hallard,
Justin Richards, Lloyd Rose, Jim Smith and Nick Wallace

The Doctor never loses.

Oh yeah, the whole concept behind [the album] came from Rick. He was into these books written by this crazy old guy. I guess you'd call it science fiction, but they weren't, not really. They were all about this broken-down planet. Real weird stuff with giant fallen statues and old temples, and eternal life and huge libraries. The people there existed in all times at once, that was their thing. We live in three dimensions, they live in four, that was how Rick explained it. That made them gods, but they were, y'know, very English, too. They'd fought all types of monsters in the past, but it hadn't worked out and they'd stopped all that. Forbidden it. One of them broke the rules, he went off and you never saw him again. Rick was always trying to get the rest of the band to read these things, but we weren't too keen. There were more than a hundred books in the series, yeah? There were like two or three hundred, and you couldn't just pick them up in the middle or anything. Danny tried to read one of them, I think, but I've never been much of a reader. I always preferred jamming over books, so I went along with what Rick said, y'know, while doing my own thing.

Interview with a famous rock guitarist, 1989

Prologue

'No doctors!'

That made a few of the relatives on the edge of the group jump, then look back at each other self-consciously. One of the aunts turned away, opened the window a little. The old man on the bed glared at her as the cold air drifted in, but said nothing.

Rachel was sitting by the bedside. The relatives were little more than silhouettes. Black outlines of people. Men in suits, women in tailored jackets, small, restless children in their Sunday best. She couldn't see how many there were. Almost all of them, though. Crowding round.

Circling.

'This is such a lovely house,' another aunt said. She was standing at the window looking down over the lush, green garden.

'Surprisingly large,' an uncle agreed.

'Too dark,' a woman's voice said.

'Cluttered,' another chipped in, to a general murmur of agreement.

There was a touch like a butterfly's at Rachel's wrist.

She looked down at the old man. Rheumy eyes stared back, unblinking. It had worn him out just lifting his hand. He'd heard every word.

'Don't let them destroy the books,' he said, loud enough for everyone to hear. 'They're my life.'

There wasn't much of that life left now. He twisted a little on the bed, the pain in his back surging for a moment, coursing through him. He opened his mouth, but no sound came out.

Rachel hadn't known him that long, but in the last month he had clearly begun to fade. He was very old – how old the agency had never told her, but she'd always thought he was in his eighties – with thin white hair and thinner white skin. He had an aquiline nose and high forehead. He had beautiful blue eyes, even if they were a little watery today. He hadn't stood for a long time, he barely even sat up now. When she'd first given him a bed bath, she'd been struck that he was smaller and lighter than she had thought.

She'd seen his picture on the inside of one of the dust jackets once. Before, there had been so much dignity.

'A good innings,' one of the grandsons said softly.

'He was a friend of H.G. Wells,' another whispered to his wife. 'Wrote science fiction before it was even called that.'

'Do you have any of his books?'

'I *have* some of them, it doesn't mean I've read them,' the man replied, eliciting a guilty chuckle from a couple of the other relatives.

'Not all of the new ones were published,' the old man tried to explain.

'No,' the grandson said, sympathetically. 'But that didn't stop you writing, did it?'

'Pen,' the old man demanded.

Rachel passed him the blue biro and the notepad. A couple of the relatives glanced nervously at each other. There was still time, after all, for him to change his will.

Once again, he tried to draw it. He started with a circle. Then a sort of broken figure-of-eight inside the circle, one with little swirls at the side. It looked vaguely Celtic. He gave up trying to get it right, again. This was the furthest he'd got with the shape for about twenty pages. He was nearly through the notepad. He could fit two, three or four circles on each page.

He dropped the pen. Rachel caught it before it slipped off the bed, and tried to hand it back. The old man refused to take it, or couldn't summon the strength.

4

'No,' he said.

Rachel smiled. 'You said it was always quite difficult to draw,' she said gently.

'Two hundred feet in diameter,' he said, angry with himself. 'Machonite inlaid in bone-white marble. A circle like that... should be. It filled the whole centre of the... the hall. The big hall. The one with hexagonal walls and statues the size of tower blocks. The... *damn it*! I want to get it right. When I close my eyes, I can see it all. But I can't even remember the name of the... I can't remember it. I was born there. Spent lifetimes there. It's *important*.'

The relatives were shifting their feet. Embarrassed by the outburst or worried that he had more life left in him than they'd thought.

The old man looked around, almost apologetic.

'I only wish I could remember the name,' he explained. 'I'm the only person on Earth who even remembers. Except... except I don't. You understand, don't you?'

Rachel made an attempt to look positive. But whenever he'd tried to explain this before, there had been just too much of it to get her head round. She thought he was sincere, that was the thing, but she didn't understand him.

'I believe you, Marnal,' she whispered. It was his pen name. Since the breakdown, he had insisted on being called that, although no one ever did.

He sighed, returned his head to the pillow. Screwed his eyes closed, wringing out a tear. Drew in a breath.

'Now I don't have the time. Lord, I wish I could remember the name.'

His head slipped back a little, his face relaxed.

Rachel watched him carefully for a minute, then held the back of her hand close to his nostrils, like she'd been taught. She placed a finger on the side of his neck and waited a whole minute. One of the relatives, a man in his thirties, looked at her, not daring to ask the question.

She nodded. 'He's gone.'

One by one, the relatives filed out. Most at least glanced back at him; one of his daughters made a show of kissing his cheek, inspiring his other daughter to do the same.

Then they had gone. Rachel imagined them all downstairs, perhaps taking a room each and sorting the contents into plunder and litter.

She turned back to Marnal. He looked even smaller and older than before. Peaceful, though. It felt like she should pray for him or something. Instead, she went over to the window and closed it. The garden was so colourful this time of year. A little overgrown, but with splashes of yellows, reds and purples among the dark green. Great trees. A couple of the younger children had already found their way outside, and were climbing them like nothing had happened.

'Life goes on,' she said.

Rachel turned back to the old man. His skin had some colour to it. She hadn't expected that, but then she hadn't known what to expect. None of her patients had ever died on her before, not right in front of her eyes. She'd been told that dead bodies could do strange things.

There was something... the old man's skin was glowing. Ever so faintly, at least at first, but too brightly to be any trick of the light. She didn't think that was normal. It was like an overexposed photo now, his eyebrows and the exact lines of his nose and mouth bleached out.

She stared at the old man's face, and when it stopped glowing it was a young man's face.

Brown eyes snapped open.

'Gallifrey,' the young man said.

Notions of heroism have always been problematic, but now heroes appear quaint relics of an age when a white man could save the day just by walking into a room and imposing his moral values on the 'bad guy'. Following the attacks of September 11th 2001,[13] we all know the problems of the world aren't so easily defined, let alone solved. Heroism is not relevant to the current international paradigm, and seems out of context in domestic political situations. It is no coincidence that the 'heroes' of modern narratives, while often good family men and patriots,[14] are often troubled, flawed characters with fragmented, traumatic pasts,[15] endlessly condemned to nightmares and flashbacks of some loved one they couldn't save.[16] A post-modern hero,[17, 18, 19] then, is on a journey of self-examination and self-validation. He is darker than the world around him, condemned to enact a revenge fantasy that will merely restore the world to imperfect, pluralist normality for an indifferent general population,[20] rather than to spread his virtues to inspire a 'better society'. Rather than 'Holding Out for a Hero'[21] it is easy to conclude that most modern observers would actually find all the forms and attributes of traditional heroism old-fashioned and actively undesirable.

Extract from a book of essays by a prominent popular historian, 2003

Chapter One
New and Missing Adventures

The walls were meant to be soundproof.

Mondova had spent a great deal of time and money trying to block out the noises and sights of the vast city below. The terraces of his palace had been built miles high so that they enjoyed a cool breeze, not the mephitis that belched from the armament plants, germ foundries and war-robot factories which clung to the narrow streets. Here, although the air was thin, Mondova rose above the concerns of his subjects.

Now, though, as he stood on the edge of the very highest terrace, he could hear the loudspeakers telling people to stay in their homes. Worse, he could hear that those proclamations were being drowned out by cheering crowds. Laughter and insolence. Music was being played. Mondova hated music, and had banned it as his first act as monocrat, over two hundred years before. Slogans were being chanted. He could hear what sounded very like a vast statue being toppled. On this planet, there were only statues of one person. Was it the one in Victory Square, Mondova wondered, where he was holding a spear aloft in one hand, a peasant's head in the other? That was his very favourite.

'Crallan!' he yelled. 'Crallan, what in the name of the Seven Systems is happening?'

His chancellor ran into the room, already cowering, almost tripping over his dark grey robes.

'My Lord Mondova.'

'Where are my bodyguards?'

'They've fled, my lord.'

'Scum! I knew they would be unreliable. That's why I had my Kyborgs built. Deploy them in the streets. Wipe out this resistance.'

'The Kyborg legion changed allegiance to the rebels, my lord. That's why the bodyguards fled.'

Mondova hesitated.

'Then I have no choice. Call in the space fleet. Order them to atomise the city.'

'The space fleet has gone, my lord.'

'Gone? Gone where?'

Crallan shrugged. 'We haven't managed to figure that one out yet.'

'It is the most powerful space navy in the galaxy. It has snuffed out stars, Crallan. Civilisations spanning whole sectors of space have surrendered at the mere thought I would launch my fleet against them. It has campaigned, unbeaten, for over two centuries.'

'No longer, sir. It's… gone.'

The cybernetic regulators of Mondova's stomach skipped a track. He lurched at Crallan, grabbed him with one armoured hand, lifted him into the air.

'We have to regroup. Gather those still loyal to me, bring them here to the sanctum! I'm not defeated, you hear me?'

He dropped Crallan, who picked himself up and dusted himself off. 'Of course, my lord.'

'Find my daughter,' the monocrat growled, concerned with little else now.

'I'm here, Father.'

She was so beautiful. The slits, folds and colours of her exquisitely tailored outfit contrived to make her long legs longer, the curve of her back more graceful, the blue of her skin more delicate, the white of her hair more vivacious. Her eyes burned with gold fire, just as her mother's had done.

'I have been persuaded of the error of my ways, Father. For

10

twenty decades you have bullied your subjects, killed them on a whim, sent them across the universe to die in your name.'

It was impossible to see Mondova's face behind the burnished-steel mask, so he didn't seem to react as Crallan pushed his way past his daughter to flee the room.

The monocrat's voice sounded calm, when it came. 'Persuaded by whom, may I ask?'

She smiled. 'He only arrived here this morning, but... he opened my eyes, Father. He showed me what was really going on in the city. He's given the people down there hope.'

Mondova watched her carefully. There was defiance in those opened eyes. A joyfulness he'd never seen before.

He had lost her.

He toyed with the idea of reaching over and snapping her neck.

'Who?' he asked instead.

'The Doctor,' she said simply.

'Doctor?' Mondova roared. 'Doctor who?'

A man stepped into the room. He was not an old man, but neither was he really a young man. His long face was oval, with an aristocratic nose and a full mouth. He had a high forehead, framed with long, dark-brown hair. His skin was milky-pale. He wore a long, dark velvet coat that flapped behind him.

'I think that's my cue,' he said, a little shamefaced. 'There comes a time when you have to accept it's over. It's over, Mondova. Your power base is destroyed, your people have spoken. There's no place in the universe for tyrants like you.'

Behind the Doctor were his companions.

'Hi, I'm Fitz, this is Trix. Glad we caught you.'

Fitz was a scruffy, tall man in his thirties and Trix was a little younger, slim and elegant. They had grabbed Crallan, and were leading him back into the room.

The Doctor held up a small silver device, some sort of tool. It emitted a whirr so faint it could barely be heard.

'No...' Mondova managed, before gravity caught up with him.

The armour crumpled to the floor, the man inside sagging with it.

11

'Too heavy,' he wheezed.

The metal plates that cocooned him had been kept weightless by the generators. But now the mechanisms he had designed and built were broken, fused. The armour was just ordinary scrap metal. The Doctor was pulling it off him, piece by piece. Mondova looked down at his own bare arms and chest as the armour came clear of them, surprised to see how slight and pale he had allowed his body to become.

Finally, the Doctor tugged off the helmet. He held it up for a moment, looked into its empty eye slits. Then he tossed it over the edge of the terrace, to the city below.

The Doctor looked down at the naked old man at his feet.

Then he held out his hand, to help him up.

'It's over,' he told him. This time, Mondova believed it.

An hour and a half later and very far away, a police box that wasn't a police box sped through a place where there was no time and no space.

As with a book, you couldn't judge the TARDIS from what it looked like on the outside. It appeared to be an old wooden police-telephone box with peeling blue paint, but (again like a book) inside it was far larger, more grand and complicated. And, as with the best novels, you couldn't always tell where it was going. The TARDIS was a machine capable of travelling to any point in space and time. That alone would be enough to make it special, but what really made it unique was that it was the place the Doctor called home.

As with his ship, there was more to the Doctor than met the eye. He was an adventurer, a bookworm, a champion, a detective, an explorer, a father and grandfather, a historian, an iconoclast, a jackanapes, a know-it-all, a lord, a meddler, a nuisance; he was old, a physician and a quack, a renegade, a scientist, a traveller, a utopian, a violinist, a widower, a xoanon; he was youthful and he was a zealot.

One thing he wasn't, though, was human. Two hearts beat in his chest. He'd lived for centuries, at the very least. The Doctor didn't think much about his past; he rarely talked about it, even with his friends. He lived in the now, the only time that meant anything to someone who could spend yesterday in the far future and tomorrow in the olden days.

Now he stood at the central console, right in the middle of the cavernous control room, the very first room you'd come to if you'd just stepped inside the TARDIS. The console was hexagonal, the size of a large desk. Thrusting out from the centre right up to the ceiling was a powerful piston, encased in a glass tube. It rose and fell, pulsing with blue light as it did so. The Doctor watched it, almost hypnotised. He was still wearing his frock coat. He would occasionally break away to start operating controls, check readouts and generally fuss about. He wasn't steering the ship, though, so much as trying to decide where it was heading.

The Doctor was smiling to himself. A tyrant toppled was always a good day's work. The planet Mondova had taken control of had been a beautiful world of orchards, sculpture and music. Now it could be all those things again. That would be for the people there to decide.

In another part of the TARDIS the Doctor's two companions, Fitz and Trix, were smiling too. They had also been celebrating the fall of Mondova and his regime. Unlike the Doctor, they had done this by going to Fitz's room, by downing a couple of bottles of wine they'd liberated from the monocrat's wine cellar, by turning up a record player and dancing, then by grabbing each other and kissing.

While they had known each other for some time now, and had both been living in the TARDIS all that while, it was the first time Fitz and Trix had done any of these things together.

'A day can be an awfully long time, can't it?' Trix noted, rolling on to her back, still a little breathless.

Fitz's head had ended up somewhere around her midriff. He

mumbled what sounded like an agreement.

'What was that?' Trix asked.

Fitz's rather unshaven face emerged from the bed sheets. 'I said you've got a flat stomach.'

'Thank you. You could get one too, if you did a few push-ups.'

'When did you first think we would...?' he began.

'I hoped we might when you put the record on,' she said.

'Really?'

Trix smiled. 'Really. Why, have you been holding a torch for me for months, or something?'

'No. Not like that. It was... it was this afternoon. When we were splashing around down in the catacombs. I thought that Kyborg had drowned you. When I saw you again, I realised then how much I'd missed you. How much you meant to me.'

Trix shifted, a little uncomfortable.

'Hell,' Fitz said quickly, sitting up. 'Look, if this was just a, y'know, a thing, then it's a thing. There's a lot of lust in there. On my part, I mean. Those legs of yours... they're long, aren't they? Not freakishly long, obviously. But, well, what I'm saying is that if you want to keep this superficial, then I'm a pretty superficial person.'

Trix smiled. 'I never doubted that for a second.'

'Good, cos I mean it.'

'What are you doing?'

Fitz pointed to the cigarette he'd just put in his mouth and turned his other hand to show her the lighter.

'I know what you're doing. What I meant was don't do it.'

'Not you as well. Does no one smoke in the future? Do you all just go straight to sleep?'

'I'm not from the future, I'm from the present. You're from the past, remember?'

Fitz smiled. 'Yeah. Old enough to be your dad. I need a ciggie. Even though this is my room, and my record player, and my bed, I'll go and find somewhere else to smoke. Happy?'

Trix sank back into the pillows. 'Ecstatic,' she assured him.

* * *

14

All his memories had come flooding back.

Rachel had done what Marnal had asked: shooed the relatives away, explained that she'd made a mistake and that he'd got better, and that, no, they couldn't see him. It had taken over an hour to round them all up, convince them and herd them out to their Rovers, Audis and Lexuses. She'd gone back upstairs to find him in one of the many spare bedrooms.

'Time Lords are the ruling class of the planet Gallifrey,' Marnal began to explain. He vanished into the huge wardrobe, but his voice carried on. 'All Time Lords have increased cranial capacity, blood with a vastly superior capacity to carry oxygen compared with haemoglobin, a body temperature of sixty degrees, a respiratory bypass system, a lindal gland, a reflex link...'

Rachel had started fidgeting halfway through the list, and had tuned out long before Marnal had finished.

'Most importantly, Time Lords have the ability to regenerate our bodies if we are mortally injured.'

'Are these characters in your books?' she asked.

'No,' he said coldly, returning from his journey with an armful of clothes. 'This is what I am. The Time Lords are my people. Shortly, I will be rejoining them. I have to look my best.'

He started pulling on a pair of trousers that were a little too baggy on him.

'They sound like your books, that's all. I read some of your stuff when I was a kid. All about the Time Lords and their adventures, that was you, wasn't it? I was never really into science fiction. I prefer real stuff.'

'That was "real stuff". That was my life. The early stories flowed so easily, I remembered some things, you see. But there came a point where...' he paused for a moment, then started again. 'I wrote everything I remembered down. There were always gaps, but I had to keep going. I was the only person who knew anything about Gallifrey, you see. I couldn't ask. And I didn't even remember its name.'

He was wearing a frilly Mr-Darcy-style shirt now. Over that, he pulled on a dark-blue blazer. It was a peculiar ensemble. He hurried over to the mirror and examined himself, pudging up his face with his fingers.

'Um... This is all right, I suppose,' he said to himself. 'A little scrawny. A little young, but I'll grow out of that.'

He shrugged off the blazer and found himself a velvet jacket.

'And so what you did before... that was *regeneration*?'

'That's right. This' – he pointed down at his own body – 'is my thirteenth incarnation. The process renewed me, a surge of artron energy restored my damaged synapses. Gave me back all the memories I had lost.'

'You were suffering from post-traumatic retrograde amnesia,' Rachel said. 'It's rare, but it happens. In people, I mean.'

Marnal looked impressed as he discarded the jacket in favour of a light blue knee-length coat.

'I got my degree,' she reminded him. 'And because of that, I know that there's no such thing as a lindal gland or any of the other things you mentioned.'

'You saw me change,' Marnal reminded her. He was turning, admiring himself in the mirror. Then he threw away the coat, scowling at himself, and put the blazer back on.

'I've been thinking about that. It was a dark room, and I was on my own in there. It could easily have been a trick. You're one of the old man's nephews or something.'

Marnal turned to her, stared at her.

'You were the one that believed me,' he said, a hint of cruelty in his voice.

Rachel hesitated, thought about it for a moment. 'I do believe you,' she said. At the very worst, it was a harmless fantasy.

'Every word?'

'Every word.'

'It's all true, I promise you. The world you know is just one of an infinity of worlds.'

He took her hand in his, pressed it against first one side of his chest, then the other. A heart beat on each side.

'How are you going to get back?' she asked.

He pulled a small cube from his pocket.

'It was there all along, only I didn't know what it was.'

He pressed it to his forehead, screwed his eyes shut.

'There we go.'

He put the cube back in his pocket.

'A telepathic signal. The miracle of time travel is that whenever they receive my message, they can dispatch someone to this exact point. We won't have to wait.'

They waited.

The Doctor frowned and put down his book.

There was something there. He could hear it over the sound of the time engines.

He slipped out of the control room, through one of the many doors that led to the depths of the ship. He walked past the workshop and one of the smaller libraries, carried on down a winding corridor.

This was the corridor that led nowhere. You walked through a couple of doors, then after the last turn there was another fifty paces to walk, then there was just a wall, covered in the same round indentations as most of the other walls. The Doctor knew that his time-space machine was very large, so large he hadn't been able to explore it all. But he knew this corridor well. He thought of it as the back wall of the TARDIS.

Sometimes, when his companions were asleep, he would come down to the back wall. The Doctor knew Fitz had discovered this place too. Fitz had never tried to discuss it with him. The Doctor didn't know if he'd ever heard the strange noises. If Fitz spent any time down here, he would have heard the scratching. Today was no different. He must have wondered if an animal was trapped on the other side. Or perhaps a person, their fingernails grown into claws over the centuries they'd been down here.

'Oh… Hi.'

The Doctor turned to see Fitz. His companion was wearing a

tatty dressing gown, and had one hand stuck in his pocket. The noises behind the wall had stopped.

'Come down here for a smoke?' the Doctor asked.

Fitz removed the hand, and the packet of cigarettes that had been in there with it, from his pocket.

'Yeah... er... you weren't waiting down here to catch me, were you?'

'No. I often come down here.'

'You mind?' Fitz asked, taking out a cigarette. Then: 'I mean if you want one, then of course...'

The Doctor looked pained.

'Yeah, all right, just being polite.' Fitz lit the cigarette and took a draw from it to get it going. 'How did you know?'

The Doctor pointed to the pile of around a hundred cigarette butts on the floor. 'Elementary, my dear Fitz.'

His companion nodded thoughtfully. 'Yeah, well, this ship may be full of stuff, but there's not one ashtray.'

'Cigarettes will be the death of you,' the Doctor said.

Fitz took the cigarette from his mouth. 'You know that for a fact?'

The Doctor looked askance at him.

'Hey, look, sometimes you know the future, yeah? You being a time-traveller. I've seen you do that "I know you" stuff, and then you tell someone their destiny.'

'I've not done that for ages,' the Doctor laughed.

'So you don't know how I die?'

'No. There are some things it's better not knowing.'

'Yeah.'

'Are you all right? You look like there's something on your mind.'

Fitz looked distinctly uncomfortable. 'Er... look. Didn't mean to interrupt. I'll get back to... I'll go back to my room.'

It had been an hour. Marnal had been sitting in the same spot, the same look of expectation on his face the whole time. He'd been writing up today's events in his diary, scribbling away happily. He'd not once asked Rachel for her side of the story.

'I don't think they're coming,' Rachel said gently.

'I don't understand why they haven't shown up. There must be a good reason.'

'So how did you end up here on Earth?' Rachel asked.

He was clearly a little irritated by the question. 'I'll explain later.'

'Don't you have a rocket or a flying saucer or something? You could go to them.'

Marnal shook his head sadly. 'My TARDIS was taken from me.'

'TARDIS?'

Marnal took a deep breath before starting. 'It stands for Time And Relative Dimensions In Space. TARDISes are semi-sentient dimensionally transcendental time-space machines created using block transfer computations and powered via the Eye of Harmony. They dematerialise from one point expressed as a set of relative space-time coordinates and travel via the time vortex until they rematerialise at another point. My TARDIS was a Type…'

Rachel listened carefully, wondering if she should take notes.

'So you're stuck on Earth?' she asked, when she was sure he'd finished.

'Yes.'

'No alien technology at all? Not, of course, that you'd think of it as alien.'

'Nothing.'

'Is there no other way to get in touch?'

Marnal thought for a moment. 'There may be,' he concluded. 'We need to check the library.'

The Doctor was back in the control room, sitting in his chair with his book.

There was a chime from the console. The Doctor finished the scene he was reading and headed over. The computer display was scrolling data too fast for human eyes to take it in. The Doctor read it carefully, then read it again to make sure.

He reached out, a little tentatively, and flicked a couple of switches. He waited for this to take effect, then adjusted a dial.

There was an anomalous reading coming from Earth. He tried to pinpoint the time zone.

Trix was sneaking past him.

'I can see you,' he told her, without looking up. 'Getting itchy feet?'

'Eh?'

'Can't wait to land?'

Trix relaxed. 'No, sorry. Looking for something in the fridge.' She was in silk pyjamas. '*The Doctor's Dilemma*?' she asked.

'Yes. I met Shaw at one of Wilde's parties.'

'I didn't think Shaw drank.'

'He didn't drink spirits or beer. He drank champagne. "Doctor," he told me, "I'm not a champagne teetotaller."'

'That gives me an idea,' she said, resuming her journey to the TARDIS fridge. 'Wait a second. Oscar Wilde?'

The Doctor smiled and nodded. 'March 1895. Around the time of the McCarthy murder. Sherlock Holmes solved the case before I could, as I recall.'

'Sherlock Holmes is a fictional character,' Trix pointed out.

The Doctor grinned. 'My dear, one of the things you'll learn is that it's all real. Every word of every novel is real, every frame of every movie, every panel of every comic strip.'

'But that's just not possible. I mean some books contradict other ones and –'

The Doctor was ignoring her. 'We're heading to Earth, 40 BC. We've had to change course to avoid resolving a quantum storm front. We should have landed any minute, but it'll be more like three hours now.'

'Oh. OK. Three hours?' she asked.

'You don't mind?'

Trix had a bottle of champagne tucked under her arm. 'Not at all. I'm sure Fitz and I will be able to fill the time somehow.'

'Jolly good,' the Doctor replied, returning to his study of the readouts as she hurried away.

* * *

Marnal was pacing around the library now. He kept playing with the lapels of his blazer, and clearly loved it. Rachel wondered if it was a little too tight for him.

Most libraries consisted of books written by other people, but this one was different. There were a dozen bookcases, packed with volumes of all sizes from big leather-bound books to yellowing paperbacks. There were also papers, pamphlets and notebooks stuffed into every available space, and countless magazines, comics and journals. Every single thing here had been written by Marnal. How many words, Rachel wondered. Tens of millions, easily, she thought, although she had no real idea how many words there were in a novel.

She had looked him up a few months ago, when the agency told her that her new patient was an author. She had a vague feeling that she recognised the name, but she couldn't place it. She hadn't found 'Marnal' in *The Oxford Companion to English Literature*, between *Marmion: A Tale of Flodden Field* and Marney, Lord. Or in *Cultural Icons*, between Marley, Bob, and Marsalis, Wynton. She'd gone online. There weren't any books in print on Amazon, although *The Emergents* and *The Kraglon Inheritance* were listed. Bookfinder was little better – she put in an order for *The Witch Lords*, the one book her search revealed, but was emailed back by the seller and told the copy had just been sold. On Google she got a list of autoparts and vitamin retailers. When she added 'science+fiction' she got one hit: a page in Spanish that she decided was best left untranslated. It had taken her a couple of days at a library, and a brief correspondence with a science-fiction society, to find out anything more tangible. This had sparked off some memories. She'd read a couple of his novels, but couldn't remember very much about them.

There was something sad and strange about finding all these forgotten books here, together in one place, gathering dust. It was the literary equivalent of the lost gardens of Heligan. That's what everyone thought of Marnal, if they thought of him at all: a rich, colourful mind that had become overgrown, tangled as it grew old. An author of popular adventure fiction who had succumbed to senility without realising it, whose books had become an impenetrable jungle, alienating even his most loyal fans.

'Where do we start?' she asked.

She reached up, moved aside a Hugo Award and pulled down a copy of *The Strand Magazine* that had almost fallen apart.

Carefully, she opened it, and flicked past pictures of Moriarty and Holmes and the falls at Reichenbach until she found the story she was looking for. '*The Giants*, by Marnal,' she read. 'Once, long ago, on an island in a sea of clouds, there was a land where giants walked. The giants lived amongst the other peoples of that land, and they used their great strength to help them. But the power of the giants was too great, their hands were too strong, their tread too heavy and the more they tried to help the people, the greater was the destruction that they caused. Until the people that they had tried to help were no more.'

Marnal took the magazine from her. 'The first myth of the Time Lords, and my first foray into the Terran literary world.'

Rachel sifted through a pile of *Pearson's Magazine*, *The Idler*, *The Graphic* and more copies of *The Strand*.

'These are all over a hundred years old,' she told him.

'George Bernard Shaw was first published in 1884,' Marnal replied. 'He was still writing when he died in 1950, and the obituaries said his was the longest literary career this world had ever seen. Since 1960, I believe that honour has belonged to me. I don't think anyone ever noticed. These books represent the longest-running science-fiction series anywhere in the world, an exercise in world-building that –'

'Well, no one's written your obituary,' Rachel interrupted. 'And they probably think "Marnal" is a pseudonym like, I dunno, Hergé or Saki or Iain M. Banks or something.'

Marnal waved his hand. 'What I need is in one of these books, but I can't remember which one.'

'What? I thought you had your memories back?'

'I have a good memory, but not total recall. That's one of the reasons I wrote all these. There had to be a record. Help me to look. I think it's in one of the Arrows. A paragraph describing the main temporal monitoring chamber.'

He reached up and pulled down an armful of colourful paperbacks. Rachel took them. They all had lurid covers variously depicting bronzed men in flowing robes standing over scantily clad (but not too scantily clad) women, spaceships shaped like egg timers, monsters that looked like trolls, vampires and icky worms.

'Whatever the books' literary merits, their covers were always a problem,' Marnal conceded. 'Come on – we have work to do.'

There was structure, the universe was a web made not of spider's silk but of space and time.

But in such a cosmos, one of fluxing quad-dimensionality, who was to say what was cause and what was effect? Even the newly woven children of his world understood the solution to that solemn inquiry: there was no history, don't you see, only established history. Time was an ocean of broth, rich in elements and possibilities. Observations could be made to spot trends and to predict, for the oceans of time were subject to the laws of temporal mechanics. But these were projections of reality, not the reality itself as long as the Lords of Time remained in their Citadel, merely watching. Yet, if a single one among them were to cease observation and to step out into the universe, they would freeze time wheresoever their feet touched the ground, wheresoever they drew breath from the atmosphere. At that moment, their mere presence would change time, from a fluid to a solid thing. If one of the Lords of Time but glanced into the night's sky, the stars would become true in the instant they were seen, and thence back for every picosecond of the ten thousand years of the stars' photons' journey. When a time-traveller swam in this ocean, it solidified around them, crystallised, became transmuted into that which could never change. And so was written the most sacred law of all – for even the softest touch of a Lord of Time could condemn a man to existence or non-existence, bring empires into being and destine them to ruin, and blot out the sky or fill it with heavenly radiance. Observe. Never interfere.

Extract from *The Hand of Time* (1976) by Marnal

Chapter Two
Gone

Rachel put the book down. She wasn't sure that 'destine' was really a word, or that 'flux' was a verb, but they might have been. Marnal had been a writer for a hundred years longer than she'd been alive, so she was willing to give him the benefit of the doubt.

She was skimming through the gaudy paperbacks, looking for the words 'temporal' (which appeared a lot, almost as often as 'anomaly' and 'eldritch'), 'monitoring' and 'chamber'. It was like a one-armed bandit, she thought – every so often one of the words would spin into view, but not all three of them at once in a row. So she hadn't hit the jackpot. Marnal was making slow work of it. Reverentially lifting the books, opening them ever so carefully, treating them like medieval parchment.

'This is the entire history of Gallifrey,' he explained. 'Or at least everything I remember. A record of the greatest civilisation the universe has ever seen.'

'If they're stories,' Rachel began, 'then, er, how true are they?'

Marnal glared at her.

'Because every time you write something down you, er, well it's like you say here. You crystallise it. If you do that, you change it. Yeah?'

Marnal was still giving her that stare of his.

Rachel dug herself in a little deeper. 'You have to change it a little, to make it a story in the first place. Tidy it up, make sure it's entertaining. Your own opinions inevitably seep into the story, don't they?'

'Everything happened like I said it did,' he told her firmly. 'Everything. That's the whole point of writing it down. Humans might not be able to write what happened down without skewing it and ruining the truth of it. I can, and I did.'

He continued his search, in silence. Rachel made a half-hearted effort to do the same. Almost straight away, though, she found what they were looking for.

'*The Time of Neman*, page 127,' she said.

Marnal snatched the book from her, and scanned it quickly. 'Yes,' he said. 'Well done.'

'Er... Now what?'

'We build one of these,' he said, stabbing his finger at the page and passing the book back to her.

'A temporal monitoring chamber?'

'Yes.'

'Er...'

'If you know the true way to read it, this book contains codes and hints for building a pocket universe that maps every aspect of the real one. Using such a device, we'll be able to see Gallifrey.'

Rachel looked down. 'That book?' she said.

Marnal's eyes glinted. 'If you clear a space on the dining table, I'll show you.'

After half an hour Marnal had assembled all sorts of things from the garage and various piles of junk around the house. A big glass bottle from a home-brewing kit, an old portable television, what looked like a section from a recording studio's mixing desk. After about an hour's work connecting them up with cables to a row of smelly old car batteries, he stood back.

To Rachel's amazement, the inside of the glass bottle had gone dark, then tiny bright dots had started to resolve.

'Galaxies,' Marnal assured her. He was twiddling with the mixing-desk controls, checking the television screen, which was full of what looked like Greek symbols.

'Greek?' she asked.

He smiled condescendingly. 'No, these are letters of the

Gallifreyan omegabet.'

'Which is like an alphabet, but superior?'

'The last word, you might say.'

Rachel peered into the bottle. Wherever she looked, she was able to focus in and in and in and in and in. So the galaxies became stars, became planets, became patches of land. It made her eyes go funny, and she had to blink and start again a couple of times. She saw something that looked like the moon, only the rocks were more jagged and there was a strange purple sky. Things that looked like woodlice were burying themselves in the soft sand.

Aliens, she realised. She was looking at alien life forms.

Then the contents of the bottle faded away, and she found herself staring at Marnal's face on the other side, distorted in the clear, curved glass. He was holding the power cable, which he'd unplugged from the car batteries.

'These will go flat in a matter of minutes. I need a better power supply,' he told her. 'I'll construct a cold-fusion reactor. Shouldn't take long.'

'But no one knows how to do that,' Rachel said.

'No one on Earth. It's child's play to my people. Your human children rub sticks together to make fire?'

'I was a Girl Guide, but I was useless at all that.'

Marnal gave her a forgiving smile. 'Well, fusion is just a simple matter of rubbing helium nuclei together to make energy.'

'And it's safe?'

'Oh yes. Completely clean.'

'You could solve loads of problems on Earth,' she told him. 'The energy crisis, the dependence on fossil fuels, air pollution, cheap space travel...'

'Yes, but there are more pressing matters. I have one last car battery.'

He connected it up and started scanning star systems.

'Now, it's towards the galactic core, it should be around...' He paused. 'I don't understand. It's gone.'

'What do you mean gone?'

'If I could answer that question... I can't find Gallifrey. I can't even see Kasterborous. Anywhere in space or time.'

'You don't want to go to a genuine Roman orgy?' the Doctor said, astonished.

They were standing in the marketplace. The farmers and merchants had all gone home for the night, cleared their stalls and tied back the bright awnings. The fountain was still playing, though. A beggar was sitting at it, dipping a cup into its trough for a drink. A small statue of Ceres looked over the scene.

'No,' said Fitz, apparently cheerfully. 'You do that, we'll follow the old washerwoman.'

The Doctor looked at him suspiciously. 'Not like you to turn down wine, women and song. Wait, are you...?'

Without warning, he grabbed Fitz's head and stared into his eyes, as though he was trying to get a look at his brain.

'Gerroff!' Fitz complained, shaking him away. 'No, I admit it's not like me. But on this occasion – I mean... you're OK going instead?'

The Doctor nodded, and checked his toga one last time. 'Needs must. Good luck, the pair of you.'

He hurried off and disappeared between two columns of the colonnade.

It was a pleasant Italian evening, so a little too warm for Fitz and Trix.

'I'm very proud of you,' Trix told Fitz as they made their way back to the villa they'd cased earlier that afternoon.

'You owe me, that's all I'm saying.'

Trix kissed him on the cheek. 'I'll repay you with interest.' He blushed in a very endearing way.

'So, what do you think's up?'

'That face-grabbing was a clue,' Fitz said. 'Someone's in disguise. And we're in history, so I'm guessing the baddy is trying to alter the time line or something like that. Mount Vesuvius is probably involved too.'

Trix smiled sweetly. 'Mount Vesuvius? Fiver?'

'As ever.'

They took up a position at the back of the villa.

'You're thirty-five quid down so far,' she pointed out, 'after seven bets.'

'I'm due for a change of luck, then.'

'Look!'

Trix pulled Fitz out of sight as one of the back doors opened. An old crone shuffled out, carrying a basket of clothes and linen that was almost the same size as she was. Trix and Fitz followed her a little way to where she had a mule tethered. With a bit of difficulty, the old woman attached the basket to the mule's saddle. She slapped its shoulder and it clip-clopped away, with the old woman half-guiding it, half-led by it.

Trix followed, slipping from shadow to shadow. Fitz wasn't far behind.

'I'm getting too old for this,' he said.

'Oh come on, it's fun.'

'Hey, I'm not denying that.'

The washerwoman was a hundred yards away and about to disappear down an alleyway with her mule. They hurried to catch up with her.

They were back in the marketplace. The old woman was unloading her basket, and looked befuddled by the attention she was getting from Trix and Fitz. The mule was drinking from the trough of the fountain, presumably taking the opportunity before the washing went in.

'Get her!' Trix shouted.

Fitz grabbed the washerwoman's arms, and held her in place. The woman didn't say a word; she just looked shocked.

'I know your secret,' Trix said, confronting her. 'You're no washerwoman. You're a spy.'

'She's not a washerwoman?' Fitz asked, one eye on the basket of washing.

Trix grabbed the washerwoman's face. 'She is not even a she, Fitz. This is a man, one with an obviously false nose.'

The nose stayed in place, despite Trix's best efforts. The washerwoman yelped and whined, finally slapping Trix hard on the face and running off.

'Damn. She looked so butch. You'd think I would know a disguise when I saw one. Could have sworn it.'

'No,' said the mule, 'you were on the right track.'

They watched as the mule stood on its hind legs and started to shift form, gradually settling into a smooth bipedal shape not wholly unlike a mule's, but with smooth grey skin like a dolphin's. It had glowing red eyes and wore a distinctly fascistic black uniform.

'Christ on a bike!' Fitz exclaimed.

'So, you are time-travellers.'

'No,' lied Fitz, badly.

'Then could you explain how you know the name of a deity who is not yet born and a mode of transport that has yet to be invented?'

'Yeah, well, OK, we're time-travellers. We're one step ahead of you, and we're here to foil your plan.'

The alien gave a braying chuckle. 'You don't have a clue what I'm planning.'

'Are you going to trigger Mount Vesuvius?' Trix asked mischievously.

The creature frowned. 'By your human calendar it is 40 BC. The eruption of Vesuvius doesn't happen until 79 AD. Furthermore, we're over a hundred miles away from there.'

Trix smiled. 'Yeah, I knew that. He didn't, though.'

'Damn,' said Fitz. 'Now I owe her a fiver. So... what's your plan?'

The creature looked at them suspiciously, then clearly decided they weren't a threat. 'I am Thorgan of the Sulumians. Three hundred and seventeen thousand years from now, your human species will encroach on our domain in the eighth dimension. I have a sacred vow to deflect the course of human history to stop that incursion. And what I will do tonight will prevent the Treaty of Brundusium from ever being signed.' He gave a triumphant laugh.

'Eh?' Fitz replied, speaking for both himself and Trix.

'If the treaty isn't signed, Octavian will never divorce Scribonia!' the monster explained.

'Eh?'

The creature's eyes narrowed. 'So he won't marry Livia.'

Fitz shrugged. He looked over to Trix, who shrugged in turn.

Thorgan waved a hoof impatiently. 'Don't you see? If that happens, then Antonius won't be allotted the eastern imperial territories, and won't abandon Octavia for Cleopatra VII.'

'I've heard of Cleopatra,' Fitz said helpfully. 'I didn't realise there were seven of her, though.'

'Oh, come on – none of this is exactly obscure,' the creature growled.

Trix was also puzzled. 'Brian Blessed!' she exclaimed finally.

'Eh?' Fitz repeated.

'He played Augustus in *I, Claudius*,' Trix told him.

'Eh? I thought he was on about Octavian?'

'They're the same person,' the creature said, clearly aggravated. 'After he wins the Battle of Actium, he renames himself Augustus.'

'That's a gross simplification of the history,' the Doctor said. He was standing behind the creature, and had changed back into his normal, velvet frock-coat. 'But exactly what I've come to expect from a Sulumian.'

'Doc-tor!' the creature snarled. 'I might have known.'

The Doctor moved to shake the monster's hoof. 'Hello, Thorgan. I'd offer you a jelly baby but, you know: gelatine.' He glanced at the hoof then let go of it, a little embarrassed. 'Gosh, it must be – what? – minus twelve hundred years since I saw you last.'

'Pisa,' Thorgan replied.

'There's no need to be like that, he was only saying –' Fitz chipped in.

The Doctor pointed at the mule-man. 'Thorgan was trying to kill

Fibonacci before he wrote the *Liber quadratorum*. Imagine it, Trix: western culture without the ability to solve diophantine equations of the second degree.'

'Why, the whole face of human history would have been changed,' she deadpanned.

'Yes,' Thorgan cackled. 'And I vowed when you defeated me then, Doc-tor, that there would be a reckoning.'

He tugged a small silver box from his belt and held it in his hoof.

'Before I discreate you, Doc-tor, I will allow you to watch as I detonate the strontium grenade I planted in the peristyle of Octavian's villa.'

'I understood some of that!' Fitz announced happily. 'Watch out, Doctor, he's got a bomb!'

'Don't do it Thorgan.'

'Too late… Doc-tor!' The mule-man squeezed the control box.

'Run,' the Doctor suggested to Fitz and Trix, already practising what he preached.

There was a huge, sharp explosion behind them, and they were showered with a combination of mosaic tiles, plaster and a smattering of minced mule.

'You usually give a bit more warning than that,' Trix complained, brushing debris from her shoulder and turning back to look at the crater.

'Sorry,' the Doctor said sheepishly. 'I managed to plant –'

'– the grenade on Thorgan when –' Fitz interrupted,

'– you shook his hoof,' Trix finished.

The Doctor looked a little crestfallen. 'Oh.'

'As long as he didn't see it coming,' Trix said. 'That's all that matters.'

'We should get back to the TARDIS,' the Doctor said.

'Don't you want to check the villa, to make sure everyone's OK?' Trix asked.

Fitz brightened. 'Yeah, perhaps we could go to the org– the villa, after all?'

'Fitz…' Trix warned gently.

'Don't worry. We'd only observe, not interfere,' he assured her.

The Doctor ushered them away. 'No, they'll all be fine... Besides, there's a young lady called Fulvia waiting for me back there, and I've already given her quite enough of my attention for one night.'

Six hours of searching and Marnal's voice had an edge of panic, now. He'd built his cold-fusion reactor from things he'd found under the sink, and connected it up. He'd not found Gallifrey, but he'd found that some of the stars and planets nearby had disturbed orbits. This was a sign that something catastrophic had happened.

'It's been attacked. It's the only explanation. The scrolls said that... no. What's done is done. It can't be undone. It's written. We have to find out who did this terrible thing.'

Rachel frowned. 'It can't have gone. It's a planet. Don't you think you should recheck your results again?'

Marnal turned on her. 'A terrible injustice has been done. The planet of the Time Lords, a civilisation twenty thousand centuries old, the one you loved to read about as a child, a place of such beauty and power that it makes your heaven seem profane, has gone, and gone forever. Someone destroyed it.'

'Who?'

'I don't know, not yet. But now I have my memories back, I know of many who might have wanted to do it. There are so few with the necessary power. It could have been the Klade, the Tractites, the Ongoing. It could have been Centro, but... no. In the end, none of them operate on such a scale. None of them would dare do such a thing.'

'But you can find out who did it?'

'Yes. I know ways I can track down the culprits.'

'And then what?'

Marnal paused to put his blue blazer back on, then: 'I told you. We'll hunt them down and destroy them in turn.'

'You said that. But if they can blow up whole planets, how can we stop them?'

'I'm not sure I can. Not this time. But I have to try.'

Marnal was stalking around his dining table, talking to himself but expecting Rachel to listen to what he was saying.

'Whatever destroyed Gallifrey would have to be time active, and very powerful. It – or they – could be anywhere in time and space. I need to put some thought into how I can find them.'

A flash of inspiration hit Rachel. 'Couldn't you just tune in to history and look at the destruction of Gallifrey itself? See it happen, then follow whoever did it?'

'No. The destruction of the planet unleashed a vast ripple in the space-time continuum, one that makes it impossible to navigate or even see the area of devastation. Gallifrey cannot be observed, at any point in its history. Not any more.'

'Oh. Shame.'

Marnal was pacing around the room.

'What's all this about the fourth and fifth dimension?' Rachel asked.

She'd brought a couple of his novels with her to the dining room. If they really contained the secrets of the universe they might be worth struggling through. She'd started on *The Beautiful People*. So far, though, it was just *The Da Vinci Code* all over again.

'Time and space,' Marnal said. 'Relative dimensions, you see.'

'Oh,' Rachel said again.

Marnal slapped his head. 'Wait! That's it! There will be a trail in the fifth dimension.'

He started adjusting the mixing-desk controls again.

The bottle grew dark again, the stars came out.

Marnal peered in. 'It's a question of seeing things in five dimensions. Yes. I think...'

He stepped back.

There was a swirling psychedelic pattern in the bottle now, instead of the galaxies. A column of grey light that broke up into lines, then a colourful mass of concentric squares, a howling tube of blue light and what looked like stars, then a lurid purple galaxy.

It struck Rachel that it would make a great screen saver.

All the time, Marnal was adjusting the settings, twisting dials on the mixing desk and then checking the bottle, as if he was tuning a television set.

'We're going to see who destroyed Gallifrey,' he announced.

Images started smearing across the screen. Ghostly half-pictures, pictures of nothingness, of insectile things and abstract mechanisms. Something that looked like an orchid briefly flickered and faded.

'Nearly there,' Marnal called out.

The picture was resolving.

'It's a... What is that?' Rachel wondered. It looked like a phone box, floating in space.

A fresh solar wind breathed over the battered police box. Harsh starlight dappled it, picked out the blue paint. It sat in a hard vacuum, with temperatures little above absolute zero, and in a belt of radiation that would instantly kill anyone who stepped from it. Nevertheless, it sat there nonchalantly as though it was a perfectly normal place for it to be.

Inside, the Doctor pulled up the handbrake, locking the TARDIS in position, then activated the scanner. They'd left Rome eight hours ago now. They'd moved on, and had a new problem to solve. Don't dwell on the past, that was his motto.

The Doctor wasn't sure why the TARDIS had materialised here. He wasn't sure where 'here' was yet. It was well within a solar system, several hundred million miles away from the star. He had a quick look round using the scanner. The sun here was dimmer than Earth's – the Doctor guessed the absolute magnitude would be about 13.5 – but the night sky was much as it appeared from Earth, with all the familiar constellations, give or take a few. So they weren't very far from Earth, relatively speaking. He couldn't see any gas giants. The star flared slightly.

'Ross 128,' the Doctor concluded.

It was a little under eleven light years from Earth, in the

constellation of Virgo. The Doctor checked the instruments, and – belatedly – they were coming to the same conclusion. He'd never been to Ross 128 before, as far as he remembered, but had heard only nice things about it.

Setting the coordinates of the TARDIS was like sticking a pin in a map. Not every landing was in a place of great interest or historical importance. The TARDIS usually ended up on a habitable planet, but not always. He checked the instruments. The TARDIS had picked up a signal of some kind.

The Doctor turned his head.

A man in a blue blazer and a blonde woman in jeans were watching him. The woman was saying some wordless something. She looked agitated. The man was more calm. He replied, silently, then leant in, blocking the woman's view – and the Doctor's view of the woman. The two men stared at each other for a moment, across time and space. The Doctor recognised him... not by name, not even his face, but he knew him from somewhere.

Something terrifying crossed the Doctor's mind, for the merest moment. The scratching at the back of the TARDIS seemed to be inside his brain. Fuelled by raw panic, he hurried to the console and flicked the rows of switches that activated as many of the TARDIS defence systems as he could think of, one after the other.

He moved around the console, his hands reaching for and tugging at controls on instinct. He slammed down on the emergency dematerialisation button. The central column started rising and falling, and its rhythm had a soothing, lullaby effect on the Doctor's hearts' rate.

The link was broken and Fitz had his hand on the Doctor's shoulder.

'What the hell's the matter with you?' Fitz asked him. 'You look like you've seen a ghost's ghost.'

'Did you see them?' the Doctor asked, aware there was a tremble in his voice.

Fitz shook his head. 'There's no one here. Pull yourself together.'

The Doctor stepped away from the console, and used his new

vantage point to look around the control room.

'There was someone here?' asked Fitz, clearly concerned.

'Not physically. Not… not in three dimensions. They were just watching us.'

'Looking inside the TARDIS? Is that possible?'

The Doctor nodded thoughtfully. 'Evidently it is.'

'Thank Christ they were looking in here, not my room. Could have been a bit embarrassing otherwise,' Fitz noted.

'What?' The Doctor scowled.

'Nothing,' Fitz said quickly. 'Why are you so freaked out?'

'This is serious,' the Doctor snapped.

'Yeah, all right. So what do we do?'

'You go back to your room.'

Rachel stepped back as the bottle went empty again. There had been something about the face of the man they'd seen.

Marnal was still peering into the bottle as though he could somehow reassemble the picture. He reached over to the controls, and started to adjust the levers. 'I can't lock on again,' he said to himself.

'The reactor's gone flat,' she told him.

'No, it's still working at full power. He saw us and boosted the force fields protecting him.'

'But you know where he is?'

'He will have moved, and he'll have obscured his trail,' Marnal scolded himself. 'He was 3.35 parsecs away. That's practically next door.'

Rachel glanced out of the window at the side of the neighbouring house, the Winfields'. Marnal was shaking his head. Something was troubling him. Something was troubling Rachel too, but it was ridiculous. She decided to ask Marnal what he was worried about instead.

'Do you know who it was?' she asked.

'I never thought it… I never…'

Rachel gave him a moment.

'The background,' he asked, 'did you see it?'

'It was like a flight deck. There was a control panel on a podium with a big column rising up out of the middle of it.'

'Yes. It was the control room of a TARDIS.'

'TARDIS? You said that word before. That was the name of your time machine.'

'Yes.'

'So the man who destroyed Gallifrey was a Time Lord?'

'No... How could it be?'

'So he must have stolen a TARDIS?'

'All the TARDISes would have been lost when Gallifrey was destroyed. They draw their power from Gallifrey itself.' But Marnal clearly wasn't comfortable.

'If they're time machines, could it be from a time before your planet was –'

Marnal gave her a withering look. 'Time travel occurs in relative dimensions. Weren't you listening before? A TARDIS can travel into the past and future, but not its own past and future. That would be a theoretical absurdity.'

Rachel glowered at him, but he was completely oblivious.

'Would every single one of your people have been on the planet when it blew up?' she asked instead. 'We know the answer to that: you weren't. So there could have been others.'

Marnal wasn't happy with this line of inquiry. 'There were always renegades and exiles,' he said. 'Right from the earliest days. But not one of... them was capable of this. Not one of them would, well, would dare.'

'Perhaps the Doctor wanted revenge on the Time Lords.'

'Perhaps,' Marnal muttered. He turned to Rachel, looking at her properly for the first time since he'd changed his appearance. 'What did you just call him?'

'Forget it.'

'No. What did you just call him?'

'It's silly, OK? But he reminds me of someone I knew, once.'

Marnal was watching her.

'It's not him,' Rachel said, uncertainly. 'How could it be?'

'Where did you see this man?' he asked.

Rachel took a deep breath. She might as well say what had been on her mind.

'There was a girl in my class, back in primary school. We were both on the chess team. She was really clever – she moved away, down south and we lost touch. Anyway, I think that's her dad. It looks just like him. And her dad called himself "the Doctor".'

Marnal had returned to his book. 'Coincidence,' he said sharply.

'That's what I think. It's just... Well, he did have a police box in his garden.'

Marnal looked up.

'Give me the exact time and location,' he ordered, heading back over to the glass bottle.

Rachel swallowed. 'Well, I'll do my best.'

Interlude
The Girl Who Was Different

A snowy winter's night, in a back street on the edge of the Derbyshire village of Greyfrith.

A tall shape loomed up out of darkness – the helmeted figure of a policeman, trudging from his panda car. He moved along the little street to where it ended in a brick wall. He shone his torch onto the barrier. He paused for a moment, listening – there seemed to be some kind of electronic hum, like a generator. It was very faint. Perhaps he was imagining it.

Now, though, he definitely heard something behind him. He turned, and caught the young girl in the torch beam.

She was about ten years old, a very slight figure. She wore a woollen bobble hat, with red curls snaking out from underneath it, but other than that she was in her school uniform – a blouse and knee-length skirt. It was far too cold. And there were no houses around here, she must have walked a long way like that.

'Aren't you frozen?' he asked.

She didn't look it. Someone might have dropped her off here. But why?

The young girl smiled and said something, but so quietly he couldn't hear.

The policeman moved over to her. 'What's your name, miss?' he asked.

She indicated that she wanted to whisper it to him. She was half his height, so he had to bend down to her. As he did so, he gave her an encouraging smile.

'>:-(' she said, before lunging at him, grabbing his throat and crushing his Adam's apple under her thumbs.

The policeman made an attempt to get up, but she was a dead weight around his neck. He tried calling for help, but no sound came out. Now he tried to breathe, but he just couldn't suck air into his lungs – the grip around his throat was too tight. He felt himself weaken, saw everything going black. If he hadn't bent down, he realised, she wouldn't have been able to reach his neck. She was about ten years old.

He was dead before he hit the snow. The girl stood over the body, her Clarks sandal pressed down on his windpipe, for more than a minute just to make sure.

They'd gritted the paths around Greyfrith County Primary School, and that had taken all the fun away. Miranda had been hoping she could slide the length of the playground, but its surface was now a dull red-grey mush that was getting into her shoes.

Her friend Rachel was shivering. 'They should let us inside.'

'No one else looks that cold,' Miranda noted. She rarely felt cold herself, but the Doctor, her father, told her she should always be careful to wear a coat, to blend in.

The Doctor had been her father for almost a year. It was the second time she'd been adopted. Her original adoptive parents had been killed in a car accident. She wanted to stay with the Doctor, and the Doctor was keen for her to do so. Even with the backing of her teacher, Mrs Castle, and a number of character references from some of the people the Doctor had met over the years, like Graham Greene and Laurence Olivier, it had taken a long time to become official.

But Miranda always thought of the Doctor as her father.

Like her, he had two hearts. Like her, he would often stare up at the night sky, and feel some strange sense that up there was home and living down here was just a temporary thing.

'What are they playing at?' Rachel asked.

She meant the question literally. Two of the boys, Adrian and

Chris, sat next to each other on a step, each with some sort of electronic device in their hands.

Miranda went up to them, but they didn't even look up. They were staring intently into the little screens, their thumbs working away at the buttons beneath. Every so often there would be a furtive bleep or buzz. The boys seemed totally absorbed. Their conversation rarely sparkled, but it was usually better than this.

Miranda bent over to get a better look, but all she could see was a set of seemingly random letters, numbers and other symbols. It was like a code of some kind.

'What are those?' she asked.

Adrian looked up, as if it was the first time he'd registered she was there. 'They're giving them out,' he said.

'But what are they?'

'They're giving them out,' Chris echoed. He'd always been one to follow his friend's lead.

It looked like a walkie-talkie, or a toy telephone.

'Can I have a look?'

'Get your own,' Adrian said.

Chris just glared at her. Miranda stepped back.

'Where from?'

'New girl.' He pointed to a small redhead in a bobble hat. There were a handful of kids around her, and she had a black bag on her shoulder that was almost the size she was.

'What's her name?' Rachel asked, but the boys were absorbed in the latest craze.

By the end of the day, every kid in the school had one of the electronic devices, and every one of them had ended up as antisocial as Adrian and Chris. During classes no one played with their devices, but it was eerily quiet. You could sense the phones there, nested in everyone's schoolbags, waiting for the next break.

As soon as she got home Miranda took hers straight to her father.

He was in his study, filling in forms. He smiled, glad to be able to finish them.

'What have you got there?'

'The latest craze. It's a portable telephone, but it does other stuff.'

He picked it up and weighed it. 'This is a telephone?' He seemed surprised.

He put it next to his own mobile phone, which was about four times its size and weight. It was only now that the two phones were side by side that Miranda realised just how weird hers looked. It was all liquid curves, with a strange pearl-like sheen to its silver casing. The controls were dotted around, not laid out in neat rows. It didn't have an aerial, let alone one you had to pull out.

The Doctor picked up the new phone and turned it over in his hand. 'I don't see how you get into it,' he told her.

'It recharges and repairs itself,' she told him. 'A few people dropped theirs, and they just... fixed. You can throw them against walls and run them over with cars and they're fine.'

The Doctor looked impressed, then worried. 'Where did you get this?' he asked.

'They were just handing them out.'

He frowned. 'This is worth hundreds of pounds. Who was handing them out?'

'A girl. She's quiet, but someone else said her dad's just taken over an electronics factory.'

'Provider Electronics? On the Buxton Road?'

'That's right. Was I right to take one?'

The Doctor tapped his lip thoughtfully. 'As I said to King Priam, you should beware of geeks bearing gifts. If only he'd listened. Of course, I also told him not to look a gift horse in the mouth...'

'Dad...' Miranda said impatiently.

'Did this come with a box or instructions?'

'No. It's meant to be easy to use. I can't get it to work, though.'

'You can't?' He pressed a button. 'That turns it on, and –'

'I know that. But –'

'And I place it to my ear and... Oh, it's gone dead.'

'That's what I'm saying.'

The Doctor tried again. 'Perhaps I'm pressing the off button with my ear,' he suggested. A third attempt yielded the same result. He laid it down on his desk and looked at it for a moment. 'This was free?' he asked.

'Yes,' Miranda told him again.

The Doctor picked up a metal paperweight and smashed it against the telephone, neatly breaking open the casing.

'Dad!' Miranda cried out.

'Merely the first part of my careful scientific investigation,' he assured her.

He peered down into the mass of circuits and wires. Something caught his eye. He reached into the jumble with a pair of tweezers.

It was a glowing blue wire, and it wriggled in the grip of the tweezers like a worm.

'It's alive?' Miranda asked.

'No... I don't think so. But it's not a product of human technology, either.'

The Doctor dropped the 'worm' back into the mass of circuits. As he and Miranda watched, wires in the two halves of the telephone started twitching, reaching out for each other. A couple managed to grope blindly across the divide. They latched on to other wires, and started to pull together. Two minutes later, and the phone was back in one piece, and on standby.

'I think I'll pay that factory on Buxton Road a visit,' the Doctor said, quietly.

'I'm coming with you.'

The Doctor hesitated, then nodded.

They had parked close to the factory, then walked the rest of the way. It was in the little industrial estate right at the edge of town and was an old mill building with a slate roof. There was a ten-foot wall all the way around it. Flecks of soot and dirt had washed into the brown stone over the years.

'I'm amazed no one's noticed that,' the Doctor said, waving his hand towards the factory.

It was dark, but Miranda could see what her father was pointing at: a radio mast, taller than a tree, gleaming silver. It ended in three prongs, making it look like a gigantic trident planted in the ground.

'Can you hear something?' the Doctor asked.

Miranda could, right on the edge of her hearing, like the sound when you first turn a television on or blow on a dog whistle. This wasn't a continuous tone, more a series of bleeps and blips.

'Is it Morse code?'

The Doctor concentrated for a couple of seconds. 'No,' he concluded. 'It's a regular pattern, though. We need to get in there.'

The Doctor and Miranda walked all the way round the building, but there wasn't a gate.

'Perhaps we missed a bit,' Miranda said, but the Doctor pointed to their tracks in the snow.

He was examining the wall. Miranda turned her attention to the ground. The Doctor's Trabant wasn't the only thing that had left tracks in the snow. There was a set of footprints that came up from the main road, and led off to the left.

'Dad, look at the snow.'

'Not really the best time for that, Mir,' he called back.

Miranda pulled a face at him, and followed the trail. There were several sets of prints, all converging at the same point on the wall. It wasn't a gate, though – it just looked like bricks. A big lump of snow had drifted up nearby, as though it was covering something. Miranda stepped towards it.

A hand grabbed her shoulder.

It was the Doctor.

'No,' he said.

'OK,' she replied. 'Do you see the prints?'

They led right up to the wall. The Doctor bent over to take a closer look at them. 'Small shoes. More your size than mine. Boys and girls.'

He placed his hand on the wall, but it was solid.

'There's a hidden door. How did they open it? Oh, of course.'

He took the phone from his pocket and waved it towards the wall. There was clicking sound, then the wall swirled away like water down a plughole.

'Phased molecules,' the Doctor said knowledgeably.

He stepped through. The wall swirled back up into place behind him.

'Dad!' Miranda shouted.

'I can't get it to open again,' he told her, glad she was on the other side. 'Go back to the car.'

Miranda, sulkily, agreed. She was sitting back in the passenger seat before she realised he could have thrown the phone over the wall to her, and by then she knew it would be too late to go back and get him.

The Doctor made a beeline for the radio mast. It must have been a hundred feet tall. It would be able to broadcast over a wide area – hundreds of square miles, at a guess. He'd never seen an aerial with this exact configuration before. There were plenty of footprints in the snow, leading to a small building at the base of the mast.

Before going to the mast, he took a peek through a window in one of the main factory buildings, where a light was on. Sitting at a wide workbench were a dozen boys, all working to construct telephone handsets with blank-faced determination. They made a miniature production line, nimbly taking a component from the tray in front of them, fitting it into place, then passing it to the boy on their right. The last boy dropped the handsets into a large black bag, overseen by a small red-haired girl. It all happened in perfect unison. None of them was speaking.

The Doctor took a closer look at the girl. Her telephone was clamped to her ear. Now, he saw that all the boys had handsets over their right ears, as if they were glued there.

He tapped at the window. As he suspected, not one of the children even looked up.

He made his way round to the smaller building at the base of the radio mast, keeping in the shadows. It was a more recent structure, like a Portakabin, constructed from the same metal as the mast. There were no windows, but there was a door that opened when the Doctor tried it.

He found a single room, lined with computer banks. Three girls around Miranda's age sat at control stations, all of them staring at screens. They didn't react to the Doctor's arrival. They sat playing with their phones; thumbs hooked around them, pressing the buttons almost instinctively. As the Doctor watched he could see that they were compiling machine codes. Endless lines of letters and numbers were being displayed on the screens in front of them. He recognised one of the girls as Rachel Rowley, a classmate of Miranda's. Then the monitors cleared, and a new message flashed up.

UPLINK READY

'XLNT:-)' the girls said with one voice, sounding disconcertingly like a church congregation.

The Doctor pushed one of them out of the way to get a better look at the screen.

CONNECTING

'W8! Who R U? >:-('

The Doctor looked around curiously. The girls' voice had no trace of puberty, but it did have a slight electronic warble. It reminded the Doctor of a couple of the seances he'd attended in the 1920s – the girls were possessed. But what was doing this?

'I am the Doctor,' he told the girls gently.

'Dr? Dr ??' came the confused reply.

'Indeed.'

The Doctor hesitated. He decided to pick on the girl he recognised. 'And you're Rachel, aren't you?'

'nt rachL n e more we r d Netwk'

'The Network?' the Doctor echoed. He thought for a moment, then snapped his fingers. 'Intelligent software that runs on a human brain instead of a computer. Self-replicating telecommunications technology. It was only a matter of time.'

'u knO of us'

'Not specifically. But already the telephone network of this planet has as many individual connections as there are neurons in the human brain. It's only one step from that to behaving like a brain.'

'Y D age of orgnic lfe is over 2moro b lgs 2 us :-)'

'But you're not of this Earth, R U? I mean... Are you?'

'N. We hve Xisted 4x10(2d8) yrs. Netwk Coverage will b universal.'

'Broadcast from one planet to another, spreading out in irresistible wavefronts at the speed of light, picked up by any planet with sufficiently advanced technology. Ingenious.'

The Doctor moved around the control stations, trying to work it out.

'So those are the ends, but what are the means?'

He glanced at the cables. There was the mast outside. Why children? Every screen was flashing the same message:

CONNECTING

'You're just the advance party, though, aren't you? You're going to try to receive a signal from space. Then what?'

'N1 cn stop us not evn U Dr :-)'

'You're probably right. So if you'd just explain your plan to me, omitting no detail?'

'N'

'Hmmm... Are you sure?'

'Y'

'Fair enough. No harm in asking. Saves a bit of time, that's all. Right, I'll have to work it out for myself.'

An instrument was confusing him. A Geiger counter. The Doctor recoiled.

'Children's brains are more susceptible to radiation than adult brains. Mind control via radiation emissions. Total mental domination of the human population.'

'UR > clver thn U : dr'

51

'Do you mind if I…?'

The Doctor grabbed Rachel, pushed her off her chair, took her place, snatched the phone from her and started working at the controls.

Rachel picked herself up, grabbed the Doctor's wrist and squeezed so hard he had to let the phone go. He tried to pull away, pushing his wrists down between her thumb and fingers, the weakest point of any grip. But he could barely move his hand.

'And you are stronger than you look,' the Doctor noted ruefully.

She threw him across the room.

'Limin8 d dr :-)'

W8!!

The great booming voice seemed to come from high above them. The Doctor looked around, trying to identify the exact source.

'Y Gr8 Provider?' the three girls chorused, without looking up from their phones.

d Dr s kwn 2 me of old. We hve f0 aX time & spce. He has of10 cut us off :-)

'You know me?' the Doctor asked.

Y

'And you call yourself the Great Provider?'

Y

'I don't remember you, I'm afraid.'

d dr hs gr8 knwledge. We s%d + his memries 2 our d8abase.

'Oh, I don't really have memories. I've misplaced them somewhere. A long story, at least I assume it is. How can I explain this to you? Well, I suppose you could say that my memory tapes have been wiped.'

d dr tries 2 DCve us. Attach d h&s free headset.

'If d dr tries 2 resist :-(?'

normal terms & conditions apply.

The Doctor tried to stand up, but two of the girls put their hands on his shoulders and forced him back down.

The third girl was bringing over a pair of chunky silver headphones. She clamped them over the Doctor's ears. He could hear a screech, then a high-pitched burble. A string of digital information, he realised.

'Calling,' the Doctor said. 'Connecting…'

He could feel a new presence. It was as though his brain had swallowed iced water and he could feel it working its way around. A mind of extraordinary clarity that divided the universe into binary states. Yes or no, to every question. Quite unlike an organic mind.

The intruder vanished from his brain.

The Doctor grinned.

WS!

'What's the problem, O Great Provider?'

Now it was the Doctor's turn. His mind surged down the headset, into the computers then out to the boys' and girls' handsets. As he ran through the electric labyrinth of the printed circuits, he carefully shut down the Great Provider's mind, dismantling and deleting it. The Provider had run a simple set of instructions to each of the children. The Doctor undid every one of them, line by line.

CONNECTION FAILING. SIGNAL LOST. NO CARRIER.

'Don't call us, we'll call you,' the Doctor shouted up at the ceiling.

The girls had collapsed on the floor, their phones melting as though they'd been dipped in acid. He'd have to call the police and get their parents to take them home. The computers were sparking and fizzing, their tapes unspooling and fraying. The mast was silent.

The Doctor headed out, back to Miranda and the car. She was waiting for him at a new gap in the wall. She ran over to hug him.

Behind them, the mast disintegrated in a mass of blue sparks.

'What did you do?' Miranda asked.

'The person behind this wanted the contents of my brain. But my mind is… Well, let's just say there's more to it than meets the eye.'

'He's gone?'

'Oh, he won't be in any position to bother Earth again for decades.'

The Doctor and Miranda drove away, ready for their next adventure.

Chapter Three
The Time Trap

Rachel swallowed. It was very strange seeing herself as an eleven-year-old. These days a lot of new parents bought camcorders, so many people would end up with such a window on their past, episodes of their lives recorded as though they were characters in a soap opera, but they'd know they were being watched.

She'd always wondered why she'd been wary of getting a mobile phone.

'That was the man we saw,' Marnal confirmed.

'Do you know he's a Time Lord?'

'Yes. He had two hearts. So... he calls himself the Doctor?'

'Do you know him?'

Marnal shook his head. 'There was no reason to think I would know him personally. So, he had a daughter. And he seemed to be trapped on Earth at the time. No TARDIS? And he said something about not having all his memories. Interesting. I will have to do more research.'

'Could you look at anything using that bottle universe?' Rachel asked.   Everyone had things they didn't want other people to see. For that matter, everyone had plenty of things they didn't want reminding about.

'Anything,' Marnal said, busy scribbling in a notebook. 'Now I have his trail, I should be able to follow his entire time-stream.'

'It would change the world,' Rachel said. 'To see the past like that. Instead of trying someone in a court you could just play the tape.'

'It doesn't just view the past,' Marnal said offhandedly, 'it shows the present and future too. It's all relative.'

'The future?' she said. She was getting that twitch in her leg that she got when she was really scared. 'I could see my future?'

Marnal turned the notebook over. He'd filled the second half of it with impenetrable equations. 'It's a little more complicated than that. You have free will. If you could see your own future, you could alter it.'

Rachel nodded, a little relieved. 'If I knew I was going to be run over by a bus when I was still a young woman, I could avoid buses for a few years.'

'You could certainly try,' Marnal agreed.

'This... thing,' she said, waving her hand over the bottle universe. 'It's like magic. Cold fusion and going to other planets? We've at least heard about those. We can't do them yet, but it can't be much longer before we work out how. But... this?'

Marnal gave her a condescending smile. 'Your race hasn't even reached Type 1 on the Kardashev scale. It doesn't control the resources of this one planet, let alone a solar system or a galaxy. The Time Lords were the Type 4 civilisation. We had no equals. We controlled the fundamental forces of the entire universe. Nothing could communicate with us on our level. Most races pray to lesser beings than the Time Lords.'

'Yet my planet is still here, and yours isn't,' Rachel said.

Marnal's face seemed to grow dark. 'Indeed.'

'And you really think the Doctor did it?'

'I know it.'

'But he was helping mankind there. Without him, the Network would have conquered the Earth.'

'He was interfering, don't you see that? Breaking the most sacred law of the Time Lords.'

'He saved lives. Including my life.' She hesitated. 'And yours, for that matter. You were on Earth then too.'

'Who is to say the Network shouldn't have conquered this planet? What gives the Doctor the right to pick a side and fight for them?'

'Those aliens would have killed us.'

'No. They wanted you alive. They'd have made you smarter and stronger. United your species, given them a great purpose, made you part of a vast and ancient civilisation.'

Rachel considered this, then said, 'He saved my planet.'

'And destroyed his own.'

'We don't know that for certain.'

'We know it. We just don't know the exact circumstances. What I'm interested in is that if the Doctor was telling the Provider the truth, and he really has amnesia, he himself may not know the reasons why he did it himself.'

'Well,' said Rachel, thinking aloud, 'who's to say that the Doctor shouldn't have destroyed Gallifrey? Perhaps he picked the right side and it was meant to be.'

Marnal was clearly angry at the thought. 'No.'

'How can you know?'

'I know. I know what was meant to happen. It wasn't that. With that one act, the Doctor has done untold damage to history.'

Rachel looked over at the bottle universe. 'And now you've picked up his trail again.'

'I can track him, yes. I will use this device to find out what I can about him. He's the enemy, Rachel. We must know our enemy.' Marnal hesitated, then smiled. 'It seems we may be able to know him better than he knows himself.'

'God, I hate Mars,' Fitz said, not for the first time. 'This is even worse than the last time I was here, when Anji –'

'As I said to Dr Johnson, "When one is tired of Mars, one is tired of life",' the Doctor retorted.

'Yeah, shut up, Fitz. This is brilliant!'

Trix was bouncing along in the light gravity. Her catsuit looked great on her. Emma Peel in sequins. Electric-blue wig and lipstick matching her eyes. Exactly the way a bird from the twenty-first century like Trix should dress, in Fitz's book.

It wasn't, on the other hand, a look that suited Fitz at all.

'It's 2097, Fitz. When in Rome...'

'When we were in Rome, Doctor, you wore a toga. Here, though, I notice you've opted for the old frock coat and poncey shirt ensemble. Your normal clothes.'

'What of it?'

'Well, I can't help but notice that you're the only one of us not wearing moon boots and false eyelashes.'

'You look very fetching, Fitz,' Trix assured him. 'In fact, I really want to take a photo of you.'

She waved the 3-D camera she'd just bought at him.

'Get lost.'

It was the middle of the day, but it was about as warm as a winter's afternoon. The sky was dusty pink. The Doctor stopped in his tracks.

'You'll be inside the dome but I need to be out here. So I need to dress up warm, and you need to dress formally. We know there's going to be an assassination attempt on the pope, but we don't know where, or how.'

'That's another thing. It's always that lot these days, every second time we land somewhere. They're always doing the same sort of thing, and you always beat them.'

'Practice makes perfect.'

'Yeah, but it's boring. Who'd want to fight them when we could be taking part in a yacht race across the whole world of Selonart or seeing an astral flower bloom? What about when we fought crystal skeletons across time and space, defeating them at the end of the universe? I'd watch a movie of that, I'd even read a book about it.'

The Doctor had a serious expression. 'This is a crucial point in Earth's relations with alien species. The very first papal visit to Mars. The pope is going to consecrate the first cathedral here, and anoint the first native Martian archbishops, and if she's ext –'

The Doctor whirled round. 'I think I heard something. Hang on a second.'

He disappeared over a nearby ridge, but was back within a minute.

'There's only about six hundred of them. You two, get back inside. You know the plan?'

'Yes,' they both chorused.

The Doctor had already hurried away, and the shooting had started

'"When you're tired of Mars, you're tired of life",' Trix reminded Fitz.

'Perhaps I am.'

'Tired of life?' she looked suddenly, gratifyingly, concerned.

A flying disc screamed overhead, its pilot on fire.

'No. Not life. This life. My life.'

'You're ready to settle down, you mean?' Trix's laugh almost drowned out the sound of the explosion.

'Why not? The two of us.'

She stopped in her tracks. 'Fitz...'

The ground shook like an earthquake, breaking an awkward silence.

'I don't mean straight away.'

She looked at him. 'When do you mean, then?'

He had meant straight away, but even as he'd spoken he'd realised it was too much. 'Next time we're on Earth.'

'You think that next time we're back on Earth, we should... what?'

A great patch of the night's sky was white, the stars points of black, for a second.

'I don't know,' Fitz admitted. 'We should be normal for a bit. Together. Make a go of it.'

Trix giggled. 'Settle down on Earth?'

'Earth in the twentieth century,' Fitz clarified. 'I'm not getting stuck in the olden days, or after they drop the Bomb or whatever.'

They laughed.

There was a grating metallic scream, loud but a long way off.

'Early twenty-first. That's where I've got my credit cards.'

'Either way, it's got to be England.'

Bits of metal started raining down.

59

'The United Kingdom,' Trix said, stepping aside to avoid a falling hemisphere of bonded polycarbide the size of a car.

'It won't happen,' Fitz said. 'We'll spend our whole time in alien galaxies or in the far future.'

They grinned at each other. In the distance, there was a low rumbling explosion.

'Did that sound like a flying saucer kerploding to you?' Fitz asked.

Trix checked her watch. 'Four minutes. I think that's a new record.'

'Have you found him again?' Rachel asked. She'd brought Marnal his first coffee of the morning.

A month had passed since she'd seen the old Marnal die and the young one take his place. The agency was still paying her to look after him, and it wasn't as though she had anything better to go to. So she came round every day, still in her carer's uniform, to make sure he was all right. He seemed grateful for the company, in his way, especially after she managed to fob off his relatives. His family weren't interested in Marnal, they were interested in his money, and when she'd told them he'd recovered and looked better they stayed away. Which was probably just as well.

Marnal had spent the last month piecing together episodes in the Doctor's life, using the universe in a bottle. Rachel had seen some of this – the Doctor speeding around San Francisco on a motorbike, confronting a bulky reptilian creature at the Tower of London, attending an arms bazaar on the moon, punting down the Cam. Marnal had documented hundreds of landings. The Doctor's was a long life, and he was trying to review everything he could.

At the moment, he was poised over his bottle universe, peering into it. The Doctor was looking up at a flying saucer exploding over a red desert, an expression of quiet satisfaction on his face. Marnal had scribbled notes on pad after pad of paper. He'd asked Rachel to stop off at Smith's on her way over to him to pick up some more, but Rachel had forgotten. He still had a few spare sheets.

One of the ones he was working on caught her eye.

'What's this list?' She read from part of it. '"Lorenzo, Delilah, Frank, Claudia, Deborah, Jemima-Katy, Miranda, Nina, Anji, Beatrice".'

'His companions, in the order he first met them.'

'A lot of people.'

'Indeed. He's dragged them all into his criminal lifestyle. It should be possible to trace at least some of these people.'

'Using that device?'

'No, the telephone directory. All of these people are from Earth, from this time zone, give or take. Now look at that,' he said, holding up one of the sheets of paper and pointing at what looked for all the world like a scribble. 'That's the course of his travels. There's also a list of all the planets he's visited. I tried to put them all in chronological order, but it's impossible.'

Rachel looked for patterns. Marnal had carefully marked points on the line with numbers. He sipped at his coffee as she studied it.

'There's a long straight line here,' she ventured.

'After he destroyed Gallifrey, he hid out on Earth for over a hundred years. That was when he started to claim his memory had been erased. It was during that period that the incident with the Provider happened.'

'What's this gap just before that?'

'There's a discontinuity. A piece missing. Right at the moment Gallifrey was destroyed. Three minutes seven seconds' duration. It's like an area of space-time has been boxed off.'

'Because of the temporal warp... factor thing?'

'The violence of the destruction of Gallifrey, yes. It must be. Look at the rest of the Doctor's time-stream, though. It's meant to be a neat line. The entire history of this incarnation is one of temporal orbits, retcons, paradoxes, parallel time lines, reiterations and divergences. How anyone can make head or tail out of all this chaos, I don't know.'

Rachel certainly couldn't, not from this.

'As for his future… he has three ninth incarnations. I've never seen anything like it.'

Marnal was rubbing his eyes.

'Have you slept?' she asked. 'I mean… do you even sleep?'

'So much to know,' Marnal said. 'So many facts to keep straight.'

'You're a writer,' she reminded him. 'I know your novels were all based on reality –'

'They were reality,' he snapped. 'They were perfect unless some damnfool editor got his pen to them and –'

'Yeah. OK. But you're thinking about it like, I don't know, a novel. A biography. At the moment, you're writing a biography. What you want is something more like a clinical assessment. You don't really care about where he's been, and who he met. It's now that you're interested in. You want to understand how his mind works, you want to know who he is, and why he did what he did.'

Marnal looked at her for a moment.

'Obviously,' she continued, 'his past and his background and all that are factors in making him who he is. But you're getting obsessed with history. If you want to know your enemy, you don't worry about what presents he got for his tenth birthday, or what he had for breakfast three weeks ago. You want to know how he'll act. He has things he values, he has strategies for achieving goals, he has strengths and weaknesses. A psychology. You're asking "Doctor what?" when you should be asking "Doctor who?" Does that make sense?'

Marnal nodded. 'Yes. There is a certain pattern to his behaviour.'

'There is for everyone. It's psychology.'

'You've studied this discipline?'

'Well, a bit, yes, as part of my nursing. I don't have a degree in it.'

For the first time, Marnal looked interested in hearing from her.

It was dark and raining.

Fitz stepped out of the TARDIS and splashed mud over his shoes and trousers.

'Where are we now?'

'The TARDIS detected a complex shape here.'

'A shape?'

'One end of a five-dimensional object, according to the instruments. A vastly long, very narrow tube, sculpted from history. Some kind of wormhole.'

'Uh-huh.' That didn't sound very interesting. Not worth, as the expression went, getting out of bed for. Fitz glanced over at Trix, who was looking around and trying to get used to the dark.

'What's causing it?' she asked.

The Doctor had some sort of Geiger counter-type thing in his hand and was half-heartedly waving it around. 'The signal's not very strong, but there's a huge amount of disruption in hyperspace and I don't really understand why. It may be evidence of another time-traveller. On the other hand, there's always a chance it could have been an echo, or some fleeting piece of rogue energy. Or... er... well, it might be caused by us travelling here to investigate the phenomenon.'

'We could be chasing our own tails?'

'Yes.' The Doctor at least had the decency to sound embarrassed.

'Terrific,' Fitz said. 'Where are we?'

'One of the London churchyards, I think,' the Doctor said, making a show of sniffing the air. '2005 by the smell of it.'

Fitz and Trix glanced at each other.

The Doctor was checking the device in his hand. 'There's definitely something. It seems to be stronger facing north. I'll head up this way and try to triangulate the signal.'

He strode off, oblivious to the rain.

'England in the twenty-first century,' Trix said quietly.

'We didn't, y'know, mean it,' Fitz said. 'What we said on Mars.'

'It was a figure of speech,' Trix agreed.

'I mean, I do like you, but...'

'And I like you. But we don't really even know each other.'

'I mean, we're kind of living together already, in the TARDIS. And that's working. Don't get me wrong, but if we go too fast, then –'

63

'It's OK, Fitz. I agree.' Trix hesitated. 'We're living together. I hadn't really thought of it like that.'

The rain pelted against the side of the TARDIS.

'We should go and find the Doctor,' Fitz said.

Trix agreed, and they headed off.

They found the Doctor propped up against a tree, adjusting the detector.

He angled it one way, then another. Finally, he walked off. Fitz and Trix followed. It had stopped raining, but it was still muddy. Fitz wasn't enjoying himself.

'Yes. Here we are,' the Doctor announced.

There was a tiny plastic ball, faint blue light pulsing from inside it, nestled at the base of a gravestone. The Doctor knelt down and picked it up.

'The signal is coming from this,' he told them. He scrutinised it carefully. It was about the size of a marble.

'Any idea what it is?' Trix asked.

The Doctor shrugged. 'Nor who put it here.'

Fitz was more interested in the gravestone itself. A recent one. Trix read the inscription.

SAMANTHA LYNN JONES

1980–2002

'She was young,' Trix said.

'Younger when we knew her,' Fitz said softly.

Trix looked over to the Doctor for confirmation. 'You knew her?'

The Doctor looked impassive. 'I don't remember.'

Fitz looked up from the gravestone. 'Drop the act.'

'Pardon?' The Doctor was taken aback.

'It's Sam.'

'Fitz, I don't –'

'The three of us spent years together. You'd been travelling with her for years before you met me. She grew up travelling with you.'

'You know I don't –'

'Oh, I know all right,' Fitz spat. 'You don't remember anyone or anything, except when you do, of course. You can't operate the TARDIS any more, except when you can. You don't know what happens in the future, except when you do. Drop the act, it got old years ago.'

The Doctor was still smiling, but there was a flicker of uncertainty there. The hint of a facade. 'Fitz, whatever terrible thing happened, it happened to you. Your memories went too.'

Fitz gathered his thoughts before replying. 'Not straight away. They faded. We were going to talk, we were going to have a conversation, and when the time came, you said "No".'

'I wasn't ready.'

It was a quiet night. The only sound was a lorry in the distance, reversing. It had gone before Fitz spoke again.

'If I woke up without my memories I'd be keen to get them back. Wouldn't you, Trix?'

'You leave me out of this.'

'No. Wouldn't you say the Doctor exhibited curiosity?'

'Fitz...' the Doctor warned.

'You've just chased a flashing plastic ball halfway across the solar system, but for years now you haven't shown the slightest desire to find out who you are, where you're from, if there are others like you and where they all are. Isn't that ever so slightly odd? Isn't it remarkably like there's something you have to face up to, but you daren't do it? Two hearts and no balls, is that it?'

'That isn't it,' the Doctor said.

'No? What is it, then?'

Trix grabbed Fitz's arm. 'You're upset.'

The Doctor had taken a step back. He still had the signalling device in his hand. He was finding it hard to look in Fitz's direction.

'The TARDIS laboratory has equipment that will be able to analyse this and...'

He didn't finish the sentence. Instead he turned round and headed back to the ship.

Fitz sat for a moment, not saying anything.

'Sam was a schoolgirl when they met,' he said, finally.

'He wouldn't put a kid in danger, would he?' Trix asked.

'He puts us in danger.'

'We're old enough to understand the risks, though.'

'I was thinking about this the other day. He can go into the future, he knows everything about it when he gets there. So who's to say he didn't know the exact date Sam died?'

Trix's mouth twitched. 'You've been to the future. As far as you're concerned, this is the future. So have you ever looked for your own death certificate or gravestone?'

'No, but...'

'Would you want to? Don't you feel just a little uncomfortable knowing the things you do about the future already? It's weird, but you get used to it. We all die, Fitz. It would be a bit depressing to –'

'Sam was so young when she died, Trix.'

'She'd left the Doctor. However short her life was, think of all the places she went and people she met. We do more in a week than most people do in a lifetime.'

'Think, Fitz, that she'll reappear in the future, as part of our travels. She wasn't confined between 1980 and 2002, whatever that gravestone says,' the Doctor agreed.

The Doctor's words hung in the night air for a moment. Neither Trix nor Fitz were sure when he'd returned, or what he'd heard.

'I thought you were going back to the TARDIS,' Fitz said.

'Um, I was. It's just that it seems to have gone.'

Matrix projection, extrapolated from current time line. History has been altered following the destruction of the cicatrix. In the first draft, the creatures evolved to became an advanced, benevolent race. In the redraft, the creatures have scattered, and migrated. They have swarmed across and occupied much of the galaxy, evolving along aggressive lines. First draft, they were not a threat to Gallifrey. Now the Matrix projects a final stand between the Time Lords and these creatures. Time Lord fatalities were 20 to 40 per cent of the total population. This is a possible Last Contact.

Matrix Projection
date index 309456/4756.7RE/1213GRT/100447TL

Chapter Four
Acquisitions

The lorry, Trix realised.

They'd heard it while they'd been over by Sam's gravestone, and she knew now that they'd walked straight into a heist. Someone had lured the TARDIS here, then led its crew just far enough out of the way for it to be loaded on the back of a lorry and driven away.

There were tyre tracks in the mud, right next to the square imprint the TARDIS had left. No footprints. The lorry must be one with a hydraulic grabbing claw on it. It wouldn't make a very good getaway car, and it was probably still within a couple of miles of here. But it was dark, they didn't have any transport, and so the thieves might as well have beamed the TARDIS to Pluto.

The Doctor didn't seem unduly concerned. 'We'll find it,' he assured them.

Fitz and Trix exchanged glances.

'Like that?' Fitz asked.

'We've just walked into a trap,' Trix said.

'And we're still standing,' the Doctor pointed out.

'Aren't you worried?' Fitz asked, speaking for both himself and Trix.

'Whoever's taken the TARDIS can't get inside. We'll find it.'

'You hope.'

'What do we do now?' Trix asked.

'We find somewhere to sit down, I think.'

* * *

The warning siren of the lorry as it reversed into Marnal's garage would wake up all the neighbours, Rachel was sure of it.

Marnal had never learnt how to drive, so she'd been behind the wheel of the lorry. Rachel imagined it counted as a heavy goods vehicle, meaning she didn't have a licence to drive it, and she knew for a fact that she hadn't been insured. Marnal had spent the entire return journey glancing back at the police box they'd stolen, and was practically salivating.

Now they were home he was straight out of the cabin and on to the back of the lorry. When Rachel caught up with him he was running his hand down the front door of the police box. He tried the handle, but it wouldn't budge. The lock looked like a Yale, but Rachel guessed it was going to be a lot less straightforward than that.

'Why did we leave the Doctor there?' she asked.

'This is his time machine, we –'

'I know what this is. But the Doctor was right there.'

'With his companions. Three against two. Our opponents are a team, one used to conflict. If we had confronted them they would have beaten us. Without his TARDIS, the Doctor can't get far.'

'I suppose,' Rachel conceded. They'd spent two weeks coming up with this strategy, talking it through, checking the Doctor's previous behaviour to see what he would do.

'My plan worked. We didn't just take his TARDIS…'

'… We drove a wedge between the Doctor and his companions in the process.'

'It's difficult to keep track of how many birds we killed with one stone,' Marnal said gleefully.

'The Doctor is still dangerous.'

Marnal wasn't listening, though. He held his hand flat against one of the wood panels of the police box. 'Hello, old girl,' he said.

Rachel must have had a scathing look on her face.

'Try it,' he suggested.

Rachel did, placing a hand on the door. It wasn't humming like a boiler or a computer. It felt more as though she was stroking a cat. 'It's alive!'

'Yes.'

She looked up at it. 'It's locked?'

'I can get in,' Marnal assured her. 'I have the key.'

'What about the Doctor?'

'What about him? There's no way he can find us here.'

'Well, actually, we've got two ways,' the Doctor replied. 'First, we have this little device.'

He put the glowing plastic ball down on the melamine counter in a little café they'd found.

'We can't analyse it without the TARDIS lab,' Trix pointed out.

'Well, which leads me to the second clue.'

'The lorry,' she said.

'Indeed. Now, unless we've made enemies of a bunch of builders, whoever stole the TARDIS must have hired the lorry.'

'Or bought it.'

'Possibly. But the key thing is that it was acquired recently – the tracks it left looked as though the tyres were very fresh. It's a specialist piece of equipment.'

'Not that specialist.'

'No, but there can only be a finite number of places where they could have got one.'

Trix didn't think it would be easy. Finite encompassed a lot of numbers, and if she was doing anything like stealing the TARDIS she'd have paid a little extra to buy some silence.

'They knew who we were,' Fitz said gloomily. These were his first words for a while.

'An old enemy out for revenge?' Trix wondered.

'Who knew Sam,' the Doctor added. 'I'm not so sure. It's not as though there's a shortage of candidates, it's just… Well, the chief suspects must be the two people I saw in the control room a couple of days ago. Do you remember, Fitz?'

Fitz shrugged. 'Look. I need a cigarette. I'm going outside.'

He patted Trix on the shoulder, but it was clear he didn't want her following him.

'Two people in the control room?' Trix asked.

'A man and a woman. I didn't think I recognised either of them, but I may be wrong. There was something familiar about both of them, and that's nagging away at me a little.'

'Is Fitz all right?' Trix asked.

The Doctor looked up from the plastic ball. 'Oh yes. He's upset about Sam.'

'And you're not?'

'I don't remember her. She was young, and clearly she travelled with me, so... yes, I feel something.'

Trix had a sudden image of a tall, middle-aged woman with blonde hair standing alone in a space station at the end of time. It had happened a few months ago. They'd watched her die. Just one of many deaths they had seen, but this had been someone special. 'Miranda,' she said.

The Doctor looked up.

'You didn't mourn her after she died, either. You hardly reacted at all when she was killed right in front of your eyes. She was your daughter, Doctor. Not that you ever talked about her, let alone went to visit her. When we got back to the TARDIS, when you had some time on your own, did you cry for her then?'

The Doctor shook his head. 'The two of us spoke beforehand. Afterwards, I stayed in my room and thought about our time together, and that I was now a grandfather. I didn't cry.'

'And... do you think that's right?'

'I can't afford to dwell on my past.'

'You're avoiding something nasty. Something you know you shouldn't have done.'

The Doctor looked her right in the eye. 'Takes one to know one, Patricia.'

Trix turned away.

'Do *you* think Fitz is all right?' the Doctor asked.

Trix looked at him and considered the question for a moment. 'I don't know,' she admitted.

The Doctor nodded. He scooped up the plastic ball and slipped it into his coat pocket. 'He's upset with me, but not with you. See what you can do to cheer him up.'

'So how are we going to find this lorry?'

'Well,' the Doctor said a little sheepishly, 'I thought we might call the police.'

They'd unloaded the police box, and then Rachel had returned the lorry to the plant-hire yard. There had been a token argument about small scratches and repayment of the deposit, but she'd got her money. Then she'd caught the bus back to Marnal's house.

Marnal had spent the time in one of the upstairs rooms, looking for a key. He'd found it just a minute before she returned. Now, with Rachel at his side, he was back in the garage ready to open the police box.

'It looks like an ordinary key,' she told him.

'The Doctor and I look like ordinary human beings,' he replied.

'I've been meaning to ask why a time machine looks like a police box. I mean, what is a police box anyway?'

'We Time Lords are a cautious people, as a rule. This ship is camouflaged as an Earth object so that it doesn't draw attention to itself.'

'It's nine feet tall and bright blue, with a lamp on top of it.'

Without replying, Marnal slotted the key into the lock and twisted it. The thin door creaked open.

And, as never before, when Rachel stepped through the door it was like stepping into another world.

Inside the police box, which was just a few feet wide, was a space only a little smaller than Marnal's whole house.

Walls stretched out and away, then swept back round to mark out a hexagonal space. They were covered in shelves, instruments and alcoves, and were seemingly held up by iron pylons and what looked like stone buttresses. The ceiling arched up like a vault. The floor was covered with various rugs and carpets, and a few chairs and small tables were scattered around. Every surface was covered in piles of books, candlesticks, Tiffany lamps and other odds and ends. The overall effect was as if a Victorian steamship had crashed into a Gothic cathedral, and someone had opened an antiques shop there.

It wasn't that different from the clutter in Marnal's house. Presumably, immortals ended up with a lot of junk.

In the centre of the room, on a small dais, sat a control unit made from mahogany and wrought iron. A large column shot up from the centre of this, disappearing into the stonework of the ceiling.

There was a faint hum, coming from all around.

It was like that holiday in Italy, when she'd wandered into a small church. From the outside, it had been a fairly plain wall with a big wooden door. Inside, it was almost absurdly large and ornate. Mysteries hiding in niches and unexplored corners. Echoing footsteps and diffuse, weak lighting.

She felt nervous about touching anything here, and didn't feel that she understood it at all.

Marnal was perfectly at home. He strode up to the control console and circled around it. Rachel joined him, careful to stay out his way.

'Is it what you expected?'

Marnal nodded. 'He's redecorated, but everything I need seems to be here.'

'Um... Now what?'

Marnal was studying the instruments. He scowled, flicked a switch, then tried flicking it again. He pulled a couple of levers, checking a readout panel after each adjustment.

'Half the systems aren't working,' he said. 'Most of the other half don't seem to be turned on.'

He twisted a dial rather violently. Deep, deep beneath them the pitch of the hum changed slightly and the lights brightened a little.

'I'm going to have to recalibrate a lot of this before I do much more. That's not difficult, but it might take a day or two. It isn't safe to fly until then.'

'I'll look around,' Rachel told him. He didn't acknowledge her; he was too busy tutting over the controls.

Rachel quickly found an alcove containing what looked for all the world like an MFI kitchen. She didn't touch anything. If an old man could be an immortal alien and a police box could be a time machine, then a fridge could be a nuclear reactor or something. The bookshelves in another area looked innocuous enough. She plucked a book at random. *Harry Potter and the Philosopher's Stone*. This was worth a bit of money if it was a first edition, which it was. She opened it to check for damage. The first page had been crossed out, and someone had scrawled 'No, no, no, no, it didn't happen like this at all' in red ink. Rachel sighed, and put the book back on the shelf with its nine sequels.

Marnal was heading out of the door.

'You're not leaving me in here?' Rachel asked.

'I need some of my books and notes,' he called back.

Rachel was alone in the time machine.

She went over to the console, both hands tucked behind her back – she wasn't going to risk pressing anything. There were hundreds of switches, levers, buttons and dials. Various displays too, from blinking lights to a small television screen. It was all brass and polished wood, almost self-consciously Jules Verne. The Doctor wore clothes from the same period too, she recalled. And Marnal had been here long enough to have met Verne. Either Victoriana had been the fashion on Gallifrey, or the two of them shared an affectation.

She paused. There was a handbrake, clearly labelled – in English – as a handbrake.

The only other thing she recognised was a display giving the time and location: Humanian Era, Earth, 6 June, 11:23:05, 2005. Each of the displays looked as though it could be adjusted. If she reached her hand out, just changed one setting, she could make it 2004 or 2006. She could go anywhere.

Her hand had snaked out and was heading for the console.

Rachel pulled herself away, then took a couple of steps back.

Marnal had returned with an armful of books and notebooks.

'You haven't touched anything, have you?' he asked.

Rachel shook her head.

Fitz was a fairly cosmopolitan bloke nowadays, he thought, equally at home in the muddiest huts of history or the soaring plastic towers of the future, but 1963 would always be the present. Some things about the twenty-first century baffled him. Take the advertising hoarding opposite the police station. Fitz couldn't even work out what it was for. Adverts were meant to tell you what they were advertising. 'Drink beer.' Not 'Here's a hummingbird wearing boxing gloves hovering over a volcano, you work it out'.

Trix had found him.

'Not staying in there?' he asked.

'The Doctor can deal with all the formalities. He's getting nowhere at the moment.'

Fitz nodded.

'So, what's up?'

He glanced down at his cigarette packet. 'Smoking kills, apparently. And there's a hummingbird over there who can stop me getting Spam all over my computer. Something of a specialist product, I'd have thought.'

'You don't know what spam is, do you?'

'It took me a while travelling with the Doctor before I got used to the idea that someone could own their own computer. It's not the meat stuff, I take it?'

'Spam spam spam spam,' she sang, not as helpfully as she clearly thought.

Fitz shrugged.

Trix huddled up to him. 'What's the matter?'

'I don't care if this is the future. Let's do it. Let's leave.'

She took a deep breath.

'Why not?' he asked.

'Because you're upset. It's a big decision, and it needs both of us to sit down and talk it through.'

'This isn't about Sam.'

She looked at him.

But it wasn't about Sam. 'I liked Sam, of course I did. I didn't think of her like that. A little young for me. Well, y'know, I'm male. And there was that one time with that parallel universe version of her when we ended up –'

'You should probably shut up,' Trix suggested.

'It's not Sam,' he told her firmly. 'It's the Doctor. I think... I think I've grown out of him. The more I think about the future – my future, I mean – the more it seems silly to be following him around. He doesn't change. He'll still be there in another forty years, bouncing around saving the universe. He'll have some new bit of top totty with him, he always manages that somehow. Am I meant to follow them around with a walking frame?'

'If you want to.'

'You're not planning to be there, though, are you?'

'Where you come from, people have jobs for life. Here, we have careers. I was planning to hang around for a year or two, then move on.'

Fitz tried to do the maths, but he had no idea how long it was since he'd met Trix. His best guess was that she'd been around more than a year, less than two.

'I don't think of it as a job,' he said. 'It's my life. Last time we were here, the Doctor asked me about it. We were walking through the woods and I think he was hinting that I should go.'

'He's not really the subtle-hint type, is he? If he wanted to get rid of you, he'd tell you.'

'Even then, I didn't want to leave. Couldn't even imagine it. But I've changed.'

'You haven't, though.'

'I've changed by not changing at all.'

'Is this about him or you?' Trix asked.

Fitz thought about that. 'Both,' he said. 'He's hiding things, I know it.'

'We all do that. Everyone nudges things about their life under the carpet. The Doctor may have some skeletons in his closet, but –'

'I know what he did,' Fitz said, clearly surprising Trix. 'And I've spent so long biting my tongue. I've known for a while. I got my memories back months ago on Espero. I know why he'd want to avoid the subject – it's hard for me just to think about it.'

'You think he has all his memories?'

Fitz nodded. 'I think so. I get a hint of it every so often. He's avoiding the subject – but how can you avoid something so well if you don't know what it is?'

'We all have secrets.'

'Not like this.'

Trix gave an uncertain smile. 'Er… How bad could it be?'

Fitz shook his head. 'No. I can't. Just… of all the horrible things we've seen, all the dead bodies and atrocities. Everything we've been fighting against. It was worse. And he knows it. But that's not the worst of it…'

She was looking at him, but he held up his hands.

'I'm not going to tell you,' he repeated. 'I shouldn't have said anything about it in the first place. Sorry, I didn't mean to…'

She seemed to accept that. 'What about Mars?'

It took a while for Fitz to remember what she must mean.

'Make a go of it? Take it slowly. Be normal for a bit. I'd need to get a job, of course, and –'

'You wouldn't need to get a job.'

'I wouldn't?'

'Oh, look at your eyes light up. No. I have a little nest egg tucked away, for when I was ready to settle down.'

'You've found time to set up a savings plan?' Fitz asked. 'I barely have time to eat breakfast, let alone put aside any of my wages… Hang on a second, what wages?'

Trix looked at him, forgivingly. 'If we're going to set up here, we should make an appointment with my financial adviser. I'll go and tell the Doctor we've got something to do.'

* * *

Trix found the Doctor sitting at a desk in a back office in the police station, working on a computer.

'Five minutes ago, they were about to arrest you for being a nutter who was wasting their time.'

'I talked them out of that, and now one of their PCs is letting me borrow their PC. Very PC of him, I thought,' the Doctor explained. He was typing frantically, but barely seemed to be concentrating on what he was doing.

'And they brought you a coffee.' Trix had just noticed the plastic cup on the desk.

'If it's any consolation, it's not very nice coffee.'

'So, do you think whoever did this will have a police record?'

The Doctor shrugged, and finally stopped typing. 'I just needed access to the Internet. I'm hacking into the CCTV cameras around the churchyard.'

'You think there will be one there?'

'There are four million CCTV cameras in the UK. The average Londoner is seen by three hundred of them a day.'

'Police stations don't have direct access to CCTV systems, do they?' Trix asked.

'Not normally, not yet. The rules governing them are all over the place, though. If you know what you're doing, it's easy enough to hack into some of them.'

Trix felt very self-conscious suddenly. 'Er... Fitz and I were just going to pop into town.'

'I don't blame you. This is going to take a while. Cheer him up, would you?'

'I'll do my best. Are you going to be all right?'

'Yes. I'll chase this up and find you later.'

'How?'

The Doctor tilted his head towards the screen. 'Probably best if neither of you do any shoplifting.'

As Trix left, the Doctor returned to his work.

Fitz felt distinctly scruffy as he and Trix entered the lobby. It was a vast, light atrium which Fitz could say with some authority was larger than the one in the palace of a Roman emperor. The building was new, and they'd already passed a display telling them exactly how many architectural awards it had won. It was in the heart of the City of London. It wasn't quite the tallest building, or the most showy, but there was something about it that exuded power, confidence in the future and – above all else – money. It was like a nuclear reactor that generated cash instead of electricity.

'We have an appointment,' he assured the supermodel receptionist, who clearly didn't believe him.

As she phoned someone, Fitz was getting a little nervous. He'd never really thought of himself as one of the daily worker crowd – that always sounded rather an arduous schedule to him – but he felt as though he didn't belong in here.

'What?' snapped Trix. She, of course, looked gorgeous in her new outfit.

'It's a big deal going to see your bank manager.'

Trix rolled her eyes. 'I keep forgetting you're from the Middle Ages.'

'I think I'd rather be with the Doctor.'

'Looking at computer records?'

'Well, it's bound to get more lively than that soon, isn't it?'

The receptionist pointed the way to the lifts. 'You're to go straight up.'

'No sitting around in a waiting room?' Fitz said. 'I like that.'

The two of them crossed the floor to the lifts. Outside, it was a cold and grey midday. In here, it was bright and sunny. There were dozens of people, men and women, every nationality, all in their perfect suits, almost strutting.

They moved out of Fitz and Trix's way. At first, Fitz assumed they were avoiding him. Then he realised they were deferring to him.

'This way, Mr Kreiner,' an athletic man in a dark suit told him, indicating the express lift.

Fitz followed Trix into the lift, which started going up without them having to press anything.

'OK,' he said. 'You clearly don't think this is weird.'

Trix kissed his cheek. 'All will be explained,' she added.

The lift slowed and stopped. The doors opened, and they were on the top floor. There were panoramic views of the City, and indeed the city, from here. Fitz stumbled, a vestige of vertigo warning him to stay away from the windows.

There was a large desk at the other end of the office. Behind it sat a very pretty young Indian woman in a designer trouser suit.

'Hello, Fitz,' said Anji. 'Trix.'

The Doctor checked the address he'd written down.

A large town house that looked as though it had been built just before the First World War. Red brick, with a high-sloping roof and a mock-Tudor frontage. It had a large, slightly overgrown front garden and gravel driveway leading up to a large, separate garage. It was secluded from its neighbours on both sides. But this was a perfectly ordinary-looking house.

It was the end of his trail. After an hour or so working through CCTV footage, he'd glimpsed a lorry with a grabbing arm, and a time code that was only a few minutes after they'd been in the churchyard. It wasn't possible to see the number plate, but the name of the hire firm was clearly visible. He'd rung them up, and – with only a little trickery on his part – had persuaded them to pass on the details of the person who'd hired the lorry.

This was the address he'd been given. If this wasn't the place, then the trail had run cold.

He couldn't sense the TARDIS. He was linked to the old girl, attuned to her. He often thought he could sense when she was close by. It was an erratic ability at best, though. That he didn't feel anything now didn't mean anything.

Large tyre tracks in the gravel. Not conclusive, but circumstantial evidence that the lorry he was tracking had been here.

No obvious sign he was being watched, or that there were guards inside the house. No obvious signs of activity.

The Doctor trudged up the drive, staying alert. He reached the front door, and nothing had happened to him.

He knelt down and peeked through the letter box. A perfectly ordinary hallway.

The Doctor unlocked the door with his sonic screwdriver and went inside. Thick green carpet, and lots of pictures all over the walls – sepia photographs, old maps, generic country landscapes.

He picked up the post. Six items, all addressed to Marnal Gate. It sounded more like a place than a person. Nothing important by the look of the envelopes, just bills and junk mail. The air was full of dust. The smells were more like a library's than a home's – no cooking smells, or pets, or bathroom, or bedroom, or washing. The Doctor followed his nose towards the back of the house.

An impressively large room full of packed bookshelves. Dark and a little musty. Paper and leather. Magazines and books of all shapes and sizes. The Doctor had always been one of those people whose eyes instinctively go to the bookcase in a room. This time, though, his attention was caught by a piece of apparatus on a table in the middle of the room. A large glass jar connected up to pieces of electrical hardware, including an old television set.

It was the only thing he'd seen in the house so far that wasn't dusty.

He tapped at the glass.

Upstairs, a floorboard squeaked.

The Doctor looked up at the ceiling.

Fitz was looking around. Anji was another of the Doctor's former companions. She'd travelled with Fitz and the Doctor for a couple of years, and had left only a few months ago – as the TARDIS flies – to go back to her job at some international bank.

'You… er… got a promotion?' he ventured.

'I'm on the board now,' she told him.

'Isn't that... er... a little fast track?'

'It's about right, given my proven ability to boost the company's profits.'

'Some more stock tips for you, boss,' Trix said, handing over a compact disc and a handful of other items. 'There's also a 3-D camera, a bag of ancient Roman coins, a biomechanical gauntlet and this is a wig made of some new type of plastic.'

Anji walked over to a bare patch of wall and opened a concealed panel. A scanner popped out and slipped over her eye. Then there was a click and a small safe opened. Anji put the items in there and closed everything up.

'Oh come on,' said Fitz. 'That's *cheating*.'

'No, just a sensible arrangement,' Anji said. 'Everything this company does depends on what will happen. Will a new company succeed or fail? Will a new product sell or flop? How much will insurance companies have to pay out? What will the price of oil be in a year's time? If a futures trader could see the future, her job would be a lot easier.'

'We cooked this up between us,' Trix said, grinning from ear to ear. 'I send information to Anji, she bases investment decisions on that data.'

'It occurred to both of us independently,' Anji added. 'It's pretty obvious, when you think about it. It needed one of us in the TARDIS and one of us here.'

'I wondered why you left in such a hurry.'

'That wasn't the only reason. But it's like any career opportunity – you know when it's the right move.'

'Why don't you find out who won the Grand National and bet all your money on a sure thing?' Fitz asked, aggrieved.

'It would take all the fun out of going to the races,' Anji replied easily. 'It's not as straightforward as you'd think. You have to know the rules and regulations. We can't overplay our hand, and it would look very suspicious if we committed all our capital on risky ventures but never put a foot wrong. It's quite hard work convincing my employees they're brilliant analysts.'

'This isn't right,' Fitz said. 'Would the Doctor approve?'

'He knew I was doing it,' Anji said. She paused to loop her hair back behind her ear. 'I mean, he caught me with a copy of the *Financial Times* once, in the future. He didn't seem to mind too much.'

'Before you have a crisis of conscience,' Trix told him, 'the deal is that I get a cut of the profits.'

'A big cut?' Fitz wondered.

'At the moment, Ms Macmillan's fund is worth around a hundred and fifty million,' Anji said. 'We guarantee 20 per cent returns on investment per annum. Tax-free – and that's something a time machine's no help with.'

Fitz considered this for a moment. 'Pounds?' he asked, eventually.

'Pounds,' Anji confirmed. 'It's almost all in stocks, shares and bonds.'

'Ah, not cash,' said Fitz. He knew there would be a catch.

'We can liquidate any of it. You'd need a day's notice if you wanted more than spending money, but I can get you two hundred now, if you need it.'

'Pounds?' Fitz asked. That was three or four months' wages back in 1963.

'K,' Anji told him, and a moment later had to explain what she meant.

Fitz gave an exaggerated nod, intending to appear nonchalant. This scheme wasn't, perhaps, unethical. Anji was a good sort, after all, and could be trusted with the knowledge.

'Where do I sign?' Trix asked.

Anji buzzed for an assistant, who arrived before the buzz had died down and led Trix away.

Fitz stood there like a lemon.

'You two are a couple?' Anji asked Fitz, to break the silence.

'Yeah. I think so.'

'For how long?'

'Er... Three days, I think. Something like that. Early days.'

Anji raised an eyebrow. 'And you've already got your hands on her fortune. Seriously' – Fitz hadn't been sure it was a joke – 'well done. You've gone up in the world. She's a good catch. I can't work out what she sees in you, though.' She smiled.

That question hadn't even occurred to Fitz. 'Thanks. I think. How about you?' He'd noticed the ring.

Anji nodded. 'Greg. He's a journalist. My parents are delighted. We've been together for nearly a year now. Engaged, married next year.'

'Wow.'

'What about you?'

'I'm exactly the same as before, and that's the problem.'

'You've always been exactly the same.' He must have looked hurt, because she quickly added, 'Which was always part of your charm.'

'You might need a new business partner. I'm thinking of leaving, and I'd need Trix with me.'

Anji nodded. 'Don't worry about me. If you want to leave, well, you'll know when it's the right time. Whirlwind romances... well, I didn't exactly dawdle with either Dave or Greg. If it's right, it's right and you go for it.'

That last bit sounded like she'd heard it on a course somewhere. 'You never wanted to join us in the first place.'

Anji smiled. She'd been whisked away from a successful, fulfilling life and into the TARDIS by a series of events, rather than out of any choice on her part.

'And I'm sure I complained and had a sour face a lot of the time, but I don't need to tell you it was the most incredible experience. We had a life that most people don't even have the imagination to dream about. I used to think all that stuff was for children, and anyone over the age of ten should have grown out of it. No. What's the expression again? There are some things money definitely can't buy.'

'And it doesn't buy you happiness.'

'Oh, it doesn't hurt, trust me.'

'I'm not sure I can settle back into an ordinary life.'

'Then be extraordinary.' She grinned. 'Do you think the Doctor will manage?'

'Oh,' said Fitz, 'I'm sure he'll be fine.'

It was difficult for the Doctor to judge, but from the footsteps it sounded as though there was only one person upstairs, and that it was someone who was quite light. A woman? Possibly. A little early to assume that it was the blonde he'd seen watching him in the TARDIS.

He hadn't crashed around the place, but she might have heard him. It wouldn't be easy to get away from the house unseen. Besides, he had business here.

It would also be a bit rich for someone who'd stolen his TARDIS to complain about a little trespassing. The Doctor straightened up. He was in the right here... or not so very far into the wrong.

He strode from the library and up the stairs, heading for the source of the footsteps. Right at the top of the stairs was a bathroom with an open door that revealed a cheap, green suite that probably thought it was 'avocado', not 'snot'.

The house was clean, but cluttered. The carpets were thick with dense, rather unaesthetic patterns. The next room was full of boxes of all shapes and sizes. In a house where every room was a junk room, this was the junk room.

'Hello there,' the Doctor said to the woman he met in the next room along.

It was a spare bedroom, and she was lying face down on the neatly made bed reading a yellowing science-fiction paperback. There was a pile of them on the small bedside table.

She jumped up and shouted something. It was only then that the Doctor realised she was wearing tiny headphones and had been listening to a portable CD player.

'I'm not going to hurt you,' he said, holding his hands up. 'I'm the Doctor. I believe you have something of mine?'

The woman was young, a little prone to puppy fat. The jeans and unflattering blue top she was wearing looked like work clothes, not something she'd wear from choice.

'How did you get in here?' she asked nervously.

The Doctor smiled. A fair question, but not one he was going to answer. 'You first. I saw you watching me. I can tell you recognise me, and you have my police box.'

She glanced down and behind the Doctor, to his left, and didn't even realise she was doing it.

'The garage,' the Doctor concluded, without looking round. 'The first place I should have looked.'

'Are you reading my mind?'

'No. Would you like me to?' He smiled. 'You don't have anything to be afraid of, I wouldn't harm a fly. Not unless it was a particularly wicked one.'

He stepped into the room.

'Stay back!' She was almost shaking.

The Doctor took a step back. 'Is this your house?' he asked. 'Do you live here with your parents?'

'How old do you think I am?'

'What a terribly rude question to ask a lady. Twenty-seven.'

'I'm thirty-three.'

'Really? You really do seem younger. You still live with your parents, though, don't you? Not here. This doesn't seem like your sort of house.'

'You don't even know anything about me.'

'No. But this is very clearly a spare room. The bed hasn't been slept in; I doubt those dusty old pictures are the ones you'd choose to put up; there's nowhere to put your CDs or books; from the marks on the glass you've tried to open the window but gave up because you don't know how to; that old wardrobe hasn't been opened for years; your book, bag and keys are on the floor there; there's no dressing gown hanging on the back of this door, and you've not taken your shoes off. All of which is suggestive.'

'You're Sherlock Holmes, are you?'

'No, but as I was just saying, I met him a few –'

The young woman was trying very hard not to look over his right shoulder.

A floorboard squeaked behind him.

The Doctor saw something in the corner of his eye.

The world filled with crackling green energy that surged through him, filling his body with agonising pain for a moment. Then he collapsed into the dusty, thick carpet.

One particularly obscure text from the period comes close to fulfilling the criteria listed, but does not in all honesty provide much to discuss. Published in 1899, *Marnal's Journeys or the Modern Crusoe* purports to be the diary of a traveller from a distant, highly advanced civilisation, washed up on the shores of 19th century England. The conceit is a clever one – while Defoe's Crusoe was stranded from 18th century European civilisation on a desert island, Marnal is similarly forced to subsist in the 'primitive' culture of Victorian England. Unfortunately, the novel is let down by the preoccupations of its narrator: Marnal expends many thousands of words deriding the culture he finds himself in, but references to his own background are maddeningly opaque and inconsistent. It is as a worldbuilding exercise that the text's unknown author (the book is credited to the fictional Marnal) fails, denying him or her a more significant position in the history of fiction by neglecting imagination in favour of heavy-handed satire. The premise of the novel may seem like science fiction, but the content is more mundane.

Footnote from an undergraduate essay, 1981

Chapter Five
Deadly Reunion

The Doctor's eyes snapped open.

His back was burning. His nervous system felt like a bell that had just been struck.

He was in a bare, windowless room, one that felt like a cellar. He was tied to a metal chair with what felt like three-ply plastic twine. This sort of thing always gave him a terrible sense of déjà vu.

The man in the blue blazer was standing over him.

'Hello, Doctor. I am Marnal,' he announced, bowing his head a little.

'Delighted to hear it,' the Doctor replied.

'Don't you recognise me?'

The Doctor shrugged, as much as he could in his circumstances. 'I take it you're the person who stole my TARDIS, but beyond that, no.'

'The TARDIS is quite safe.'

'And you killed Samantha Jones.'

Marnal looked taken aback. 'No, Doctor, I had nothing to do with that. Don't you know what happened to Ms Jones?'

'You'd be surprised at the things I don't remember.'

Marnal shook his head. 'I've been watching you for a while. I know all about your amnesia.'

'You know, I'd forgotten I even had that.'

Marnal wasn't smiling, not even one of those thin, cruel smiles. 'You were responsible for her death. If you hadn't met, she'd be

91

twenty-five now. A graduate, working for an inner-city charity. Engaged to be married. She would live to be a hundred, a political activist until the day she died, dedicated to making her world a better place. Not just a guess, Doctor. I've seen the time lines overwritten as you met her, peeled them back to see the way things should have been.'

He paced around the chair. 'But that is a minor offence. It is the grand scheme of things that concerns me today. Would you like to save us both some time and confess?'

The Doctor frowned. There had been something odd about this from the beginning. Here was a man – a being, let's not assume anything for the moment – who knew what a TARDIS was, and casually talked about time lines and wasn't of this world, but whose level of technology stretched no further than hiring a lorry and buying some rope. There was no sign of the young woman.

'You've done something terrible,' Marnal continued, 'and deep down you know you have. You might not want to face up to it, but you no longer have a choice.'

'I don't know what you're –'

'You're a coward for not facing up to this sooner. Do I have to say the word, Doctor?'

The Doctor felt a shot of anxiety. 'Marnal… all I know is that you shouldn't –'

'You'll pay for what you did, Doctor. What you did to *Gallifrey.*'

Marnal was bent over the Doctor, watching very carefully for his reaction. He clearly wasn't happy with what he saw.

The Doctor sighed. 'Look, sorry. If you really have been spying on me, then you'll appreciate that I'm tied up by some git with a grudge every single week. So, if you'll excuse me…'

The Doctor stood up and handed Marnal the rope.

Marnal drew a nasty-looking pistol and shot him.

'He'll be able to track us down,' Trix assured him.

He shrugged. 'Aren't you enjoying yourself?'

'It feels like we're bunking off.'

'We quit, remember? By now he's probably found some new dolly bird and given her my room.'

'I hope for her sake he opened a window and changed the sheets first.'

They were in a large music store. Fitz had spent a good hour now just clacking his way through row after row of CDs. He was clearly irritated to be reminded about the Doctor, but quickly cheered up once he returned to his task.

'There's nowhere better than the future if you're shopping for music,' he said. 'Well, except for parallel universes. You think you've got all the Beatles albums until you've been to a few of those.' He hummed a few bars of 'Little Girl'.

'You could pick all this stuff up online.'

'You're joking, aren't you? I'm still wondering how they get all the music on one little disc like this. Look: shiny. The record players here use lasers for needles, you know that?'

Trix smiled. 'I'd heard a rumour.'

'Can you think of anything cooler than that?'

She was going to have to explain iPods and HVDs to him gently, she could tell. 'We really ought to start looking for clothes for this evening.'

Fitz sighed. 'Yeah, OK. I don't like clothes shopping.'

'You surprise me.'

'If you've got a look, you should stick with it, yeah?'

'You've got a look, have you?'

He flapped his suede jacket and looked down at himself. 'Yeah. This is timeless. Classic. Retro. Better than a frock coat. Did you even know what a frock coat was until you met him? It's like he's constantly off to a wedding.'

'The Red Fort, the place we're going tonight... it's not fascist about it, but it does have a dress code. Smart casual. You're about halfway there.'

'You always dress nicely,' Fitz conceded. 'I'll let you pick an outfit for me. But I get a veto, OK?'

* * *

The Doctor's eyes snapped open.

He was still in the cellar, still tied to a metal chair, this time with what felt like home-made manacles.

Marnal was standing over him. The Doctor had been hit three times, the stun bolts forming a neat equilateral triangle on his left collarbone. He'd been conscious until moments before the third shot hit.

'Touché,' the Doctor said quietly.

'There's no escape this time, Doctor.'

'There never is,' the Doctor sighed. 'We don't have to go through these theatrics. If you've got something to say, we can sit down like men and discuss it. Pull up a chair.'

Marnal paced around the room. There was a small pile of books by the door that the Doctor didn't think had been there before, which was odd. Ten books, a seemingly random collection of old and relatively new paperbacks and hardbacks. They were turned – deliberately? – so that he couldn't see the titles.

Finally, Marnal was in front of him again. 'I spent a lifetime trying to remember that name. Just one word, right on the tip of my tongue.'

The Doctor let him speak, tested the manacles. Steel, welded, and they weren't going to budge.

'I've lived here for a long time.'

He looked to be in his mid-thirties.

'How long, out of interest?' the Doctor asked.

'A hundred and twenty-two years.'

'Really?' the Doctor said, nonchalant. 'This house is a little older than I thought, then.'

'I've watched the trees in the garden grow from saplings.'

The trick with these sort of bonds was to create a little wriggle room, but as things were going there wasn't a huge amount the Doctor could do now. The weak link was the chair. It was made from metal, but it was quite spindly and wouldn't last long against the concrete floor down here. But breaking it up would be very noisy.

'It was all so frustrating. I knew all that time that if I could just say the word everything about my life would make sense. It would all fall into place. There would be meaning.'

Marnal was leaning over the Doctor, who smiled politely.

'Have you felt like that? Oh wait... I see from your expression that you have. You and I are –'

'Strangely alike?' The Doctor completed his sentence for him. 'That is what you were going to say, isn't it? Or was it going to be "two sides of the same coin"? If you've spent an entire lifetime sitting around in this house, waiting for something to come along, to hear some magic word that will solve all your problems, hoping someone walks in and knows it all already and gives you all the answers, then no, sorry, no we're not the same.'

'I always thought there was more to it all than this.'

The Doctor looked up. 'Doesn't everyone feel like that, from time to time?' he asked.

'You think that a human being could feel emptiness like we do?'

'I don't feel...' But the Doctor couldn't finish the sentence. 'I'm half-full, not half-empty. I don't feel sorry for myself, I don't dwell on the past.'

'You wouldn't want to remember, would you?'

The Doctor felt as though something dark was fluttering above him.

'Not when there's so much more in the present and the future, no.'

'I had fragments of it,' Marnal said. He'd walked over to the pile of books, and now picked up a handful of them. 'But I was like a man dying out in the snow, recalling the flicker of a match.'

The Doctor squirmed a little in his seat. It wasn't physically uncomfortable.

'My life had great purpose, once,' Marnal said, waving the books. 'I always knew it. I had bathed in the light of heaven, and now I was in darkness, but I knew that I would come back, yes, I would come back. Until that day –'

'You thought you'd go back?' the Doctor asked.

'Yes.'

'I... didn't,' the Doctor admitted. 'The way I saw it, my purpose was to be the match. To carry the torch, to be the torch. The spark of heavenly light in the cold and the darkness. To go forward with all my beliefs and –'

'That,' Marnal said, looking weary, 'was because you knew what I didn't.'

He turned and left the room, locking the door behind him.

'I didn't,' the Doctor said quietly.

Fitz strummed the new guitar he'd somehow acquired during the course of his clothes shopping.

'I'm going to miss the TARDIS wardrobe,' Trix said. She'd buttoned up her shirt and was walking around his hotel room, looking for the skirt she'd bought this afternoon. It was the casually miraculous, Fitz thought. Sharing a life with such a woman, just turning your head to see her there.

She frowned. 'You have the strangest look on your face.'

'You're a beautiful person,' he told her.

'There's a lot you don't know about me.'

'And I have hidden depths too,' Fitz countered. 'Or, at the very least, I have a lot of hidden shallows.'

Trix sighed. 'Are you ever going to get changed?'

'The restaurant isn't ten minutes' walk away and we've got an hour before we have to be there.'

He plucked at the guitar again.

'Are you getting hungry? You've not eaten anything today.'

'It's OK, Trix, I can look after myself.'

She smiled. 'Sorry.'

'What for?'

'I don't want to nag.'

'You weren't.' He put the guitar down and patted the bed, trying to look seductive.

Trix was too busy putting on her skirt to notice.

Fitz wondered how best to attract her attention. 'Remind me to ask her about Jamais and Chloe. I forgot before.'

'I'll try to remember. So what do you think Greg will be like?'

'Tall, dark and handsome, I'm guessing. Like me.' He gave what he hoped was a sweet smile and patted the bed again.

'Anji's one of the richest women in Britain now,' Trix said, failing to take the hint.

'Takes one to know one. It's weird. Like we won the pools or something. What's that thing they always say?'

Trix grinned. '"It won't change me." I've always thought they should take the money off anyone who said that, and give it to someone who could do with a change.'

'No. I was thinking more like "It hasn't sunk in yet". A lot's happening all at once.'

Trix's smile faltered.

'No,' Fitz said quickly. 'It's not a problem. Just that I've spent so long being the same old Fitz, it's strange that everything's changed. But it's changed for the better.'

He patted the bed again.

'I saw you the first time,' Trix told him. 'But it really is time you got ready.'

The young woman had come in to feed the Doctor. She wasn't saying anything.

She was something of an expert at serving him. She'd given him some juice, tipping it into his mouth at just the right angle. Then some soup and bread, the soup not so hot it burned, just enough bread each time to get a good mouthful. She'd done this before, and she really didn't look like a professional kidnapper.

'You're a nurse?' he guessed, once the bowl was empty.

She nodded.

'What's your name?'

The young woman spent a couple of seconds calculating whether to answer. 'Rachel.'

'Hello, Rachel. I'm the Doctor.'

She clearly didn't want to get into a conversation.

'How long have you known Marnal?' he tried.

Again, she was very wary of him.

'It's not a trick,' the Doctor said. 'If it was a trick, I'd tell you.'

A wry smile. 'I've known him a few months. I mean, I'd read some of his books. They're like Tolkien, aren't they? Everyone reads at least one of them when they're fourteen.'

The Doctor raised an eyebrow. 'He's an author? That explains the books he was waving around. He wrote them?'

Rachel nodded, but it was her turn to look puzzled. 'He told me you'd recognise his name.'

'He's preceded his fame, I'm afraid,' the Doctor admitted. 'So those books are science fantasy?'

'They're about his planet.'

The Doctor sat back, a little surprised. 'I don't suppose you could read me a bedtime story?'

She was back to being wary. 'I shouldn't be telling you anything. Have you had enough supper?'

So, it was evening. He'd lost all track of time down here.

'I'm a light eater. Thank you.'

She barely nodded.

'Some days, do you feel empty inside?' the Doctor asked.

'No,' Rachel replied, before looking away. 'Some days I don't.'

'That's –'

'Stupid thing to talk about. Makes no difference.'

'Of course it does.'

'Not when everyone feels like that.'

'Everyone you know?'

'Everyone in the world. In the universe, probably.'

'I've got friends. They don't think like that.'

'Yeah, well, I learnt in psychology that they do, they're just better at coping or hiding it. Or they're on pills. A lot of us are on pills. More than you'd think. No one ever talks about it.'

'My friends aren't,' the Doctor insisted. 'I'm not. I don't think like that. Not often.'

'Freud had a word for it.'

'Transference,' the Doctor replied automatically.

'Denial,' Rachel corrected him.

She collected the crockery, and left the Doctor alone.

Fitz had even managed to shave, although he'd missed the bits he always missed.

His new outfit was essentially his old outfit – rubbish suede jacket, white shirt and jeans – lovingly reconstructed with newly bought clothes, any slight variation because they hadn't been able to find an exact replica. He reminded Trix of a penny that had come out of the washing machine a little too clean and sparkling to look quite right. This, though, was the smartest he was ever going to get.

The restaurant was walking distance from the hotel. It was a clear night.

'No stars,' Fitz said.

'Too much light from the street lamps,' Trix said.

'It's odd to think that we've been to some of them.'

'You just said there aren't any,' she laughed.

'They're all still there, though.'

'You're the expert. I've not been to many other planets, not really.'

'I've been to hundreds,' Fitz said.

'I know, no need to rub it in. I've been to about ten.'

'But... I've been to hundreds of alien planets. Places that the astronomers don't even know are there. That's pretty incredible, isn't it? Even ten's a pretty good score. Substantially better than the average.'

'We've both got a higher than average number of legs,' Trix said.

'What?' He thought about that for a minute. 'Oh, I see. Yeah. I suppose we have. Unless you take all those three-legged aliens into account.'

'That's cheating.'

'How about creatures on Earth? All those millipedes. What's the average number of legs? It's got to be more than two.'

'Are you counting fish? They don't have any legs.'

'Hmmmm... Good point. There are a lot of fish.'

They'd arrived at the restaurant, an Indian one called the Red Fort.

'Looks fancy,' Fitz noted.

'I think it's in our price range.'

Fitz held the door open for Trix, then followed her in and up a flight of stairs. Warm, and the air was thick with the smell of spices and meat. Strange, thought Fitz, that he'd once have thought this was exotic.

A waiter hurried over and told them that Ms Kapoor and her partner were already there.

Anji had seen them arrive, and waved. She and Greg were at what must have been the best table, one near the window. The waiter led them over. There was a good view of Soho from here. A part of London barely recognisable from Fitz's time, immeasurably cleaner and nicer. This was a very elegant place; it felt Indian without being a parody of Indianness. It was late, so not as busy as it might have been.

Anji had changed into a silk evening dress and, for her, looked pretty sexy.

'This is Greg.'

He wasn't what Fitz had been expecting. He was expecting someone very something. The first impression he had was of someone who was quite. Quite tall, quite slim, quite smart. No grip to his handshake. Which probably didn't mean very much. Anji's phone rang, and she apologised.

'The moment you walked in, I knew you must be the famous Fitz and Trix,' Greg said easily, while Anji got rid of her caller. 'You're just like Kap described.'

The waiter took their drinks order, delaying an awkward silence for a moment or two. Fitz mentally rehearsed breaking the ice with a joke based around Greg being a West Indian and Anji being an actual Indian, then decided against it.

'Er... so. What's the music like nowadays?' Fitz asked. 'I'm going to have a lot of catching up to do.'

Greg looked a little lost at the question.

'There's no use asking him.' Anji smiled nervously. 'Greg's more of a film buff.'

'Like –' Fitz slammed the brakes on the sentence. He was going to say 'Like Dave', Anji's previous fiancé. Who'd died the day she met the Doctor. 'Like so many people are,' he finished, weakly.

Greg still looked lost.

Trix was studying the menu rather too furiously for Fitz's liking.

He decided on a new line of inquiry. 'So, Anji, we were just talking about this on the way over: how many planets do you think you went to?'

Greg had gone from mild bewilderment to total confusion. 'Planets?' he frowned.

It was about ten hours since Rachel had given the Doctor his supper.

He was sore from sitting in one place for so long, and the few movements he could make weren't quite enough to keep the stiffness out of his joints. He had managed a little sleep, and that was all he needed.

The door was unbolted and Marnal entered, pistol raised. He relaxed when he saw the Doctor still secured to the chair, and tucked the gun back in his blazer.

'I have been reviewing more of your interventions,' he began.

'Good morning to you, too,' the Doctor replied.

'You repeatedly claim to have lost your memory as a result of what happened. How convenient.'

The Doctor did his best to shrug, given his restraints. 'I don't know why I lost my memories, and I don't think I ever claimed otherwise. I don't think it's particularly convenient or inconvenient. I've got plenty of new memories now.'

He paused for a moment, unaccountably worried.

Marnal took advantage of the hesitation. 'Do you know what happened to our race?'

'So... you're from the same civilisation as I am?' He'd known

Marnal had lived a long time without ageing, but he'd met more than his fair share of immortals in his time.

Marnal nodded. 'I thought I was the only one.'

'Well, so did I for a long time. Yes, sorry I never called. I must have missed any number of your birthdays. I owe you a card and a book token, at the very least.'

'You don't seem surprised that you are not alone.'

'There were four of us left, apparently. You'd be number five.'

Marnal rounded on him. 'Left after what?'

The Doctor hesitated. 'I don't know. Some disaster. I've picked up hints, seen the odd vision, but I was never able to follow up on anything.'

Marnal leant over him, sensing a moment of weakness. 'Weren't you, now? Not terribly enterprising of you. So you have no idea?'

The Doctor shrugged apologetically.

Marnal raised his hand, and the Doctor thought he was going to hit him. Instead, Marnal touched the Doctor's temple with a fingertip.

'Contact.'

For the briefest moment, the Doctor saw himself as Marnal saw him. Then back to vice versa. Then rapid alternations between the two viewpoints. It was dizzying.

A man with a sallow face and small, pointed black beard, who wore a blue rosette; a young woman with long blonde hair in an extraordinary piece of haute couture; a tall man with a bent nose wearing a cravat and holding a pair of dice; the Doctor himself with close-cropped hair, sitting on an ornate throne, a newborn baby girl in his arms.

Marnal was attempting telepathic contact. Memories were flitting from one mind to the other.

Nothing.

Parts of the Doctor's brain that he wasn't even aware were there came to life, repelled the attempt to link up.

Nothing.

Nothing.

Marnal took a step back, jerking his head from side to side, as though he was trying to loosen something that had got stuck inside it.

'How?' he asked, when he had recovered.

'I'm not even sure what,' the Doctor admitted cheerfully. He looked more carefully at his captor. 'You wanted to read my mind. Over the years, quite a few people have tried. They've also come away empty-handed.'

'Your amnesia is genuine enough,' Marnal conceded. 'It changes nothing.'

'I don't know how I lost my memories,' the Doctor told him. 'But I know it was right that I did so.'

'Right? You can say that without any idea what you did?'

'Yes. I don't know why, but I know it.'

'No,' Marnal said. 'You feel unease.'

'I am often faced with serious decisions,' the Doctor said. 'Life or death decisions. I know that I am not infallible, I know that I am not all-powerful.'

'You have killed people.'

'As a last resort, but yes. My actions have led to the death of others, including innocent people. I have always tried to minimise the loss of life. That is usually not the case with those I oppose, which is one of the reasons I oppose them.' The Doctor straightened up. 'Am I on trial here, Marnal?'

Marnal thought about it. 'Yes. Yes, you are.'

'Does this look like a legitimate court to you? I don't know what my crime is. I don't know what the evidence is against me. And you seem to be judge, jury, gaoler, chief prosecution witness... As well as being an interested party in the case. I've travelled across the universe, Marnal, and if I've learnt one thing it's that trials are never fair unless they have to be.'

'You don't know what your crime is,' Marnal quoted back to him. 'You know a crime was committed, though, don't you? Ever since you woke up in that carriage, having lost everything you once were, you've known something was wrong. You've felt unease whenever you've tried to think back. You've known it was you.'

The Doctor couldn't deny it.

'It's a court of your peers, Doctor.'

'Marnal. Whatever happened, it happened for a good reason. I lost my memory of it for a good reason. It's the past. It's a done deed. I can't face it.'

'You *won't* face it – there's a difference.'

'I know what I said.'

'I think it's time for you to find out what you did,' Marnal snapped back.

Trix and Fitz were lying facing each other, noses about an inch apart, on top of the hotel bed sheets. They were both a little drunk, but only a little. It was nice and warm in the room.

'Why didn't Anji tell him?' Fitz asked.

'She covered your little faux pas very well, I thought.'

'But why hadn't she told him?'

'You've not told anyone here, have you? You didn't say to the waiter, "Hey, that chicken korma was almost as nice as the poached nightfish I had last week on planet Venus, can I please pay the bill in Andromedan euros?"'

'I'm not engaged to the waiter. She's been seeing Greg for a year now. Do you think she is going to tell him?'

'Perhaps she's waiting for the right moment.'

'Like what?'

'I don't know. Perhaps when they go to see *Revenge of the Sith*, and he says, "Half of the monsters looked like men in rubber suits and half of them looked like CGI" she could go, "Yeah, but that's about the same ratio as real life, and I speak from experience."'

'I don't think you're taking my point seriously.'

'No kidding. It's her choice, isn't it?'

'I suppose. But… well, wouldn't you want to boast about it? Or at least share it with someone? Isn't it, well, the biggest part of her life?'

'Different people do different things. I don't need to tell you what happened after the Second World War. Most men who came back from service abroad never, ever talked about it again. Even if it wasn't that bad, it was nothing like an ordinary life, nothing like they'd ever see again. So they put it in a box in their memories. Even when they met up with other old soldiers a lot of them never discussed it. Everyone has their secrets.'

'Everyone but me,' said Fitz.

'I have secrets,' she replied. 'There's a lot you don't know about me.'

'We saw a lot of death,' Fitz said. 'I always think of what we did as adventures, but so many people died.'

'More than the average number of deaths,' Trix said quietly.

'Yeah. But it's not that with Anji, it's that she's somehow ashamed of her time with the Doctor.'

'She's got a new life now. Come back down to Earth, to coin a phrase.'

'Does she really think that – what was it they were talking about? – offshore unit trusts and the European Declaration of Human Rights are more interesting subjects than giant robots and pyramids on Mars? We ended up talking about what colour to paint a kitchen at one point.'

'Isn't that the life we've just chosen? Normality?'

'No. We're not pretending it didn't happen. We talk about it. And I like to think we'll go places and, y'know, do stuff.'

'We both went through it,' Trix said. 'All that outer space and monsters and stuff. Could you explain what it's like to anyone else?'

'I could see how it would be difficult to share with anyone who wasn't there,' Fitz agreed, 'Like all those Hollywood stars who have to marry other Hollywood stars.'

'And is she happy?'

'Anji's the happiest I've ever seen her,' Fitz admitted. 'I don't understand why he calls her "cap", though.'

'I imagine it's short for "Kapoor",' Trix explained patiently.

'But that's her... Hang on, he calls her by her surname? That's just screwy.'

'I thought Fitz was your surname for ages. Never mind about them. How about you? Are you happy?'

Fitz shifted on the mattress, dislodging Trix a little. 'I think I will be. It's a big adjustment. I know this is the right thing to do.' He looked into her eyes. 'It's a good start, from where I'm lying.'

It had been an hour or two.

The door to the cellar opened, then whoever opened it went straight back upstairs rather than showing themselves. Then Marnal and Rachel both came down the stairs, slowly and carefully, bringing an extraordinary contraption with them.

It was the big glass bottle he'd seen in the library, now connected up to a variety of electronic pieces, most of which were everyday items. Two things caught the Doctor's eye. The first was a small metal tube that was humming to itself and had cables pouring out of its top and bottom. The other was a component from the TARDIS scanner.

Marnal had managed to get into the TARDIS. The Doctor tried, and failed, not to panic at the thought.

Rachel helped Marnal set up the apparatus about five feet in front of the Doctor.

'I thought you said we couldn't use it to look at this,' Rachel said.

'I can use this image processor to help resolve the picture,' Marnal told her, plugging it into his contraption. 'It won't be perfect, but it should be enough to at least get a sense of it.'

'If this is *The War of the Worlds*, I've seen it,' the Doctor said, trying to sound cheerful.

'You've seen this too,' Marnal told him.

The bottle grew dark. Then it resolved into the blackness of space, with a few stars and the wisps of a nebula. Filling the sky, though, was something utterly alien. It looked like a six-leafed orchid, the colour of bone, or perhaps some bizarre six-winged moth.

'What is that?' Rachel asked.

'I don't know,' the Doctor and Marnal both replied.

Marnal was working the controls. He wasn't getting a very good signal. 'The coordinates are slightly off.'

Then there was a star, much like Earth's sun. The picture moved away, to one of its planets. The world had an atmosphere, three vestiges of oceans and tiny ice caps at its poles, but the large continents seemed to be mostly desert or broken mountain ranges. The Doctor knew from this glimpse that what he was looking at was an immensely old place, practically fossilised. The wide river beds were dry, there were fields of rubble. Scratched in the rock were marks of abandoned roadways and settlements. He also thought he saw the glints of crystal domes and metal spires.

'Gallifrey, Doctor. Our home planet.'

The Doctor looked at the image again, with new interest. This time, he saw countless dots of light massed in orbit above the ancient world.

'This,' Marnal continued, 'is the day you destroyed it...'

Interlude
The Last of Gallifrey

The invaders were from beyond the future.

The Doctor and Fitz had known for some time that a war was coming. For months, as they'd gone about their travels, they had stumbled across hints and echoes of a battle fought in the future between the Time Lords and an unknown enemy. The Time Lords were losing. This was a war fought in five dimensions, across the whole of time and space. The Doctor was forbidden to see his own destiny, but the future had sought him out. He had learnt he would die, he had learnt that Gallifrey and everything it now stood for would be destroyed.

Those that attacked Gallifrey today had travelled back from a time towards the end of the war. They were not the enemy, but they were members of one of the factions opposed to the elite that ran Time Lord society. In the Doctor's time Faction Paradox was a nuisance, a secret society of renegades obsessed with symbols and ritual, with breaking the rules.

In the future, they had become an army, and one that was used to fighting Time Lords. And because they were from the future, they already knew how they'd won this battle. Today, they'd already dissected every planetary defence system. Their war fleet circled Gallifrey. Above the dome of the Capitol, the seat of Time Lord power, hovered the Edifice, a structure the size of the dome itself that looked for all the world like a rare orchid. Now, Faction Paradox troops had launched a massive ground assault.

The front-line Faction infantry wore costumes made from the

bones of impossible creatures. Thick ribs protected their chests, plates of bone covered their shins and forearms. They wore masks that looked like the skulls of enormous bats. No two sets of armour were identical, although most had fierce spikes and stegosaur plates. The gaps between the bones were filled with a viscous, oily-black substance. What they wore resembled costumes worn for a voodoo ceremony as much as suits of armour.

These skulltroopers advanced quickly through the Capitol, each squad covering its comrades, always pressing forward. There was something inhuman about the precision of each move. Where they encountered defences, they took them apart efficiently. They carried bulky guns that fired beams of shadow that never seemed to miss. It was impossible to surprise them, and they always managed to dodge hostile fire. Behind them were the officers in their flowing black robes and more streamlined skull-masks. They were searching the Capitol, catching the strategic areas of the Time Lord's fortress as they fell. Meanwhile, the Faction's leather-clad assassins, the Uncles, hunted down unarmed old men and stabbed them through both hearts.

More than one race had tried to use brute force to conquer Gallifrey, assembling vast armadas that had been hopelessly dashed against its defences. This attack was almost small scale by comparison, yet when the Time Lord tacticians ran what was happening through the Matrix simulators it was succeeding as well as the Faction's best-case scenario. The Faction were making no mistakes, yet perfectly exploiting their opponents' hesitations and weaknesses. The rumour among the city Watchmen was that data about the fight was being relayed to the invaders from the future. If one of the skulltroopers was about to miss, he was told how to adjust his aim. The officers were told where they would find what they were looking for, saving them the search. Entry codes and passwords were learnt and transmitted to the past, allowing unhindered access to the Capitol. History was being retouched and redrafted. Forewarned was forearmed.

The Gallifreyans guarding the Capitol had a few tricks of their own. They each had centuries' worth of familiarity with the battlefield, and knew all the ancient passages and secret paths. This place had once been a fortress, and now it was a fortress again. The defenders were well drilled, with near-telepathic communications. If the guards managed to cut off a group of attackers, then hit them so hard and fast that there was nothing they could do to defend themselves, it didn't make any difference whether or not the skulltroopers knew what was coming. The staser pistols of the Watch were set to freeze time around the attackers, cutting them off from the rest of the universe. They dropped out of existence when they were hit, momentary grey silhouettes visible for a moment before the universe sealed over them. So battle was joined. To an outside observer, the fighting looked weird and fantastic, full of improbable, illogical events.

Fitz was with the president of the Time Lords, an – apparently – young woman named Romana, who had herself travelled with the Doctor before returning alone to their home planet. They had been joined by Mali, a member of the Time Lord military. Romana was petite, with black hair and a snub nose. Mali was tall and solid, with close-cropped hair. Fitz wouldn't say no to either or both of them. The two ladies, however, were more concerned with the alien hordes swarming across the capital city of their home planet. Fitz himself had just been distracted by a hallucination, a vision of the walls running with blood, hundreds of screaming corpses trapped behind them. This had dampened his ardour.

'The Matrix has restabilised. The Faction influence has been woven into its databanks,' Romana said quietly as Fitz's vision faded.

The Matrix was the Time Lord's central computer; it contained every scrap of their knowledge and all the secrets of their power. Fitz thought someone had said something about how the memory of every Time Lord was loaded into its databanks when they died, but he might have been confusing this with something else. There were often a lot of things to keep track of on an alien planet.

'You were right, you stupid, ignorant primitive,' Romana was crying, 'you were right.'

'I was?' Fitz had guessed what the invaders were planning a little while ago, and no one had believed him. The satisfaction of knowing he'd worked out something that an entire race of immortal supergeniuses, every one of them more brilliant than the Doctor, had missed was tempered by the fact that Faction Paradox now had complete control of the entire universe of space and time.

'There are nine Gallifreys!' Fitz reminded Romana and Mali.

It was true. The Time Lords had copied their own homeworld and secreted the copies around time and space as back-up against just such an attack as this.

'No,' said Mali. 'There isn't even *one*.'

The Faction had found all the back-ups, then written them out of existence. Without anyone to stop them, their version of history was being imposed on the universe. Fitz could feel time itself being corrupted, but couldn't describe the feeling.

Something shadowy and unknowable was grabbing at him. At first, he thought it was just the sense that everything had gone *wrong*. Then he realised he was being removed from the action. The skulltroopers were closing in on Romana and Mali, guns raised. The two Time Ladies were trying to make a break for it, but the world was melting around them.

As the world faded away around Fitz he heard Romana sobbing. 'We can't have lost. Everything I ever did was to stop this from happening. I can't have failed. I can't let this happen to my people!'

Then he heard two shots.

High above the Capitol was the Edifice. Inside the Edifice was a control chamber, and inside the control chamber was the Doctor. He was face to face with the leader of Faction Paradox.

The Doctor hadn't been able to sleep the night he'd first heard his name.

He'd been a very small child. He couldn't remember how old he was, but he remembered his mother's long red hair and her cut-glass voice. She was sitting at the side of his bed, reading from a storybook.

It was a tale about an adventurous youth who had gone back into his own past, to before his mummy and daddy were born. He knew, as everyone knew, that this was strictly forbidden. Travelling into the past was allowed, but not into your *own* past. That part of your story had already been written, and there was no room for any new characters or incidents. But the adventurous youth didn't listen to his elders and his betters, and – without any obvious motivation – he used an ordinary knife to murder his own grandfather.

The consequences were obvious, even to a small child: if his father had never been born, the adventurous youth would never be born... so couldn't go back and murder his grandfather. If his grandfather wasn't murdered, he was free to have a son... and the adventurous youth would be born, and would commit the murder. It went around and around.

Although this was the first time the Doctor had heard it, this was a very old legend. A fairy tale that had been written to frighten young Gallifreyans, to warn them of the dangers that their great powers could bring them.

So what happened to the adventurous youth? Well, no one knew, not even the wise men of the High Council, not even the finest minds stored in the Matrix, not even great Rassilon himself. But there were stories that out *there*, wherever that was, there existed a shadowy half-man, simultaneously alive and dead, murderer and victim. No one knew what he looked like, except that he had only one arm – and no one could agree which one he had lost, or how it had happened. His name was *Grandfather Paradox*, and if you were naughty he would find you and use you and destroy you, as part of his labyrinthine schemes against the Time Lords.

The Doctor had taken the story very, very seriously as a child. For months, perhaps even years, afterwards he had worried that

Grandfather Paradox was under his bed, or lurking beneath the table in the refectory, or making the noises he could hear outside at night. Gradually, the fear had faded. For the best part of the last thousand years, the Doctor had blithely gone about his travels through time and space, and had been afraid of Grandfather Paradox roughly as often as he'd worried about being mugged by the Easter Bunny.

So it was disconcerting to have Grandfather Paradox leering down at him, wearing the Doctor's own face. The Grandfather was his future self. He was everyone's future self. This was what you became if you didn't mend your ways. Anyone looking him in the eye would see themselves staring back. Consumed not with anything as lurid as evil, but with cynicism masquerading as cleverness. Self-absorption and pettiness, pragmatism and grudges, boredom and sadness. He is the person you vow you'll never become as an adventurous youth, and he's always watching you, ready to strike.

Grandfather Paradox's heavy leather cloak was flapping as a gust of wind passed through the Edifice. He stood framed in an arch made of bone, in a pool of milky light.

'I am your fate. The game is played out, and I hold all the cards.'

'Perhaps we could have a whist drive,' the Doctor suggested disdainfully.

Grandfather Paradox smiled. It wasn't quite his own face, the Doctor reflected. It was older and more cruel. Greying hair and skin. The same frock coat under the cloak, but faded and cobwebbed. The loss of an arm had changed his centre of balance, subtly altering the way he walked and moved.

The Doctor started talking to himself. Then again, who else was there to talk to here?

'It seems to me there are three directions this little tournament could move in,' the Doctor said.

'Oh really?' the Doctor replied.

The Doctor nodded. 'One: I can run. Leave the universe to it. What can I do to save Gallifrey now?

'Two: Surrender to this third-rate god in the machine here,' said the Doctor, pointing to Grandfather Paradox. 'Beg him to change his mind, to spare Gallifrey, to temper his visions for his Paradox hordes overrunning space and time. Perhaps there's a chance.

'Or three...'

He tried to think what the third option might be. There was always another way...

They had never said how old the adventurous youth's grandfather was when he met him. When you hear the word 'grandfather' you picture wrinkles, false teeth and a white beard. But the whole point of the story was that the grandfather was a young man at the time. What if he was stronger than his opponent? What if he was *more* youthful, *more* adventurous? What if he'd heard how this story ended and didn't like it one bit? What if, when faced with a knife-wielding maniac from the future, he drew a gun and blew him away? That was one way to resolve a paradox.

And, responding to the Doctor's thoughts, a brass lever sprang out of the mouldy remains of the control console in the middle of the chamber. The sound, like a bone breaking, startled both the Doctor and the Grandfather.

The Doctor could feel time, space and gravity fraying around him. The laws of physics, of cause and effect themselves, were unravelling. This was going to be the paradox to end all paradoxes, but it would end the war to end all wars.

A moment later and Grandfather Paradox had leapt for the Doctor, his one arm stretched out like a pike. He grabbed the Doctor's throat, palm against his Adam's apple, fingers pressed into the flesh of his neck. This was not simply holding him away from the lever, this was a murder attempt.

'I don't want to,' the Doctor choked. 'If I do, I lose everything I hold dear.'

Rather than listen to the Grandfather's reply, he tried to come up with a strategy that would get him over to the lever.

Knowing he was, by definition, as strong as his opponent the

Doctor grabbed the stump of the Grandfather's missing arm in one hand, dug in until he could feel his nails breaking the skin and shoved himself and his opponent back across the room until they slammed into the control console. The Grandfather screamed out, but didn't loosen his grip. With his free hand the Doctor was searching the console. He found what he was looking for – metal cubes he could pluck out of their control panel. Stabilisers. He took one, turned it in his hand, sliced the Grandfather's wrist with one of its sharp edges. Finally, he could breathe again as the Grandfather dropped him and withdrew. But before the Doctor could even take that breath, the Grandfather was on him, and he'd been kicked to the ground and in the ribs and stomach.

Time stood still. Not a metaphor, just a moment of discontinuity as the energies swirled out from the heart of the Edifice and into its control room.

It was all a question of inner calm and outer leverage. Finding and taking advantage of the Lagrangian points in a room with a shifting gravity field. Do that, and you could find the centre, the stability, the balance.

The Doctor jumped up, hung in the air, and time stood still long enough for him to perfectly line up his first strike, a flying kick to Grandfather Paradox's jaw, using all his strength and both his feet.

'Hai!' the Doctor shouted.

But the Grandfather brought up his hand to block, deflecting him, and it was the Doctor who found himself crashing to the floor. At the last moment he used his momentum to flip over, and landed facing his opponent.

Time returned to normal, then sped up.

The Doctor launched himself forwards, and made a series of fast, fast strikes. Vertical to the head with the blade of the hand, covered by a feint with the other hand. To the chest, each hand in turn. Grip the sleeve. A stamp on the right ankle, a high kick to the side of the neck. Straight punch. Vertical to the head with the blade of the hand, no feint. Flat palm to the heart. Flat palm to the other heart. Diagonal to the neck. Straight punch. Shoulder grip and vertical to the head. Feint a straight punch, then leap over his opponent's shoulders, land, strike at the back of the neck. Stamp on the ankle. Grip sleeve. Hip throw. Horizontal to the neck.

All deflected or dodged calmly by the Grandfather, who barely needed to move. As the Doctor made his last lunge, time returned to normal. Grandfather Paradox grabbed the Doctor's wrist and threw him, somersaulting, across the room.

With no time to break his fall, the Doctor crashed into the back wall cracking the brittle material. He paused to take stock. Aikido stresses the concept of being in harmony with one's enemy, of synchronising, anticipating and defusing, rather than simply defeating. But this was ridiculous. His opponent remembered this fight, he could counter every move.

Grandfather Paradox took a step back. 'I only have to wait and you will be mine.'

It had already happened, from his point of view.

'You would use Venusian aikido against me, when I am the only one-armed being who has ever mastered it?' the Grandfather sneered.

'It seems you can beat me with one arm tied behind your back,' the Doctor said ruefully.

He could taste his own blood. He'd split his lip at some point. It didn't matter. He looked up at his opponent. The cube the Doctor had taken from the console hadn't just been a handy weapon. It was a vital component keeping the forces of this place in check. Now it sounded as though there was a hurricane outside. The walls started to creak and crack like an old galleon caught in that hurricane.

The Grandfather's confidence faltered for the first time.

'You wanted the power of the Edifice,' the Doctor shouted, 'and you're going to get it. Just one bolt fired will drain off the last of the binding energy holding the Edifice together.'

He struggled to his feet. Grandfather Paradox swooped across the room, cloak flapping. He cracked his head down on the Doctor's, but only connected with the frontal part of the skull, one of the better-protected areas of the body. Still, it was dizzying and the Grandfather was taking the opportunity to grab for the cube.

It was the Doctor's turn to parry an attack.

He was perfectly calm, perfectly alert.

The Grandfather was at no advantage now that he was on the offensive. This wasn't defending against an attack he remembered coming. This was trying to land a blow or make a grip that hadn't worked. In any event, the Doctor simply had to deflect whatever was thrown at him. He knew his opponent wanted the cube, so it was easy to block a series of clumsy grabs and swipes.

He still couldn't land a blow of his own, though. Grandfather Paradox was everything he was, with 292 years' more experience. And he would know what was coming.

Unless the Doctor changed history.

The Doctor dived to one side then elbowed his opponent in the solar plexus – just about the most obvious place he could have attacked, so, paradoxically, the last place the Grandfather was ready to defend.

The Grandfather doubled up and collapsed on to the cracked ivory floor.

The Doctor sailed lightfoot over his opponent, hands behind his back, and landed at the console thirty feet away.

'Gallifrey, Kasterborous… this entire sector of space will be torn apart, destroyed,' the Grandfather managed.

The Doctor realised there were tears in his opponent's eyes. The Edifice had lurched to one side, the floor was pitched at an angle. He started edging around the console to the right panel. 'Forever. But your entire fleet will perish along with it.'

'You will die too.'

'Just as well, I think. I'd never be able to live with the memory anyway.'

'You will destroy all Gallifrey – wipe out millions of lives.'

The Doctor had never realised just how persuasive he could be. Committing mass murder – how could that be right?

'I never thought I'd admit to choosing the lesser of two evils,' he admitted.

'You know you can't bring yourself to do this.'

The more he thought about it, the less the Doctor liked this third option. He couldn't walk away, he thought. No... But how about the second option? Gallifrey would fall to Faction Paradox, but lives would be saved. The war would be over, forever. And he had spent so long worried about a future filled with an all-consuming war, fought across infinity and eternity, that it had never once occurred to him that afterwards there would follow a peace. This way, there would be a short war, barely a skirmish, then peace in heaven, with him able to shape things from the heart of power and influence. Where there's life, there's hope.

He looked up at the Grandfather. But there was the denial of his argument: an image of himself utterly without hope. The Ghost of Christmas Cancelled. An image of the future, unless...

'I must!' the Doctor cried out. 'I will be sparing my people a war that will dehumanise them to the point of becoming monsters. I will be saving them from whatever living nightmares the Faction's technology can inflict on them.'

The two men shouted at each other, their words lost in the din of the Edifice tearing itself apart.

The Grandfather flew gracefully over to the console just as the Doctor reached the lever, and began a series of lunges with his one arm, swinging it like a club. The Doctor rolled and dodged, never more than one step in front of his opponent, unable to go in any direction but anticlockwise round the edge of the console. Every time the Grandfather's hand hit a fragile control panel it punched holes, and splinters and sparks flew out of it. Now they were inches from each other. A palm came down flat on the Doctor's chest, forcing the air out of his lungs, pinning him to the console. The Grandfather grabbed the Doctor's arm and bit right into it, through his coat and shirt, drawing blood.

As his opponent raised his cackling, twisted face the Doctor punched it with his free hand, breaking the Grandfather's nose and grip.

By now, just as the Doctor had planned, they had moved all the way round the console, right back to the lever.

The Doctor made a grab for it.

The Grandfather reached out and caught his wrist with a perfectly executed *katate-tori* that he just didn't see coming. But the Doctor had his other hand free now, and there was nothing the Grandfather could do about that.

The Doctor grasped the lever.

The Doctor pulled the lever down.

Then – as if the act had drained him of all his strength – he sagged against the console.

Grandfather Paradox was howling. A strange, anguished sound that the Doctor couldn't imagine himself making, and which he now knew he never would make. There was nowhere either of them could run. Nothing either of them could do. The die had been cast, and now the two of them simply had to wait for oblivion. It felt like defeat, not a victory.

He could hear the energies of the Edifice gathering together for one final, inevitable, release.

Why could he hear footsteps?

Gallifrey's atmosphere was swirling off into space in streams of ionised gas. The ice caps melted, then vaporised. Land and sea were boiling. As great earthquakes rippled across the surface the cities were shattering or tipping into great chasms of lava. The Capitol had been the primary target. Not even photons had escaped its destruction. The few time ships that tried to pull away were torn apart. Time and space were screaming as Gallifrey was uprooted from them. The whole planet was distorted, losing form. The ivory moon, Pazithi Gallifreya, was caught and consumed by one of the atmospheric flares. The Faction Paradox fleet had ceased to exist some time ago, unnoticed and unmourned.

There was a flash as bright as the sun for the merest moment, annihilation so profound that it stretched deep into the past and far into the future. Then Gallifrey was gone.

Chapter Six
And the Dream I Had Was True

Marnal didn't say anything for a moment. The picture had broken up. The forces released during the destruction permitted no observer. The Doctor looked drained. Rachel just stood there and watched them.

'You destroyed Gallifrey,' Marnal told the Doctor. He had known, but even he hadn't quite believed it until he saw it with his own eyes. 'It was your choice, an active choice.'

The Doctor didn't say anything.

'Does that jog your memory?'

'I get the distinct sense that jogging my memory would be like jogging into a minefield,' the Doctor said quietly.

'Do you still deny it?' Marnal hissed.

'I never denied it, I said that as a result of what happened that day I lost my memories. Seeing this doesn't strike a chord.'

'A lawyer's answer,' Marnal said, 'a politician's answer.'

'The true answer,' the Doctor insisted.

'Do you accept the version of events you just saw?'

'I have a couple of questions about it,' the Doctor began. 'It's missing a lot of the context, I think, but –'

'Context?' Marnal shouted. 'Context? The context is that you committed an act of genocide.'

'Two, if you include Faction Paradox,' the Doctor reminded him, realising, as he said it, that this wasn't the best defence. He paused, then continued: 'I don't have to remember anything. Judging from what we just saw and heard I had to act quickly, it

121

wasn't an easy decision, it was made under stress and physical danger, and I managed to save the universe, including Gallifrey, from domination by a hostile power.'

'Churchill didn't save Britain from the Luftwaffe by ordering it to be razed to the ground.'

'He hadn't already lost. It was more like Masada, where –'

'You murdered the entire population of our planet.'

'We just saw for ourselves: Faction Paradox was a virus, one that was on the verge of infecting the whole of history, ending cause and effect, destroying everything that means anything, even meaning itself.'

'And it was led by your future self.'

'I have no idea what he was. He looked like me. He may well have been what I would have become *if I hadn't made the choice I did*. What I did destroyed him, his scheme, his army and every one of his followers, and very probably prevented any of them from ever existing. I won't become him.'

'Are you sure about that?'

The Doctor looked stung, and didn't answer.

'Yet again, you're revelling in the death and destruction your intervention caused.'

'I'm not revelling,' the Doctor said, so softly Rachel could barely hear him. 'You heard it spelled out: if I hadn't acted, the Faction would have won. If I had joined the Faction, it would have won. It had already happened. You can't alter the past.'

'You would dare quote the First Law of Time to me as you boast of flouting it? What about the Second Law, Doctor?'

'It sounds like you're now the one giving lawyers' answers.'

'"Do nothing, and all will be well."'

'I've no idea about the laws of time. Perhaps I did then, *I don't remember*. I know I did what I thought was right. Now, please listen to me. I've got a couple of questions of my own.'

'No. There are no questions now, Doctor, except what your punishment should be. Your guilt is beyond any doubt.'

'For one thing,' the Doctor continued regardless, 'well, who are you, and how did you get here? But let's leave that aside for the moment. There's something very, very important missing. A vital piece of the puzzle. An evidence of absence. Something to do with those footsteps.'

'What footsteps?' Marnal sneered.

The Doctor sighed. 'The least you should be doing is paying attention.'

The pub wasn't like the ones Fitz would remember, but truth be told it was better. It served snacks and coffee as well as beer. It looked clean and sleek, not as though it was proud the walls were grubby and the floor had never been scrubbed. Trix liked the idea of sitting for a drink somewhere that women were made to feel comfortable.

'This is more your sort of place?' Trix asked.

Fitz was smiling, looking relaxed. He'd spent the entire meal at the Indian restaurant unsure of himself. Nervous around the waiters, worried about the menu, really not comfortable with Greg.

'Oh yeah. Not sure about the music.'

The barman was handing over the drinks. 'Never liked him myself, either. Into more acoustic stuff.'

'What like?'

Trix tuned out while the two men had their little conversation. This was going to work. She and Fitz knew each other well and they'd trusted each other with their lives. They liked and respected each other. They could talk about anything and everything.

'Your husband knows his Sixties music,' the barman conceded.

'It's like he lived there,' she told him, and only realised afterwards what he'd called Fitz. These days you don't assume that sort of stuff about couples.

'Do you play at all?' the barman asked Fitz.

Fitz shrugged.

'He plays the guitar and sings. He's very good at it.'

'We have a music night on Tuesdays. Would you be interested?'

Fitz hesitated.

'He's interested,' Trix said. 'You've got to be brave,' she added for Fitz's benefit.

'OK.'

'Tonight?'

'Tonight? Well, is that enough time to put the word around…?'

'No offence, but we're not really expecting people to come from far and wide. You'll be entertaining the regulars. If you'd rather wait until next week, that's fine.'

'He'll sing a song tonight. Won't you, Fitz?'

Fitz thought about it for a couple of seconds, then broke into a goofy smile. 'Yeah.'

'You know that the Vortex was irreparably damaged at the moment of Gallifrey's destruction. It was a miracle we saw what we did.'

The Doctor nodded. 'The explosion must have created an event horizon in relative time. It prevents any information escaping, and anyone from travelling back to prevent it blowing up, or anyone from Gallifrey's past escaping into the present.'

'So it's impossible to see whatever was making those "footsteps". Convenient for you that the evidence that exonerates you is tucked away in those precise moments.'

'I have no idea whether it exonerates me or not. I'm here, Marnal. Something happened between me sitting in the Edifice waiting to die and me… well, the next thing was me waking up on Earth in the nineteenth century. The beginning of the hundred years I was stuck on Earth. I suppose.'

'You never questioned who you were?'

'I did very little else for a hundred years. Something had happened, I knew that.'

'You knew you were implicated in a terrible crime.'

'I knew that whatever had happened, trying to remember made me feel uneasy just thinking about it.'

'Guilt.'

'No... although there were times when I mistook the feeling for that.'

'You don't feel guilt now you've seen what you did to your own people?'

The Doctor thought about it for a moment. 'I regret any deaths, not just those of my own people.'

'The life of a human is worth as much as the life of a Time Lord?' Marnal asked.

The Doctor glanced over to Rachel. 'Yes,' he told them. 'Why? Do your laws of time say something different?'

'If either a human or a Time Lord had to die, you wouldn't mind which one?'

'What do you mean "had to die"?. I would try to prevent both of them from dying.'

'If you could only save one?'

The Doctor was scowling. 'This is stupid. It doesn't even qualify as a hypothetical situation.'

'You would betray a member of your own race?'

'If there was no alternative, if the greater good would be better served, yes. Anyway, what's wrong with humans?'

The Doctor kept a careful eye on Rachel. If he could get her onside, he would be able to get out of here. Marnal obviously had contempt for human beings. If the Doctor could goad him into saying that out loud, Rachel would see Marnal in his true colours.

'Earth's your favourite planet?' Marnal asked.

The Doctor deflated at the change of subject. 'I have a soft spot for it, yes. From what I gather, you must have too.'

'Is that what you think?'

'You've spent over a hundred years here. You seem to have bought property. Oh, and made at least one friend.' The Doctor smiled at Rachel. 'I did the same once. Without, of course, your glittering literary career. I'm quite fond of human beings.'

'Do you prefer humans to your own kind?'

'If you're a typical Time Lord, then perhaps the universe is better off without us.'

Marnal stepped back, clutching his lapels, apparently satisfied with what he'd heard.

'Rather than trying to score debating points,' the Doctor suggested, 'why don't we work together to find out what happened? We both want the same thing.'

Marnal shook his head. 'Believe me, you don't want what I want, Doctor. One last debating point. It's interesting, given what you've just said, that Fitz managed to survive when every single Time Lord was killed, isn't it?'

He indicated to Rachel that he wanted her to help him take the glass bottle back upstairs.

'I'll leave you to think about that,' he said.

The Doctor stayed quiet. He didn't want to keep reminding Marnal about his companions. No doubt, Fitz and Trix would be trying to find him. Or perhaps they'd found him already, and were waiting for the best moment to come to his rescue.

Rachel made Marnal a coffee. His ready meal was in the oven, which took forever to heat up.

Marnal was sitting in the living room, a place as dull and dusty as the rest of the house. She sat next to him on the sofa and handed him his mug.

'Are you OK?' she asked.

'Me?'

'You saw your planet destroyed.'

'I knew it had happened.'

'That's not the same as seeing it.'

'No. I knew the Doctor was guilty before, but... now I've seen what he did. You said something before about no need for law courts, you could just play the tape of the crime.'

'That's not exactly what I said, but –'

'His guilt is now beyond any doubt. I'd thought that when I confronted him with his crime it would be too much for him. That he would break down and confess, that he would be racked with remorse and self-loathing. If anything, he seems more calm than he did before.'

Rachel nodded. 'He was subdued at first, but then he recovered.'

'That makes sense to you?' he asked.

'I don't know how Time Lords' minds work but sometimes, for human people, knowing something, even if it's horrible, is better than not knowing.'

He looked sceptical, so she gave him an example.

'Like when a child vanishes. If, after a week or so, the body is found, it's a relief in a way for the parents. They can begin the mourning process, they can start to rebuild their lives. That's better than constantly waiting for a phone call, making assumptions, but never knowing for certain whether their child is alive or dead. Or if you're diagnosed with an illness. Knowing it has a name, even if there's no cure, can be better than not knowing why you keep getting sick.'

Marnal was shaking his head, not crediting what he'd just heard. 'Human minds are so confusing.'

'Perhaps the Doctor's mind is more human than Time Lord. He spends all his time with people. He seems to have spent a lot of time on the Earth, perhaps some human stuff has rubbed off on him.'

'I have spent more than a century here, and I assure you my thoughts remain unsullied.'

Rachel sipped her coffee.

'The Doctor's guilt is now proven. The only question remaining is the manner of his punishment.'

'Are you going to kill him?' Rachel asked, a little aghast. She'd seen *Shallow Grave* and she knew how difficult it was to get rid of a body. Plus, of course, it would be murder.

'He has to suffer.'

Rachel felt a little cold. She thought about the Doctor, tied up and alone in the draughty cellar.

'It's not as though you can go for an eye for an eye,' she said.

Marnal looked miserable. Rachel went to get his meal. She took it out of the oven, and found herself mushing up the potato for him. Force of habit.

She went back to find Marnal still hunched up on the sofa.

'What punishment is there?' he asked her.

'I think you're still looking for answers,' she said. 'You need the Doctor for those.'

'I have the only important answer. He destroyed Gallifrey, he killed all but a handful of my people. Try to imagine that.'

Rachel sighed. 'I don't think I can. It's like being marooned on a desert island, then finding Hitler there. You can't just phone the police, or whoever you're meant to phone.'

Marnal was deep in thought.

'I don't know...' Rachel said. She wasn't used to thinking like this. Who would be? 'If Hitler really was the last man on Earth, would I kill him? We'd have a lot to talk about.'

Marnal looked at her, a pained expression on his face.

'You know what I mean,' Rachel said. 'If he was the last man on Earth. I don't know how I'd punish him. How did your people punish their criminals?'

He thought about that for a moment. 'That's a good question. This is a situation without obvious precedent, but there may be something in one of the books. I'll need your help to find it.'

Marnal had suggested he think, so the Doctor had decided to think.

He began to meditate. He'd tried it a few times before, searching for some clue to who he was. Always, the message had come back loud and clear from the back of his mind:

DON'T

Now, though, the Doctor had a little more to go on. He knew he couldn't avoid the truth, and he knew, deep down, that his brain contained the answers.

The cellar was dark and cold, the house above him was quiet.

His eyes should be closed, his mind opened.

There was no 'him' nor 'eyes' nor 'closed', simply 'mind'.

DON'T

The Doctor's eyes were open, as though he'd been woken suddenly. He was back in the dark cellar.

Back, back to his beginning.

There was an old myth that humans used only 10 per cent of their brains. This was a simple misunderstanding. Give or take, there was activity in every part of the human brain. But the physical structures in there were capable of ten times the activity they actually performed. It wasn't that a human being had a brain like a house with ninth-tenths of the rooms sealed off, it was more as though a road network wasn't carrying as much traffic as it was designed to carry.

He was back in the dark cellar.

It was very hard not to think about something.

Itself a thought.

He was back in the dark cellar.

The Doctor tutted to himself. He knew how to do this. He'd studied the discipline a number of times and in a number of locations. He'd been the one who'd helped show the Beatles how to do it, in Bangor of all places. Which reminded him. That had been the time he'd got into a conversation with a Buddhist vet about the karmic implications of putting an animal down. Apparently, if you are so willing to put the animal out of its hopeless suffering that you're willing to risk the resulting bad karma, and even rebirth in one of the hells, then it's a good act. He had destroyed Gallifrey, put it out of its misery. Had he been reborn in hell, left adrift? The crucial thing to remember, the vet had told him, was compassion.

He was back in the dark cellar.

He let his thoughts slip away. He let his mind go, introduced his mantra, replacing thought.

Simply mind. Something like, but more than, the vast ocean. It was like being dipped in golden light. A pure world, quite unlike the dark cellar.

He was back in the dark cellar.

He was out of practice. Trying too hard. He didn't need to go into a trance. He simply needed to return to –

Vibration not thought. Golden light, light of life. Pure mind, not where we come from but where we all go when we transcend, the community of mind. He had destroyed far more than he had created. But he was on the side of life.

He was back in the dark cellar. It was darker, more of a cellar. He screwed up his eyes to clear his head.

Why had that happened? That time it wasn't him, it was like someone else had warned him. It hadn't been a noise out here, in the real world.

Slipping back in was easier now.

Nothing had ever called to him in the gold. No voices tempting or scorning. No conversations. But there were other voices here. Ghosts yet not ghosts, they… He had never existed. He was the passing thought of a small, cunning man sitting alone reading a book, drinking his tea, listening to a gramophone record. In a dream.

No.

False.

He was back in the dark cellar.

'Damn it!' the Doctor shouted out. Then he felt a bit guilty – he'd almost certainly startled Marnal and Rachel. Guilty for disturbing his kidnappers, not guilty about destroying his home planet and killing its entire population and history.

Interesting.

Trying to explore his mind was like throwing a rubber ball at a wall.

The Doctor closed his eyes.

Strip away all the deception, uncover the truth.

And the truth is: the Doctor was the finest dream of hundreds of human beings, refined as they tapped away at their typewriters. For generations, they'd made him a hero to countless millions in over a hundred countries. Then, just once, he hadn't come back. His enemies had kept him away. But despite their best efforts he hadn't been forgotten. There were those who remembered him when they walked past a dummy in a shop window or sat on the beach looking out to sea, and every time they ground pepper. Some of those who remembered him had typewriters of their own. And, after far too long, a new generation of children were about hear that music for the first time, and they would learn their sofa wasn't just for sitting on. Before his sweetest victory, unfinished business here –

He was back in the dark cellar.

He left it again. Every time, it became easier to return.

He remembered the wall.

It was a stone wall, about twice his height. Behind heavy iron gates the small, cunning man he'd seen before, asleep lying on a bed of flowers. He was wearing a white suit, cut from the finest dreams.

'Is it... time... already?' the Doctor asked.

The small man sat up suddenly.

'That was a nice nap. Just three questions: where am I, who am I and who are you? But wait! Your shoes – they fit perfectly!' he gabbled, in a Scottish accent.

The little man hesitated, then pulled himself together. 'Oh, that's the trouble with memories. All that déjà vu. All those things you don't want to be reminded of. It's excess baggage, you know. I envy you. What could the relevance possibly be if I remember Ace's visit to Paradise Towers?'

The Doctor stayed quiet.

The little man sighed. 'This is all terribly symbolic. With the emphasis on terrible. Clear thinking, that's what's needed now.'

He came ambling over and poked his nose through the gate.

'I think you're in my mind,' the Doctor said.

'Well, I think you're in mine,' the little man replied slyly. 'Either way, there seems to be more than enough room for both of us.'

Yellow blossoms were falling like rain on the other side of the wall, in countless numbers.

'Times like this, I need an umbrella. I used to have one, but you gave it to Benny.'

'There must be millions of blossoms.'

'One hundred and fifty-three thousand, eight hundred and forty-one of them,' the little man replied instantly.

'You've counted?'

'The maths is simple enough. I'll give you a clue: you just have to remember to subtract five at the end.'

'Could you open the gate for me?'

'If you say the magic word.'

'Please?'

The little man chuckled.'Not that magic word. You've got plenty of room on that side. Certainly more room than any human being. Over a century's worth of memories, for one thing. Space for plenty more.'

'This is like talking to a wall,' the Doctor sighed.

This reminded him of something, something outside.

'Hang on a minute!' he exclaimed.

And he was back in the cellar.

Trix sighed. She'd woken, got up, showered, dried off and dressed. In that time, Fitz had managed to sit up in his bed and get the guitar on to his lap.

'Do you know what you're singing tonight yet? That pub looks like the sort of place where golden oldies would go down well.'

'Why else do you think I want to spend an evening there?'

'You could sing one of those parallel universe Beatles songs you were talking about.'

Fitz thought about it.'"Back Home"? No, how about this one?'

He played a couple of chords.'On the road to Rishikesh / I was dreaming more or less.'

'That's just "Jealous Guy" with different lyrics,' Trix pointed out.

Fitz paused. 'Yes. Hadn't even noticed that. Well, it's cheating anyway, isn't it? I'm going to do something new, I think.'

'You mean the Scissor Sisters or something?'

'No. Something I've written.'

'What?'

'Well... I haven't actually written it. Not yet. I think I've got the tune. It doesn't have a chorus. I'm not sure it needs one.'

He strummed a couple of chords and started to sing: 'I've travelled to the past, sweetheart / And I've been to the future, too.'

'It's not about us, is it?'

Fitz shook his head. 'No, that's private. This is just the opposite really.'

Trix seemed half-relieved, half-disappointed. 'You do know it's just a little pub thing, don't you?'

'Oh yeah. But I want to get it right.' He strummed the guitar again.

Rachel had brought the Doctor a coffee.

He was sitting up, alert. It didn't look as if he had slept – that would be difficult tied up like he was – but neither did he look exhausted.

'Where's Marnal?'

'Looking up punishments. Trying to, anyway.'

'You couldn't free my wrists just for a moment?' he asked. 'I just need to rub a bit of life back into them.'

'No. You'll hit me.'

'Hit you?'

'With that karate.'

The Doctor gave a beatific smile. 'It was aikido. Purely defensive.'

'You kicked that one-armed man in the head.'

'He was just about to conquer the universe.'

'I can't believe you know martial arts. You don't look the type.'

'Well, lucky for you, I'm afraid I forgot all that when I forgot everything else. Shame. It could come in quite useful from time to time. As a last resort.'

She asked him if he wanted anything for breakfast.

'Rachel,' he replied instead, 'I need to get to my TARDIS. The answer is in there. I didn't know that before, but I've just been thinking, and I realised that after –'

'The answer is in your TARDIS?' Rachel repeated.

'That's right. There's a... well... a back wall. I didn't know what it was before. Not entirely sure what it is now, truth be told. I know it's time to find out. Marnal will want to know about this too.'

'I will tell Marnal what you said. He'll decide what happens from there.'

'Let me go,' the Doctor pleaded. 'You heard him before. He doesn't care about humanity, he doesn't like human beings.'

'I'm not sure I do,' Rachel said.

'What?'

'Look at me. Look at what I do all day, and it barely covers the credit card bills. You don't even remember me, do you? Do you think I'm pretty?'

The Doctor sighed. 'I don't see what –'

'Translation: no. I used to think I was. I used to get home and still have a bit of life in me. Went out, had boyfriends. All three of them ended up dumping me after a month or two, and then saying it wasn't anything to do with me. Every time, I thought it was going well. I was telling them everything, and falling in love. I was reading the signs, I thought. Giving them more than they wanted. So why...?'

The Doctor looked as if he wanted to put his hand on her shoulder. He looked her in the eye.

'Most people don't have lives like that,' the Doctor said.

'You're joking,' Rachel hissed. '*Everyone* has a life like that. Everyone I know, anyway. We try to pretend we don't, we try to pretend it's like an advert and that if we buy a new pair of shoes, or some DVDs, or a wedding ring then we'll be happy for the rest of our lives, but before we're even home we feel more guilty than we did, because we spent all that money. So we just get on. And none of us talks about how effing miserable we are all the time, because when we do it feels so self-indulgent and self-centred and so petty. So we go out and get hammered and try to lose ourselves for just one evening, or we pray to a god we know deep down doesn't exist. But the vast majority of us, the vast majority of the time, just sit at home glued to some television show we don't even like that's showing us nothing, scared that the plane we can hear above us is about to fall out of the sky, or that the water's polluted or that some idiot we didn't even vote for is going to get us all killed, or we just worry that next month the overdraft will finally run out. Because that's the world.'

'No,' the Doctor said simply.

'No? That's it, is it? "No." ' She turned to go.

'There are marvels out there, Rachel. Domed cities, rocket ships, Technicolor jungles. Walls built with time itself. Smiling robots, flying women, reptile kings. People who look like every animal you can imagine, and quite a lot you can't. Seas of diamond water, landscapes carved from ice and gold. So much music, so much laughter. Ingenuity – races that can pluck a star from the heavens and place it in the palm of their hand. False gods and their games, machine minds with such purity of thought. But despite all that, this Earth is the most wonderful place in the universe.'

She turned round.

'Yeah, because speed cameras and cancer –'

' "There are more things in heaven and earth, Horatio, than are dreamt of in your philosophy." I heard that line the very first time it was delivered. All of us, every single one of us in that audience, listened to Burbage and knew the truth of it. I've spent a lifetime here, and there's so much more than even I have known. Have you ever seen a whale's tail-fin breaking the surface of the ocean, or the sun rise over the Great Wall of China? Have you walked with ten thousand people around you, all heading the same way? Have you sat in a forest with your eyes closed, surrounded by sound? Have you listened to Bach or sipped Château Yquem? Have you seen an insect's eye through an electron microscope or stood on the roof of a castle's tallest tower? Have you swum in a moonlit lake? You could have done any of that without me, Rachel. Think what you could do with a TARDIS. Yes, there's villainy on this Earth, but there's heroism that is far, far more than a match for it. However dark it seems, there is always more light. If you need help getting to the light, I will give you that help.'

'You want me to have faith in you?'

'Only charlatans ask for faith, just before they ask you to give them your money or die in their name. I can let you find the truth for yourself. All those things you said. You don't want to be right. You want to look at the universe with opened eyes. You've just been waiting for a chance, one spark to show you the way. Let me out of these chains, and I'll let you out of yours. I'm the Doctor – I can make you better. Come with me, and let's go on adventures.'

Rachel took one step forwards, then stopped dead.

'Nice try.'

She started to leave.

'Rachel?' the Doctor pleaded.

She turned round. 'You nearly had me going there. You're the worst of the lot of them. You killed all those people. You're Doctor Death if you're anything. Trying to get my hopes up. Manipulating me with cheap... emotional crap. You think I'd solve all my problems if I saw a whale? You've got no idea.'

'I... did what was right, I'm sure of it,' he told her. 'I've... I've created more than I've destroyed.'

'Are you sure about that?' Rachel asked. She went away, closing and bolting the door behind her.

'I wish I could remember,' he said. 'I know that if I did I could show you –' He shook his head, which was full of that sense again, that black shape just out of view, that scratching in his mind. He wasn't free of it.

'I know what I did!' he shouted out, frustrated. 'I saw what I did!'

The Doctor was back in the cellar.

There is no society on Earth where there is a clear distinction between the living and the dead. On first hearing that, one rebels. Where is there room for ambiguity? A man is alive or a man is not. But every culture has its tradition of ancestor worship and a belief in ghosts. Almost every religion preaches that there is some form of an afterlife, and many faiths claim that communication between the living and dead is possible. Across the world, there are tales of men who are the undead and living dead, like zombies and vampires. There is a belief that people can return from death to life – the only dispute seems to be whether everyone can, or just the especially virtuous. Even though these beliefs appear universal, we might dismiss some or all of them as superstition. However, modern doctors are far less clear about the point where life begins or ends than they would have been even a hundred years ago. It's not always even a question of blurring a boundary between two opposite states. A number of African cultures divide the population into three constituencies: the living, the *sasha* and the *zamani*. The sasha are the gone-but-not-forgotten. There are those alive that met them and can figuratively 'bring them to life' for others. When the last of their contemporaries dies, a person becomes zamani, or truly dead. Even then, they have not ceased to exist, they are simply in a new form, and are revered.

Transcript from *The History… of Death*,
BBC Four documentary, first broadcast 2007

Chapter Seven
The Edge of Destruction

There were about twenty people in the pub, not counting the landlord, the barmaid, Fitz and Trix.

Fitz was the only support act, but he wasn't going on first. A girl called Emma and a lad with a fiddle were playing for about half an hour before him and the same length of time after him, with his turn giving them enough time for a breather. They played every month, and the regulars loved them. He'd been told to keep his set to about ten minutes, which Fitz worked out meant three songs. This was two more than he'd planned for, and he wasn't sure what to do about it yet. He'd lubricated his thinking cap and vocal cords with a little beer.

Emma had a good voice. They hadn't had a chance to talk before the gig – Fitz had cut his arrival a bit fine. She was young, sort of all right, but nothing on Trix. She was singing folk songs, but with a bit more energy to them than normal. He'd been told her stuff went down well here. The song he'd written probably could count as folk, if you fiddled the figures a little.

His turn came racing round. He took his place where Emma had been standing, the applause for her merging into his welcome.

Fitz lifted his guitar.

'Good evening,' he said, confident. 'My name is…' He hesitated, unsure what he should call himself. He'd played a couple of places in the Sixties, called himself Fitz Fortune. It had a good ring to it, but… 'My name is Fitz Kreiner. I'm going to sing three songs, if that's all right.'

All twenty people nodded enthusiastically. There weren't many of them, but they were all keen.

Fitz smiled. He knew already that they'd like this one. 'I call this one "Contains Spoilers", and I warn you that it does, indeed, contain spoilers.'

He made a show of tuning his guitar, although it was already as tuned as it was possible for a guitar to be. Then he began his song.[1] The crowd were soon tapping their feet and cheered him at the end.

'OK,' said Fitz, 'this is a Beatles song. You won't remember but, trust me, the Fab Four brought the house down at Live Aid with it. This is called "Celebrate the Love". One, two, three…'

Rachel found Marnal in the garage unlocking the door of the TARDIS.

'Is it OK if I come with you?' she asked.

Marnal looked curiously at her, then stepped aside to let her in. He followed, the doors whirring smoothly shut behind them.

'Were all the buildings bigger on the inside on Gallifrey?' she asked.

Marnal gave a cold laugh. 'A few were.'

'Such as?'

'The Towers of Canonicity and Likelihood.' He looked down at her. 'You wouldn't understand.'

'If you told me how it was done, would I understand that?'

Marnal had reached the console. As he started working the controls, checking the progress of the recalibration, he was clearly considering her question.

'Yes, I think so,' he conceded after a moment or so. 'Imagine a sequence. Start with a point, then a line, then a square, then imagine a cube, then imagine a TARDIS.'

Happy with what the instruments were telling him, Marnal continued on his way, heading for a door in the back wall.

'I think I get it,' Rachel said. 'When you go into a TARDIS, you don't go forwards or backwards, you don't go up or down, you

[1] The lyrics to Fitz's song are on page 280

don't go from left to right. You go in a completely different direction, one you can't travel on Earth.'

Marnal turned, smiling. 'Yes, that's certainly one way to put it.'

He opened the door. On the other side a long, wide corridor raced off far into the distance. The walls, floor and ceiling were all spotless and white. Rachel could see other corridors branching off it. Every so often, there were doors – white ones, naturally. The walls had a circular pattern embossed on them. It was all brightly lit, although there were no apparent sources for the light.

'I've just been talking to the Doctor. He says he remembers something.'

'What?'

'He said something about the back wall of the TARDIS.'

'It doesn't have a back wall.'

'It must have.'

'A fully functional TARDIS is practically infinite.'

'Is infinity ever really a practical size?' she asked.

'No,' Marnal admitted. 'Even a Time Lord setting out in his youth and walking every day of his life with a minimum of rest could only get so far.'

'I thought you were immortal?'

'The Doctor and I can live for a very long time, replacing our bodies every thousand years or so as they wear out – sooner, of course, if we meet with an accident. We have a limited number of bodies. We can regenerate twelve times, after the death of our thirteenth body, we die. Even then –'

Rachel cut him off before she had to endure the whole lecture. 'Why make your spaceships so big, then?'

Marnal shrugged. 'There are legends that the first Time Lords were true immortals. But I think the reason is that a TARDIS and its operator are linked. All our minds have hidden depths, areas we will never consciously explore. That seems to go double for the Doctor.'

He strode down the corridor. After thirty or forty yards he stopped and looked around.

'You don't know where we're going?' Rachel asked, as gently as she could.

'No,' he answered. 'I'm looking for the power room. It usually isn't very far from the entrance.'

'What does it look like?'

'A power room can look like anything. Its distinguishing feature is that there will be what looks like an iron ball the size of a house in it.'

'That's pretty distinguishing.'

Rachel opened the nearest door and stepped through it.

It was a lad's bedroom. Small, with an unmade bed with a radio and broken clock built into the headboard. The sheets were almost as crumpled as the piles of jeans and underwear. An old record player sat on a chair, surrounded by a variety of LPs, CDs and what looked like square blocks of transparent plastic. There was a bedside table piled with a few books and knick-knacks topped by an empty champagne bottle.

Rachel trod on a discarded bra. She guessed this wasn't the Doctor's room.

'This isn't it,' Marnal told her, rather redundantly in the circumstances.

'How many rooms are there?' she asked once they were heading back along the corridor.

'Countless numbers.'

They'd walked some distance down the corridor and reached a wall that blocked their way.

'The power room is clearly down another corridor.'

'This is weird,' Rachel said. She wasn't talking about the cigarette butts all over the floor.

Marnal was staying a few feet back from the wall. 'Can you hear that?' he asked.

Now she could, and she took a step back. 'A scratching noise. There's something trapped behind there. I think we should get the Doctor.'

* * *

The Doctor lifted himself up and smashed his chair down against the cellar floor. It was metal, but it was quite old. The legs buckled, so much so that he couldn't rest the chair back on the ground. Instead, he smashed it down again. One leg broke off and another went without much more effort. With his legs free, it was the work of moments to smash the back of the chair against the wall.

He quickly found a hook on the wall, and prised the manacles apart enough to wriggle his hands out.

Free.

He stood for a moment, catching his breath and letting the blood reach his hands and feet. He'd not stood up for almost a day, and it was almost dizzying.

No time to hang around, though.

As he hurried to the door his eyes fell on the pile of books. He picked up the top one. *Day of Wrath*, by Marnal, a paperback published a quarter of a century ago. He flicked through the first couple of pages, then put it to one side and rummaged through the other books. All by the same author, all on the same theme. A record of Gallifrey, in almost obsessive detail. One of the books, it appeared, had no story as such; it was more like a novel-length summary of a ceremony that was conducted only once every century. It had been published in 1938 and was illustrated by Mervyn Peake. Another was an obsessive list of the annual variations of his home planet's climate. Gallifrey, it seemed, had more than two dozen seasons. Not that any of the Time Lords ever ventured outside the sealed domes that covered their cities to experience the weather directly – they preferred the safety of books on the subject. The problem, the Doctor concluded, for the writer of adventure fiction set on Gallifrey was that nothing much ever happened there.

His coat was in one corner. He put it back on, and checked to see if anything was missing. Only the TARDIS key. He slipped three of the thinner books into his pockets.

The Doctor went upstairs, keeping as quiet as he could. He

found himself in the kitchen. Rachel's book bag was on the counter. It was dark outside. He edged out into the hallway, standing perfectly still when he thought he heard something, but it was just a car going along the road outside. He could make his escape, find Fitz and Trix, come back for the TARDIS.

It felt wrong to run.

He knew he needed Marnal's help. Together, the two of them could come up with answers. More than that... actions had consequences. The Doctor had to face up to that. If you can't do the time, don't be a Time Lord.

However, this had to be done on equal terms. This was Marnal's turf, he had an assistant and he had a gun. The Doctor had to find a way to even up the odds a little. He pressed forward again, but stubbed his toe on a small table. He bit his lip, tried to steady the table, winced as the telephone directory fell on to the carpet with a thud that seemed to echo around the house.

The Doctor hesitated, and looked down.

It almost felt like cheating.

The crowd had chuckled a couple of times at the first one, they'd loved the Beatles song, but he thought it needed something a bit faster so he'd finished off with that Dramarama number he liked. He'd given Emma and her friend something to live up to. One of the university students there had said he was 'well weapon', which was apparently a good thing.

When he was younger, Fitz had dreamt of playing big concerts to thousands of screaming women, dozens of whom – even just statistically, he felt – would lust after him. There comes a point, and it's when you're still ridiculously young, when you realise you're too old to be a pop star. He'd comfortably passed that point long before he'd even met the Doctor, whatever he'd kept telling himself. But there he had been tonight, in a pub where a couple of dozen honest people had really appreciated what he'd done. And, after some of them had bought him a beer, Fitz was now on his way home with his beautiful blonde girlfriend on his arm and tomorrow morning... Well, he was living in the future now. Every morning would be tomorrow morning.

He'd been paid £10 and his singing tonight wouldn't make him famous, but Fitz didn't think he'd ever been happier, at any point in his life.

Trix was hugging him as they walked up to the hotel.

There was a large man standing just in front of the entrance. He wore a dark suit and was holding up his ID. There were a couple of uniformed officers behind him.

'Patricia Joanne Pullman?' he asked.

'Yes, I - Fitz, run!'

She turned to get away, but there was already another uniform waiting for her. He grabbed her shoulder.

'Patricia Joanne Pullman,' this new arrival was saying, 'I'm arresting you for the murder of Anthony Charles Macmillan. You do not have to say anything, but anything you do say will be taken -'

Fitz punched the policeman very hard in the face, and stepped over him.

'Come on!' he shouted.

Trix had already caught up with him. Together they hurled themselves round the side of the building. There was a tall fence in front of them, but a side door into the hotel to the left. They took it.

'Kitchen inspectors!' Fitz yelled at the chef who came hurrying towards them.

They swerved both ways round him, and were out of the swing doors and into the restaurant. They made their way to the fire exit at the rear of the hotel. A minute later they were over a small brick wall, through an alleyway and on a main road.

Trix was pointing up the street at a bus. It was just pulling away.

They caught it up, persuaded the driver to stop and jumped aboard.

'Two, please, keep the change,' Trix said, handing the driver a £50 note.

They took their seats at the back.

'I've got a question,' Fitz said.

Trix bit her lip.

'All that running away from monsters kept us fit, didn't it?' he asked.

Trix was barely out of breath. 'Er, yeah. Have I told you I love you?'

'No, but I kinda inferred it,' he grinned. 'Now what?'

'Have you got your passport with you?'

'Yes, I think so.' Fitz checked his pocket and confirmed that he had.

'Then how do you fancy a trip to New York?'

The Doctor peeked through the tiny garage window, but the curtain was drawn. The only way in was through the wooden doors at the front. He listened carefully, checked his watch, then made his way inside. The TARDIS took up one corner of the garage. The glass bottle contraption sat in the middle of the floor. Marnal and Rachel were nowhere to be seen.

With occasional glances towards the TARDIS, the Doctor set about examining the bottle. It was an ingenious piece of work, he couldn't deny that, ridiculously easy to duplicate. It didn't even require specialist knowledge. He was sure Fitz and Trix could cobble up one if they just knew –

The TARDIS door opened.

The Doctor tried to duck out of sight, before realising that there was nowhere to duck.

From Marnal's expression it was clear that the Doctor was the last thing he was expecting to see in here.

The Doctor smiled. 'Good evening.'

Marnal went for his stun gun, so the Doctor went for Marnal. He grabbed at the gun, pulled it out of Marnal's hand, then batted it to the far corner of the garage. By the time he had finished that, Rachel had emerged from the TARDIS.

'Or,' the Doctor said, 'we could talk.'

Marnal held back, looking as though he might lash out.

Rachel, though, looked more conciliatory. 'Talk about what?' she asked.

'You've seen the back wall?' the Doctor said.

Rachel nodded.

'Do you know what it means, Marnal?' he asked.

Marnal shook his head. 'You do?'

'I don't. But I know it's important we ask the right questions. Together, we should be able to answer them.'

'He's right.'

'Be quiet, Rachel. You're a criminal, Doctor.'

'I'm not. I've been accused of a terrible crime, but I've had no chance to offer a defence. So, I propose a truce. If I've done wrong, I deserve punishment.'

Rachel smiled encouragingly. 'That's good, isn't it, Marnal?'

Marnal was still suspicious. 'What are the terms of this truce?'

'We investigate what happened, together. I agree to stay in your custody – I don't leave the grounds of your house, but in return there's no tying up or waving guns. You will have my undivided attention until we've answered the outstanding questions,' the Doctor promised. 'With the investigation concluded, if I am found to have done anything wrong, I will submit myself to you for the appropriate punishment under the law of the Time Lords. I picked up a few of your books from the library to help me understand what that might be.'

He turned round, to show the book bag on his shoulder.

'We've established your hand in the destruction of Gallifrey, Doctor. What other questions could possibly be relevant?'

'Let's see, shall we?' The Doctor offered his hand.

'It makes sense, Marnal,' Rachel said.

Marnal shook the Doctor's hand.

The Doctor got down to business. 'There are all sorts of thing you haven't asked. For starters, why did I lose my memory? That's a good one.'

'If you did lose your memory.'

'Just for the sake of argument,' the Doctor said, smiling sweetly. 'Rachel?'

'Trauma,' she suggested.

'Post-traumatic stress? Something so horrible that I couldn't face it?'

Rachel nodded.

'You remember that, then?' Marnal said. He was still on his guard.

'Do you think it fits the facts?'

'Yes,' Marnal replied. 'You underwent a traumatic event. What's more, it's one that you initiated. Your guilt and cowardice conspired to make you block it from your mind.'

'You've been spying on me, Marnal, seen me on my travels.'

'Your interventions in history, you mean? Yes, I've seen you.'

'It wasn't a question. Would you say I'm usually racked with guilt?'

Marnal looked very self-satisfied. 'Rather the opposite. You have a callous disregard for consequences. You destabilise governments, but never stay to check that the new regime you've installed is any better. You instinctively take sides in any conflict. You can kiss a woman one minute, forget about her the next.'

'So, I'm not the guilty type. Cowardly?'

'Reckless, if anything.'

'I've seen some traumatic things?'

'You seem to surround yourself with death and destruction.'

The Doctor nodded, a little sadly. 'You saw Sabbath?'

'A human time-traveller who fancied himself as a Lord of Time. An ape who would be a king.'

The Doctor nodded. 'With fists the size of hams, that's what I always remember about him. He gave me quite a lot of trouble for a while. Sabbath started playing with the time lines, created whole new histories. For the sake of the structure of time and space, I had to correct that. For months on end I watched whole universes die.'

'More death.'

'Yes,' the Doctor said quietly. 'Millions of lives ended. Gone.'

'Your point?'

The Doctor perked up. 'Ah yes. So, to sum up: your theory of me is that I was racked with guilt, cowardly and couldn't stand the thought I'd killed so many people, so I had some sort of nervous breakdown and suppressed my memory of it because I couldn't cope. But all the evidence that you yourself have collected demonstrates the exact opposite. Hasn't it occurred to you that your theory might be flawed?'

Rachel was thinking this through. 'He's right.'

Marnal was trying very hard not to look worried. 'If you murder someone, you're a murderer. If you murder more people, it makes the first crime worse, it doesn't excuse it. Forgetting why you did it isn't a mitigating circumstance, and not knowing why you forgot it is entirely irrelevant.'

Rachel was struggling to keep up. 'I think you're right too,' she said unhelpfully.

'We've been asking the wrong question,' the Doctor said. 'There's a larger game being played here.'

'So you think we'd settle this if we knew why you lost your memory?' Rachel asked.

'No,' the Doctor replied. 'No. That's the wrong question too.'

'So what's the right question?'

'Ah... that I don't know. I was hoping that together the two of us – the three of us, sorry, Rachel – could come up with it.'

Marnal's patience had run out. 'I've answered the only question that matters.'

'ARMED POLICE! WE HAVE YOU SURROUNDED!'

The Doctor winced. It was to the point, he supposed, but couldn't the officer have thought of something more elegant?

'You called the police?' Marnal shouted. 'This is your idea of a truce?'

'What did you say to them?' Rachel asked.

'I just said who I was,' the Doctor said. 'And that you had a gun and a hostage, but I was fine, I'd sort it out, so there was no need for them to come round.'

Marnal was walking over to retrieve his gun.

'Look, Marnal, I meant what I said before.'

Marnal tucked the gun away. 'Only you could break a promise before you even made it,' he said.

A squad car had been three streets away when the 999 call had been relayed to them. A couple of young constables had turned their car around and come straight to the house. They'd been warned that there was a hostage situation, and that the kidnapper was armed, so while they waited for back-up they confined their activities to assessing the situation and getting the neighbours to stay indoors and away from the windows. Another two cars arrived within minutes, along with an ambulance. One of the new cars had brought an inspector, who took control of the scene and had the officers establishing an inner and outer cordon. By now, a van with officers in body armour had arrived, along with a couple more cars. The vehicles were parked to block the road off and provide a corral for the officers staking out the building.

The police knew very little. A man had phoned 999, given them this address and said that someone was being held hostage, probably in the detached garage. The hostage-taker was a man in his thirties wearing a distinctive blue blazer, and he had a pistol, a taser and possibly other weapons. There were only three people on the premises. Then the caller had hung up. The phone call had come from the landline of the house itself. The two officers who'd been first on the scene reported what the next-door neighbours had told them: there was one resident of the house, an elderly man who the neighbours thought had been at death's door. Most days, his nurse came round for a few hours.

Hostage situations took one form pretty much the whole world over – the authorities waited, did nothing to provoke, established a line of communication and tried to find out what the hostage-takers wanted. It was a game, of course. The police weren't going to give in to their demands, and only the most deranged hostage-taker thought otherwise. The moment the siege started there were only two outcomes: the hostage-takers either eventually gave themselves up or they started shooting. If the latter happened, this was the point where the authorities had nothing to lose and went in hard. Just out of sight, an armed response unit was already drawing up plans and checking automatic rifles. If it came, the assault would be over in seconds.

The Doctor was telling Marnal all this while reading one of the books he'd brought from the cellar.

'I've often thought about writing a novel,' the Doctor confessed. 'Never seem to find the time. I suppose that when I retire, I'll give it a go.'

'They say everyone has a novel in them,' Rachel said. 'I don't think I do, though.'

'Perhaps that will change after tonight,' the Doctor said.

Marnal was pacing around the garage. He had the gun back in his hand, but knew he couldn't fire it without provoking a police response.

'You could always put the telly on,' the Doctor suggested, indicating the glass bottle.

Marnal snarled at him, then – to the Doctor's surprise – followed this suggestion and turned on the device. After it had warmed up for a little while he tuned it into their surroundings. Outside the garage there were dozens of police, almost all of them kitted out with body armour and guns. Marnal panned around, looking for a way out that he'd missed, but it was a small garage with only one entrance. It wasn't that difficult for the police to cover every angle. There were armed men kneeling behind every garden wall and waiting round every corner.

'Why don't we just leave in the TARDIS?' Rachel asked Marnal.

'The recalibration won't be complete for hours, possibly not until this time tomorrow.'

'Recalibration?' the Doctor spluttered, finally putting the novel down. 'What are you doing to her?'

'Fixing her, Doctor. You've neglected even basic maintenance work.'

'If it isn't broken, you don't fix it.'

'Less than 10 per cent of the ship's systems are working as they should. Everything else is either malfunctioning, barely working or entirely missing.'

'Piffle. It may be missing a cupholder here and an optional extra there, but the TARDIS is fine. Name one thing that's important that's not working.'

'The absence detectors, all of the aesthetics gauges, the ahistorical contextualiser, the ambiguous resolver, the animal-language translation circuits, the aprioritron, the art device, the assimilation contrastor, the axiomator, the –'

The Doctor waved his hand. 'All I really need is something that gets me from A to B.'

'WE KNOW YOU'RE IN THERE. WE WANT TO TALK TO YOU.'

The glass bottle showed a middle-aged inspector holding up a loudhailer.

'We're going to be here for a little while,' the Doctor said. 'Why don't we try to work out what happened on the Edifice after the events we saw? Or what's behind the back wall. The answer's on the tip of my tongue.'

'Perhaps you've got Gallifrey behind there,' Marnal sneered.

'Perhaps I have,' the Doctor admitted. 'If I did, it would have a bearing on my case, yes?'

Rachel was looking glumly at the bottle. 'I don't think I want to know my future right now.'

'You can tell the future with that thing?' the Doctor asked.

'Come, Doctor, surely you recognise a –'

'Oh, give it a rest, will you? I thought it just showed repeats.'

The Doctor moved over to the bottle. 'We could use this to see how the siege ends,' he suggested, twiddling away at the knobs and dials.

A quiet beeping noise started up from one of the components.

'Oh, I see how you tune this in now,' the Doctor said. 'This is really rather clever.'

'Can anyone else hear that sound?' Rachel asked.

'Nothing to worry about, I'm sure,' the Doctor said dismissively.

'It's coming from the fusion reactor,' Marnal said.

'The what?' The Doctor twisted round to look at the silver cylinder. 'This is a nuclear bomb?'

'A cold-fusion generator.'

The Doctor touched the side, then withdrew his hand. 'It's hot.'

'You've broken it,' Marnal said, incredulous.

'Broken it?'

'The regulators have failed. The energy is increasing exponentially.' Marnal was already heading for the TARDIS.

'There's going to be an atomic explosion?' Rachel screamed.

'You could come with me,' Marnal offered, almost as an afterthought. 'Even immobilised the TARDIS is indestructible. We'll be able to ride out the blast.'

He unlocked the TARDIS door, and opened it. 'I'm sure the Doctor can defuse the reactor. If not, then… well, I doubt he'll feel anything.'

'Your books will be destroyed,' the Doctor countered.

Marnal's foot hovered over the threshold. 'I –'

'Don't worry about the books. One of you do something before a million people die,' Rachel shouted.

'No one dies,' the Doctor replied.

He unclipped the fusion reactor and tossed it through the open TARDIS door.

'What are you doing?' Marnal cried.

'Close the door!' the Doctor yelled.

Marnal was paralysed, but Rachel grabbed the door handle and yanked it shut.

The Doctor hurried over and patted the TARDIS.

'Brace yourself, old thing.'

They didn't hear the explosion and the outside of the TARDIS didn't so much as shake.

Inside, the heart of a star appeared just inside the door, a light so bright it obliterated everything. The books and the bookshelves and the antique furniture and the candles and the kitchen and the food machine and the fault locator and the lamps and the hat stand and all its hats, scarves, coats and the shaving mirror and the carpets and the gramophone player and the chairs and the wine rack and the chess sets and the ormulu clock and the full-length mirror and the table and the tea set on the table and the butterflies and the tool kit and the cuddly toys didn't have time to catch alight, they were simply gone.

The column in the centre of the room was made of sterner stuff – the forces at the heart of a sun were nothing compared with its usual fare – but the console blistered and caught fire. The walls were tough and swirled the energy around and then out of the room, through the one open door leading off into the depths of the ship.

An irresistible wall of flame surged down the corridor, seeking any opening.

Flames rolled around Fitz's room melting every record, every souvenir, every trace that he or Trix had ever been in there.

The fire crashed through the TARDIS laboratory, smashing every piece of equipment and the benches they were on.

A wardrobe the size of an aircraft hangar became an inferno, rack after rack of clothes catching alight, the racks themselves twisting and melting.

The swimming pool boiled dry, the cloisters were scoured clean of ivy.

The firestorm raged on.

Marnal was shaking.

'What have you done?'

'He saved the entire population of London,' Rachel answered.

'WE HEARD SCREAMING. YOU HAVE TO SHOW US THAT YOUR HOSTAGE IS SAFE.'

'There are billions more human beings – that's the last surviving TARDIS in the entire universe.'

'This is just a thing, not a person.'

The Doctor was barely aware of them. He was counting. When he'd waited precisely long enough, he turned the key to open the door.

'Wait!' Rachel shouted, but the Doctor didn't. He flung open the door and snatched the key out of the lock, then stepped aside for a second to avoid the blast of burning air. A backdraught of new oxygen fanned the flames, which quickly subsided.

The Doctor pushed his way through the door, eyes closed. The floor was crunching beneath his feet. He knew his TARDIS, and the distance to the console, but the smell of ash and the sheer heat of the air were terrifying. He was ready for the step up on to the dais in the centre of the control room, and groped his way around the console. He snatched his hand away from a red-hot piece of brass, and briefly lost his bearings. So many of the buttons and instruments had been wrecked. He risked opening his eyes, and forced them to stay open in air so dry it stung, as he found the controls he was looking for.

He slammed the palm of his hand down on a button.

It began raining in the TARDIS.

Primitive sprinkler technology, but as effective as any more exotic method of putting out a fire. The water doused the last of the flames and, most importantly, it cooled the room. The Doctor looked around to find the it gutted. The whole room was stripped empty, the walls smudged with great streaks of soot. The bare floor was a maze of fine cracks. The console was the only thing that was still there. Water was running off it, on to the floor and down the plugholes that had just opened up.

The Doctor bolted the door then wiped some of the damp ash from the panels, trying to get a sense of the damage from the ruined displays. The TARDIS was able to repair its own structure, given some time, but wouldn't be able to replace the contents he and his companions had amassed during their travels.

He slipped the book bag off, and tucked it under the console to keep it dry.

Checking what monitors he could, the Doctor was almost

absurdly grateful to discover that two of the TARDIS's three great libraries had survived unscathed. The walls of the TARDIS were strong, and the old girl had a strong defensive instinct. Emergency barriers had come down, keeping the blast away from the engines and other critical areas, channelling the energy towards...

The Doctor started running.

He followed the route the firestorm would have taken, licks of soot on the wall pointing the way like road signs. He left the console room and entered the main corridor to the depths of the ship. The walls were still warm, but there was little here for the fire to take. Where the hatches hadn't been battened down, it would be a different story. He passed an open door and had enough time, even running past, to see that Fitz's room was a mass of charred wood and twisted remains.

This wasn't his most pressing concern.

The Doctor instinctively knew some of the principles that controlled the TARDIS, and he'd picked up more on his travels. At the heart of the TARDIS was the immense source of the energy that travelling through time and space required. When the TARDIS had been built, it had drawn its power from a link with his home planet: Gallifrey. The Doctor himself had also had some connection to the place. He'd suffered physical side effects for a long time, until that business in Henrietta Street in fact, because the link with home had been broken. The TARDIS, though, had survived. The only inference was that it had, at some point long before the destruction of Gallifrey, been fitted with an independent source of energy.

He arrived in the large stone crypt that housed that power source. The blast had rushed into it, wiping away the decoration and leaving only the structure.

The iron sphere in the centre was immense. It wasn't really iron, any more than the TARDIS was really a police box, but that was how it appeared: a pockmarked globe of dark metal, around thirty feet in diameter, set into the floor. It had always reminded the Doctor a little of a closed eye.

The procedure, when there was an explosion or other energy release on board the TARDIS, was to channel the energy here, and send it down the link to the distant power source. An atomic bomb could go off on the surface of the sun without anyone noticing; the power needed to move one time machine, let alone a fleet of them, was many orders more than a mere star could muster. The forces at the other end of the link must be beyond comprehension. So the fusion explosion would be sucked safely down the link, a drop in the ocean of what was at the other end.

But this only worked if there was a link, and the TARDIS no longer had any such link.

The emergency procedures hadn't ever been changed. The energy had been channelled down here, right to the power source, but there was nowhere for it to go from there.

The iron sphere had cracked open.

An immense black eye was staring straight at him and through him, the message clear:

I know you.

The Doctor did not understand what he was looking at, though, couldn't even decide if it was a supermassive something or a perfect absence. He could think of nothing to do other than stare back and try to decipher what it was. He knew he had to get closer. As he moved towards the great eye he could see the room flickering. He held his hand up in front of him and saw a double, then a triple image. Radiation sickness? It made people nauseous, but that wasn't it – there wouldn't be any radiation. Time and space were being made to move in ways that weren't possible outside this room.

The Doctor walked around, inspected the damage carefully. The sphere wasn't fully open, he was surprised to see. Even after taking the full blast of an atomic explosion, there were only pinholes in it. But this wasn't a question of degree. Either the immense forces were sealed from the rest of the universe or they weren't. It was right that they were. Even pinhole views of what was inside the sphere filled the room.

He stepped away from the sphere and went over to the small control panel on the back wall. He reached for the lever that would seal the breaches.

The Doctor hesitated.

I can show you what you need to know.

The Doctor shook his head. It sounded like a man's voice. He looked back over his shoulder to the sphere, watched time twisting around the breaches like swirls of smoke. It was beautiful, a little hypnotic, like staring into a fire. He turned to get a better look, reached out his hand.

I know, should I tell?

This time there was no hesitation.

'Yes.'

Come closer, then.

The Doctor walked over to the sphere. He felt so small next to it.

He placed his eye over one of the pinholes, stared right into the heart of the TARDIS.

Time shifted.

Interlude
Intervention

The Shoal.

The charts describe it simply as an asteroid plain clinging to 1 per cent of the galactic rim, but this gives no sense of its scale. It is about two thousand light years long, three hundred deep, thirty high. Or, to put it another way, it has about eighteen million times the volume of a typical solar system.

The asteroid density varies enormously from place to place, with some areas almost void, some a swirling mass of boulders and icebergs. The size of individual asteroids ranges from chips to worlds larger than Earth with their own rings and moons. There are nebulae, but they are gossamer, not the great stellar nurseries to be found in the galaxy itself. There are no suns here, but the Shoal is close enough to the galaxy for there to be light. A crisp night's sky on one side, a black void on the other.

Scientists rarely studied the Shoal, and hadn't given much thought to its origins – either it was a remnant of the galaxy's formation, like the shells of comets found around most solar systems, or it was bits of cosmic debris pulled here from intergalactic space by the galaxy's gravity. There were more pressing matters to investigate than determining which was the case.

The long-held assumption is that there is no life in the Shoal, and no reason for life to come here. The long-held assumption has recently been disproved.

* * *

Three craft emerge soundless from the Vortex.

They have arrived in one of the Concentrations, sunless parodies of solar systems. A particularly large body would attract clouds and belts of rock and ice into orbit around it, and the larger asteroids would coalesce to become moons and attract their own satellites in turn. These were inert places, with nothing like the energy or elements needed to ignite a new star. The orbits were weak, prone to disturbance. Rogue planets would drift in or out of the systems with little incentive to stay. There were many hundreds of thousands of such places in the Shoal, all unchartable, let alone uncharted.

The ships' chameleon circuits start kicking in, adopting battle configuration. As they speed towards the second planet of the system they sprout long fins and weapons modules. The exact design is left to each ship, with one coming to resemble a snowflake, another a simple pyramid, the third a more chimerical, organic form. All are bone-white, perfectly smooth, with no portholes or vents. They adopt a loose formation, the flagship at the front, and start growing vworp drives and picking up speed. Navigation here is easy enough, although it occasionally requires suddenly changing course at a right angle, or barrelling evasive manoeuvres. The squadron passes through the Concentration as effortlessly as fish negotiating a coral reef.

Their detector beams are already sweeping the system. One catches an outpost, a small colony in the outlying asteroid cloud. The squadron pitches up and round towards it, bringing its weapons to bear.

The asteroid bears distinctive marks – needle-like towers of dirt, giving off a strong thermal signal. The squadron quickens its pace, taking advantage of some of the more obscure, unrepealed by-laws of physics, until it is travelling a little faster than lightspeed.

There is no way, then, that the asteroid could know what hits it. As they pass the three ships release pulses of white light, which shatter the spires, find fault lines in the rock, continue to pound away. A third of the asteroid breaks off under the bombardment, blown clear by the pulverising explosions. As one, the squadron swoops around and performs a second attack run, passing through the light left behind by their first approach, reducing what remains of the asteroid to rubble.

The pilot of the flagship stands at his console, surrounded by two overlaid realities: amplified representations of the space around the ship, and the control deck itself.

'Target destroyed, my lord,' one of the other ships is reporting.

'Reset detector beams, lock on to the next energy sign.'

The spoken command is a mere formality. The ships and their crews are already working together as one, doing just that. Command, communication and control all so fast that the ships outpacing their own photons seem almost too sluggish to respond.

'Aye.'

The squadron dives towards the next target, the outer planet.

There are small lakes of methane ice, and a rift valley system that probably marks out where a number of rocks jammed together to form the planet. The detectors are finding spires again, and there are even a few pinpricks of light. Below the surface the planetoid is squirming with mindless life.

The squadron breaks formation just above the surface, each ship independently seeking targets. Each one rains energy bolts down, felling the towers, obliterating each source of light, darting to avoid the devastation before regrouping to cause some more. Then they pull away as one, forming up again. Behind them, the planetoid explodes, the brightest light this area of space has ever seen, the shock wave racing through the system and perturbing the delicate status quo.

The ships are already far away, locked on course for the central mass, the 'sun' of this Concentration, the axis around which everything turned. The main nest of the monsters.

All three ships are scanning the planet, compiling data. There is nothing alive on the surface, but there are countless life forms under it. More than even they could count.

He had seen a dead cobblemouse once, turned it over to find it wasn't a mouse any longer, but a mass of maggots packing out the animal's pelt. That was what this planet was, a husk containing mindless, aggressive life forms who would make every planet in the galaxy like this if they weren't stopped.

There is an enormous energy trace coming from the planet.

'What is it?' he hears over the communications system. He has no idea.

Amplified, it looks like many hundreds of beams, coming from the surface and moving like searchlights through five dimensions.

'They're looking for us,' he concludes.

'Their technology is more advanced than we thought.'

'Should we take evasive action, my lord?'

'They can't harm us, even if they do see us.'

His ship is shuddering even as he finishes the sentence.

The lights in the control room flicker.

What is going on?

'Focus detector beam at the following point.'

A stream of numbers runs across his vision. He inputs the numbers, and his ship's detector beam swings to point deep under the planet's surface.

The amplified reality crashes for a moment, before reasserting itself. There is an energy source down there, something so exotic the databanks are having trouble finding a match. It is large, and the 'searchlight beams' are radiating from it.

The ship is being tugged down.

'I'm trapped in one of the beams,' he shouts, in the hope that someone can hear him. But the communications links are all down, as far as he can tell.

'I'm losing power,' he reports. 'Attempting a landing on the surface. You regroup and take full scans of this area. Then activate cloaking devices, return to Home Constellation. The High Council will need to –'

The planet is looming up in front of him.

The ship crashes into the crust at several hundred times the speed of sound, then skips out of the impact crater, cartwheeling up and then crashing down through the loose gravel and dust of the surface, plummeting into a subterranean chamber. It quickly comes to rest.

The inside has barely shuddered, but the ship has been heavily damaged. Lucky for him this is the latest model. Now all available energy is being channelled into the self-repair circuits and defences.

There isn't enough power left to operate the scanner.

It will still be possible to investigate the energy source, if he goes outside.

He heads to a number of storage lockers and removes items he thinks might be useful, like a torch and gloves.

After a little consideration he removes his robes and collar, deciding they would be too cumbersome. The instruments have enough power left to tell him the atmosphere outside is breathable, then just enough to get the door open.

The thin air is hotter than he had expected, heavy with carbon dioxide.

He moves out of the TARDIS, torch in one hand, pistol in the other.

A blizzard of dust motes passes through the torch beam. The light runs across the far wall of the rock chamber. This seems to be a natural formation, not part of a hive. There are no monsters here, not yet. His arrival has hardly been discreet, however, and they will be heading this way.

The ship had been pulled in by a beam from the energy source, but had come to rest several miles away from it. He soon finds himself in hollowed-out tubes in the rock, which are high enough to allow him to stand up.

The creatures have tunnelled these. Examining the rock, he finds
marks and gouges made by insect jaws. There is a breeze, heading
upwards. A ventilation system, he realises. The insects are warm-
bodied. Their hives would become too hot and suffocating
without some way of circulating the hot air out and fresh air in.

A leg lashes out towards him, embedding itself in the rock like
a pickaxe. He whirls round and finds himself staring into an
insect's face. It hisses at him. Its breath smells like bleach, its
mandibles are gnashing.

His pistol is already up at the creature's thorax. He fires, killing it
in a burst of red light. It slumps right in front of him. Its foot is
stuck firm in the rock.

He continues on his way, checking his wrist computer. It hadn't
warned him about the monster. The warm air moving around, the
exotic energy source and the sheer number of insects on the
planet are all conspiring to jam his detector's effectiveness. No
doubt he could have done something about that back in the
TARDIS. Out here in the field, he'll have to rely on his own senses
instead.

These tunnels aren't populated. The monster he met must have
been one of very few maintenance drones. The floor twists
underfoot. The insects are able to walk up sheerer surfaces than he
can. The gouges and teeth marks must make pretty good footholds
for them.

He continues on his way, sticking to the ventilation tubes. He
doesn't seem to have attracted any attention. This is not easy
going. He is used to life in the Capitol, where the most treacherous
surface is an age-worn step, each one of which is utterly familiar.
His ankles and calves are already in a little pain from the effort.

There are insects scurrying around, all larger than he and -
despite his fears - oblivious to his presence. As he enters a main
passageway it's like crossing a busy four-lane highway. Worse: the
creatures are running in every direction, and swerve abruptly and
without warning. They instinctively avoid each other. He has to
creep around the edges, take advantages of random lulls to move

forwards. He has an objective in sight now, a huge circular opening, like a tunnel mouth, with weird light pouring from it. It takes longer than he would credit to make his way through it.

He finds himself on a gantry, overlooking a shaft that must sink all the way to the core of the planet. He looks over the edge.

What he sees is literally indescribable. He tries:

Then he tries to describe it by what it is not. It is not of this universe. It is not something made of, or existing in, space or time. It has a shape, a size and a colour, but none are within his understanding. He can see it. Indeed, he can't miss it, although he can't tell if it's close, like a scar on his eye, or large, so that it more than fills the cathedral-sized chamber.

The textbooks refer to such phenomena as 'anomalies', or even just 'things'.

He decides not to look at it or think too hard about it.

Instead, he looks to see what else is here.

Along the gantry, around a hundred yards away, there is a young woman wearing a collarless scarlet jacket. Her blonde hair is loose, waist length. Her attention is taken by a large computer bank. She is working at it, entering a string of commands. It is impossible that she hasn't seen the thing, and she doesn't seem interested in looking at it now. She has then, he concludes, been working here a long time. She has managed this without being killed by the insects that are swarming around this planet, and indeed – he now sees – are thickly spread over the walls of the shaft. Every one of the monsters (there are literally millions of them) is staring straight down into the thing in the centre of the room. The strange non-light that pours from the anomaly glints off every one of their compound eyes. Lucky for him, it has their full attention.

The young woman leaves the chamber through a metal hatch. As she goes she leaves a trail of ghosts, tiny echoes in time. The laws of time are being broken right in front of his eyes. Whatever is at the base of the shaft is twisting time and space. He hurries over to the console, checks the instruments. The woman has just sent a signal to a set of coordinates. He runs the numbers into his wrist computer, but he can tell they describe a point near the centre of the galaxy, and he already has a sinking feeling in his hearts. Sure enough:

GALLIFREY

He moves around the control console. He cannot begin to work out its function. Is it monitoring the anomaly or sustaining it? Could it be controlled from here? The technology is far in advance of anything he has seen, and he is a Time Lord of Gallifrey – his understanding was that no other race could match his. Yet these creatures and this woman were here, plotting whatever it was they were plotting against the Time Lords.

He aims his pistol at the computer and fires three times, reducing it to charred panels of metal and melting circuitry.

Immediately, there is a change in the sounds all around him. He has affected the anomaly somehow. The ground starts to shake.

Pursued by the monsters who come pouring out of the shaft, he runs back to his TARDIS. He holds his arm straight out behind him, firing and firing his pistol. There is no chance of a shot missing a creature; nor, though, does it slow the insects down or make any apparent difference to their numbers. It is a long way back to the ship, and by the time he reaches the right chamber boulders are crashing down from the ceiling.

He hurries inside, slams the door shut. Even if the power hasn't been restored yet, he ought to be able to sit out the explosion. A TARDIS is practically indestructible, after all. That said, he is delighted to find all the power indicators back at normal.

He throws the emergency dematerialisation control, and the TARDIS doesn't need telling twice. It powers away from the planet.

Moments later, the pressures in the core of the planet prove too much and the world explodes, hurling fragments out into the Shoal in every direction at nearly the speed of light. The energy released is, for the first time in this region of space, equivalent to that of a star and it burns for several days.

Chapter Eight
WWDWD?

The Doctor pulled himself away.

'That was... that wasn't what I wanted to see,' he said.

You said you wanted answers. Those were answers.

'They may well be, but not to the questions I have. Was that who I once was?'

No.

'Then... Why show it to me?'

You feel cheated?

'Well, yes, I suppose I do.'

You wanted a moment where you opened a magic box and a set of neat solutions to all the awkward questions you have ever had came pouring out?

'No. I know life isn't like that.'

No, it isn't.

'You can give me my memories back?'

Yes. Like... that. Would you like me to?

The Doctor hesitated. 'No.'

Why not?

'I don't know. I just know that...' His voice trailed away.

He stood there for a moment.

'Now I've seen what I did, it was terrible, but I don't know what I'd have done differently.'

If you had your time again.

'You could send me back, give me a second chance?'

Yes. Like... that. Would you like me to?

The Doctor hesitated. 'No.'

Why not?

'I don't know. I just know that…' His voice trailed away.

He stood there for a moment.

'You have the power to restore Gallifrey?'

Yes. Like… that. Would you like me to?

The Doctor hesitated. 'No.'

Why not?

'I don't know. I just know that…' His voice trailed away.

He stood there for a moment.

'I know you,' the Doctor said.

This is a mere echo of me. The ghost in the machine.

'The serpent in Eden.'

The fallen angel. You did what I tried to do but never could, you swept away Gallifrey and the Time Lords. Cracked the dome of heaven, toppled its towers, put the gods to the sword.

'For the greater good.'

Booming laughter rolled off the stone walls of the crypt.

Marnal doesn't know how to punish you. You never had a problem with the pithy sentence, though, did you, Doctor? You threw me into this black hole, knowing that at the singularity there is infinite power, infinite command, everything I've ever dreamed of. More. Here, I am the master, I am the alpha and the omega. You also knew that those powers only work here, and here you imprisoned me. Condemned me to godhood, with no chance of parole.

The Doctor hurried back towards the control panel.

But you misunderstood me, Doctor, you always did. I didn't want power for its own sake. I wanted power so that I could take my revenge. You always denied that to me. Until now. Marnal may not know how to hurt you, but I do. I have, by using all my power to trigger the fusion device. An eye for an eye. Vengeance is mine, sayeth the –

The Doctor pulled the lever, cutting the voice off and sealing the breaches.

Only then did he turn back. The iron sphere was set in the floor, inert. Time and space had returned to normal.

This was his punishment? The destruction of some of his knick-knacks and being forced to watch a digressive bit of space opera? He didn't think that was so bad, he seemed to have been let off rather lightly. He didn't feel as though a weight had been lifted. Which left him wondering what he'd missed.

The Doctor checked his watch. An hour had passed since he'd entered the crypt.

'YOU HAVE TO PROVE YOUR HOSTAGE IS SAFE,' the loudhailer told Marnal.

He'd been sitting slumped in a garden chair. He was just looking at the police box. An hour ago he'd told her that entering the TARDIS had been suicidal for the Doctor, that he would be dead in a firestorm that would burn for days. That was just about the last thing that Marnal had said or done. Rachel could have made a run for it, but didn't want to be picked off by some overeager police marksman.

The police couldn't see into the garage – there was only one window, and that was behind a thick curtain. Rachel imagined that, even if it hadn't been, there would be so much dust and grime on the glass that no one could have seen in. It was dark now. She could just about see the street lights around the edges of the curtain and the garage doors. Without the fusion reactor, the glass bottle was just a glass bottle.

This meant that Rachel couldn't see out. She'd seen the police setting up, and enough episodes of *The Bill* to be able to picture what must be going on. She knew they'd cordoned off the area. There were cars with flashing blue lights, dozens of uniformed officers huddled behind them for cover. Half a dozen snipers would be in position, there would be another team on standby to storm the garage.

They wouldn't go away, that was the point. There were a number of ways this would end, and all but one of them involved her getting killed. She was staying away from the window and the doors.

Without warning, Marnal stood up and strode over to the TARDIS. He rattled the door, but it didn't budge. He didn't seem surprised.

'You'll have to show your face,' he told her.

'What?'

'You heard them: you're my hostage, they want to see that you're safe.'

'They'll shoot me.'

Marnal shrugged. 'I doubt it.'

'You *doubt* it?'

'They've got the place surrounded. They can afford to ask questions first, shoot later.'

Marnal had found an old towel and was dusting it off.

'A white flag,' he explained, handing it over to her. It was damp and smelled of mould.

'It's not white.'

'It's not a flag, either. But it's the nearest we have.'

Rachel held it in her hands as though it was a dead squid.

'Hurry,' Marnal insisted.

She went over to the door.

'I'm coming out!' she shouted.

'WE HEAR YOU. YOU'RE SAFE TO COME OUT.'

She edged the door open, waved the towel.

'YOU'RE SAFE TO COME OUT,' the loudhailer repeated.

'Keep your feet inside,' Marnal warned.

Rachel poked her head out of the door. The scene hadn't changed much since they'd seen it in the bottle. A line of policemen, a mix of uniformed, plain clothes and body armoured, was positioned behind a row of cars.

'IS EVERYONE IN THERE SAFE?' the inspector with the loudhailer called.

'Yes,' she answered.

'ARE YOU BEING HELD HOSTAGE?'

'Er... sort of,' she shouted.

No immediate response.

'It's complicated,' Rachel added.

'WHAT'S YOUR NAME, MISS?'

'I'm Rachel. I'm Marnal's nurse.'

'IS MR GATE IN THERE?'

'Who? Oh, that's who I mean: Marnal.'

'IS THERE ANYONE ELSE IN THERE?'

Rachel glanced back at the police box. 'Yes and no,' she said.

'THERE EITHER IS OR THERE ISN'T, MISS.'

'There are three of us. Two, er, hostages and Marnal.'

'WE HAVE BEEN TOLD MARNAL IS ARMED. IS THAT THE CASE?'

Rachel decided to consult with Marnal, and bobbed her head back in.

He nodded, patting the stun gun.

She returned her attention to the policemen. 'Yes, but we're all safe,' she shouted.

'UNDERSTOOD.'

Marnal came over and pulled Rachel back inside, being very careful to stay out of sight. He closed the door.

'Why did you want them to know you were armed?' she asked.

'They'll think twice before rushing in.'

'Oh... Right.'

The TARDIS had survived and was already beginning to cleanse and repair itself.

He was in no rush to leave. He couldn't be interrupted in here, and Marnal was still in his garage or in a police cell. Either way, he wasn't going to harm anyone.

The Doctor headed back to the control room. He was feeling dulled. Every so often he would pause, kidding himself that he was checking the nearest room. The air was dry, with a faint acidic feel to it. The whole TARDIS smelled of ash.

The third time he stopped the Doctor realised that he'd lost his bearings. The TARDIS was big, and every distinguishing feature had been seared away by the atomic blast. There had been a large pirate's chest marking one particular fork in the corridor. There had been things like mirrors and sculptures dotted around. Odd machines – some very odd indeed – had nested in alcoves that were now totally bare. The Doctor hadn't realised just how much he'd used these little landmarks to navigate around his own ship. Without them, every corridor looked exactly the same.

Except the one he found himself in now. This corridor led to nowhere but a blank wall. The Doctor quickened his pace. He'd wanted to come back here.

No evidence of Fitz's cigarette stubs remained.

The wall had been blasted and was cracked, some hairlines, some half an inch thick. The only part of the ship's structure – that he knew of, at any rate – that had been damaged in the explosion. Standing here he couldn't see what was on the other side, but if he got closer, and peered in, he might be able to get a look.

Some instinct warned him not to.

He'd cheerfully walk under ladders or break a mirror. He wouldn't throw a pinch of salt over his shoulder if he spilt any, he firmly believed a rabbit's foot should stay attached to its rabbit whenever possible, he'd never passed on a chain letter. This made him suspect that, whatever he was feeling, it wasn't superstition. He didn't need to stick his hand in a fire to realise it would be a bad idea. The world would have been a better place if Pandora hadn't opened that jar, as he distinctly remembered saying the time he met her.

Now that he knew he was at the back wall, it was easy enough to find his way to the control room.

What was done was done, though, wasn't it? Gallifrey was gone. He'd seen what had happened. At the crucial moment he'd had limited choices, and he'd spelled them out. Those choices hadn't changed. Run or submit? Choosing either would have been worse. Better that no one had the power of the Time Lords than it fell into the hands of those who would use it to destroy, or those who couldn't fully control or understand the forces they'd unleash. It wasn't a question of coming up with the brilliant, lateral solution with hindsight. He'd come up with the 'neither of the above' option straight away.

There was always another way, wasn't there?

That one time, no, there hadn't been.

It wasn't a very satisfying answer, but there didn't seem much purpose in picking away at it. What was done was done. If there was a better way, even with hindsight and time to mull over the problem, he still couldn't think of one.

The Doctor was back in the control room. He stepped up to the console. The room had a damp smell, but a fresh one. He was in no mood to leave the TARDIS and go back to the garage. Marnal had got into the TARDIS before, and the Doctor wasn't sure he couldn't repeat the trick.

The power levels were nominal. The Doctor dialled in the dematerialisation codes. The central column started rising and falling, sluggishly, and the time engines engaged. The TARDIS slipped into the time vortex, heading away from Earth but not towards a specific destination at the moment. He needed somewhere to get a bit of peace, not to mention some help in finding answers. It needed to be somewhere quiet for the TARDIS to recuperate.

'Klist,' the Doctor said out loud.

It was in the North Constellations, between Anquar and the Santine Rift. It was a planetary string, home to an immeasurably ancient civilisation. The Ruling Mind wasn't expecting visitors, but the Doctor was sure the Mind wouldn't... mind. He programmed the coordinates. The TARDIS was moving, but very slowly. It would take far longer than normal to get anywhere. Everything was working – everything that usually worked, anyway – but at reduced power. Checking the instruments, it was clear that there was still some power getting to the repair circuits.

'You'll have good care once we get to Klist,' the Doctor told the TARDIS.

He was going to have some time to think.

'Perhaps I'll write that novel,' the Doctor joked to himself.

Then the thought struck him that this would actually be a very good idea. He patted his pockets, but didn't have anything to write with. It didn't take him long to locate a fountain pen in one of the nearby rooms. A blank notebook took a little longer. He sat himself down at a desk in one of the surviving libraries.

'Right,' said the Doctor. 'Instead of banging my head against a brick wall, trying to remember what happened, I'm going to tell a story. It's semi-autobiographical, about a man called the Doctor who is faced with an impossible situation. He's facing his future self, and he's just pulled the lever that destroys his home planet, and he thinks he's going to die, and instead he hears footsteps and then… Well, I'm going to imagine what would have happened next.'

He put pen to paper.

A full minute later, the pen hadn't moved across the paper.

This was going to be harder than he thought.

The lamp on the top of the police box started flashing and the strangest grinding, roaring noise filled the air.

'No!' Marnal shouted, running towards the police box. By the time he'd reached the corner of the garage he was the only thing there.

He looked around, suddenly terrified. 'Can you feel that?' he asked.

'No,' Rachel admitted.

Marnal was making adjustments to his ray gun.

'What are you doing? You're not planning on shooting anyone?'

He considered the question. 'I need to be prepared. There's only one way out of here now.'

'There are dozens of police, a lot of them have guns.'

'Yes, but this is a maser.'

'Maser. What's that? Is it like a phaser?'

'I've never heard of phasers.'

'They're off *Star Trek*.'

'Oh. I wrote an episode of that once, but they changed it so much I took my name off it.' He finished what he was doing. 'This is an advanced weapon. It uses microwaves to work on the nervous system.'

'Yeah, I saw you use it on the Doctor.'

Marnal shrugged. 'That was a crude stun. The Doctor is a cunning opponent, and the irony is that means any attack on him has to swift and brutal enough to render him helpless before he can try his tricks. But this weapon has more subtle settings.'

Rachel frowned, looked at the gun properly for the first time. 'Subtle? What use is that?'

'It can induce emotional effects ranging from intense euphoria to deep depression.'

'You're kidding! Where did you get it, the planet Prozac?'

He was clearly trying to place the name. 'No. It's an old Gallifreyan weapon, military issue. Making your enemy shy or aphasic can be far more effective than a bullet.'

'And if you don't kill people it doesn't affect the time lines.'

Marnal's mouth flickered into a smile, clearly pleased with her reasoning. 'No, at least not as much.'

'What are you going to do to the police?'

'I've set it to Serious Indifference. Anyone I shoot will have no real interest in their surroundings or situation for an hour or so. They won't understand why they feel that way –'

'– or care,' Rachel noted.

'Indeed. So we should be able to exploit confusion in the police ranks. If it comes to that.'

He looked distracted.

'What is it?' Rachel asked.

She felt strange now. A funny feeling in her water, as her nan would say. It felt like a panic attack was coming, but... like it was biding its time.

'Something very weird is happening,' she concluded.

She had the sense this had nothing to do with the police; it was far bigger than that.

* * *

The Doctor had finished his novel. It was about thirty thousand words. That sounded about the right length, he thought. It had taken him just over two hours to do.

He'd drifted off the subject a little.

It opened at a literary festival, where a pair of young English professors, Edmund and Julia, were lecturing about Jane Austen. They were approached by a famous entrepreneur called Sir Thomas Bertram, and paid a great deal of money to go to his stately home on a mysterious assignment that he insisted only they could complete. On the helicopter ride there they met Rushworth, a post-structuralist who dressed in black and spouted drivel. They went on a tour of the facilities. Bertram had established a theme park in his grounds. He'd used the latest memetic engineering techniques to re-create some of his favourite fictional characters and he wanted the experts on literature to make sure he'd got it right, then to write nice things about him for the travel section of the *Times Literary Supplement*. Edmund and Julia were amazed when they saw Mr Darcy rise from a lake – it was magnificent. But then it all started going wrong – during a heavy storm, a whole pack of Mrs Bennets got out, and started marauding. Before long Edmund and Julia – and a couple of spunky kids – were being chased by wave after wave of predatory Collinses, Willoughbys and Elliots. It took all the academics' wits, and not a little luck, to avoid becoming terminally betrothed. Finally, they boarded the helicopter and made their escape.

He closed the notebook. *Mansfield Park*, by Doctor –

This really wasn't helping.

The Doctor found a scrap of spare paper, and began scribbling.

There was nowhere either of them could run. Nothing either of them could do. The die had been cast, and now the two of them had to simply wait for oblivion. It felt like defeat, not a victory. He could hear the energies of the Edifice gathering together, for one final, inevitable, release.

Why could he hear footsteps?

He paused.

Someone else was coming towards them. It was a tall man with a lot of hair.

The Doctor thought about this for a moment, then crossed out everything after, and including, 'a'.

a short, bald woman.

No, this didn't strike him as very likely either. He crossed it out too.

It didn't matter what this mystery person looked like. What would he do? That was the purpose of the exercise.

'We don't have much time, and I need your help,' the Doctor said.

'Obviously.'

The Doctor read this back to himself. Yes. So... picture the scene.

Grandfather Paradox was still in his corner, but by now he was barely the ghost of a ghost. His howl was so faint it was barely audible. The new arrival walked straight past him without even noticing he was there; and then he wasn't.

What would the Doctor ask?

'Where's Fitz?'

Concern for his companion, that seemed fair enough. Logically, that meant the new arrival wasn't Fitz.

'Safe and sound.'

'Excellent. Quickly, I need you over here.'

'In about fifty-five seconds, there won't be an "over here".'

'Good, good. Plenty of time.'

She – he'd decided it was a she – stepped over, sighing theatrically.

'For what?'

'I'm not sure yet. Give me a minute to think. No, second thoughts, make it not quite a minute. That's the trouble with memories. All that déjà vu. All those things you don't want to be reminded of. It's excess baggage, you know. I envy you. What possible relevance could it have if I remember Ace's visit to Paradise Towers?'

'What are you talking about, Doctor?'

'Just talking to myself. The important thing to remember is –'

The Doctor had run out of paper. By the time he had found some and got back to his writing desk, he'd forgotten how he was planning to finish the sentence. He sighed.

Rachel woke up, and spent the first few seconds surprised she'd fallen asleep.

She checked her watch. No wonder she felt tired, it was the middle of the night. It was cold in the garage and she was stiff. She'd been woken by shouts and calls from outside. Lots of 'What the hell?' kind of things, and police radios squawking.

Marnal was standing, head cocked to one side, like he was trying to assess the situation.

'Something's happening out there,' she concluded.

Marnal looked worried. 'They're getting ready to storm the place.'

Rachel moved to find the towel.

'I don't think that's it,' he said, after another minute.

There was the sound of a car starting, then driving off. A minute later a few other vehicles had gone, including a big one – one of the vans, or the ambulance.

'Some of them are leaving,' Rachel said.

'It could be a trick.'

'Did you fire that gun at them and make them homesick?'

'No. Why would a police unit leave the scene of an armed siege?'

'They wouldn't. At least not on TV they wouldn't. We're in London, there are other policemen to deal with another incident coming up.'

Marnal raised his gun and checked it.

'There could have been a terrorist attack,' she suggested.

'At two thirty in the morning?'

'Why not? Maybe not an attack, but a warning, or a tip-off.'

'You can feel it too, can't you?'

Dread. Unease tugging at the primeval parts of her, the oldest areas of the brain. Was this how animals felt when they sensed a hurricane or a forest fire coming? She tried to analyse it. It was only

178

through thinking hard that she realised something had gone fundamentally wrong with the light.

The Doctor hadn't been able to prevent the destruction of Gallifrey; that had happened. All the Time Lords were dead, their home planet had gone. That was a fact and it couldn't be undone.

Despite that, he had saved the day, snatched victory from the jaws of defeat. He'd done it from inside the Edifice, with seconds to spare. And the little man he'd seen while meditating had given him some clues, he was sure of it.

The Doctor started writing:

The new arrival ran her fingers along the dusty console. 'The Edifice was your TARDIS all along, then?'

The Doctor waved his hand. 'Yes. Get to station one, and boot up the library computer. I'm sure I'm forgetting something very important.'

'Forty seconds.'

The Doctor snapped his fingers. 'Ace remembered going to Paradise Towers,' he said triumphantly.

'Pardon?'

The Doctor was wiping spores and mould from another panel on the console. 'Yes, here.'

'The telepathic circuits? I've got the library computer working, by the way.'

'Good. These are still functioning. Once, I was editing out some of my memories using the telepathic circuits, when I –'

'Why?'

'I forget'

'Har har. Thirty seconds. You were clearing some space, like defragging a hard drive.'

'I suppose I must have been. It can get very cluttered up there. Anyway, a long time ago now, gosh, just before I faced the Timewyrm, I accidentally gave Ace one of Mel's memories.'

'And now you're… editing out your memories again. Can't this wait?'

'Er... no. Where's Fitz, by the way?'

She rolled her eyes. 'Doctor.'

He joined her in front of the library computer.

'You're hacking into the Capitol's computer systems,' she noted.

The Doctor looked up. 'Obviously. I need the password. You don't happen to know Romana's birthday or her mother's maiden name, do you?'

She shoved him aside. 'Here, let me. I can uplink directly.'

'I've got a plan,' the Doctor told her. 'We need twelve seconds, give or take.'

'We have eleven. Ten, nine, eight...'

The Doctor read this back to himself. His companions weren't ever that caustic, but overall it seemed a plausible account.

So, he'd done something fiendishly clever to delete his memories. That answered one question. He'd lost his memories because he himself had deliberately erased them. He instinctively knew this was what had happened. Then again... hadn't he just said to Marnal that why he lost his memories wasn't that important a question?

He tried to remember but, again, there was that sense of dread, as he knew there would be. Fear flapping its wings, warning him to keep away. Just an instinct that there were some things he wasn't meant to remember. He'd said as much before he did the deed, sitting in the Edifice, waiting to die.

'It makes no sense,' the Doctor said, to no one in particular. 'I saw Gallifrey destroyed.'

He hesitated. That way, it sounded like a denial.

'I saw myself destroying Gallifrey,' he rephrased. Then a third attempt: 'I destroyed Gallifrey. I was solely responsible. The Doctor, in the Edifice, with the binding energy.'

The fear wasn't there any more.

It just came and went, it always had. Ever since he'd woken up on the carriage, well over a hundred years ago now. He had learnt not to think back, because it only scared him. But he knew what he had done now. It wasn't quite remembering, but it was as near as he was ever going to get. If he'd been blocking it out, for fear of having some sort of a breakdown… well, that block had gone and he felt fine. Not fine, obviously, but…

'My choice,' he said, 'I pulled the lever. How many times do I have to say that I don't feel guilty? I did what I had to do. If I had my time again I wouldn't change my decision. The alternative was worse.'

Had he done something even more horrible? Ockham's razor suggested otherwise. Destroying Gallifrey was the foul deed, there was no need to come up with another heinous crime. He'd met William of Ockham once, nice man with a bushy beard. The Doctor had tried to get him to work out the history of the planet Skaro and almost given him a nervous breakdown.

The Doctor racked his brain. Panic attacks, irrational fear. That wasn't like him. What if there was a logic at work? He tried to think back and the dread came, sharp and clinical. He shook it away, then he realised: thinking back was what scared him. That's what the dread was stopping him doing. It didn't want him getting to all those old memories. He'd always assumed he was being protected from the nasty memories, but perhaps his memories were being protected from nasty old him. Why, though?

The Doctor didn't feel any sudden sense he'd got it right. A moment later he'd worked out why. He'd decided that he didn't have any old memories because he'd deleted them all.

The Doctor deflated.

Something was tugging at him, telling him to get back to Earth. A seventh sense, or a twenty-eighth, or however many it was he had. He ignored it. Earth would have to look after itself for a little while. He was so close. This had to be his priority; there couldn't be any distractions, not until he had the answers. What could be more important than settling this? Now he was sure he could work things out for himself. Take the facts, apply logic, take his time. Think it through.

The police had all gone.

Rachel turned, to see Marnal sitting hunched in the back corner of the garage.

'Are you all right?' she asked, kneeling beside him.

He was rocking back and forth. 'They're here. How?'

'The police? They've gone.'

'We need to get into my TARDIS.'

'You have a TARDIS here?' Rachel asked.

Marnal pointed shakily over her shoulder.

'That was the Doctor's TARDIS. That's gone too.'

'It's not important. Not now.' Marnal suddenly seemed very old again.

Rachel looked around. Well, she was supposed to be his carer.

'Let's get you back into the house,' she said. 'It's warmer in there, more comfortable.'

She helped him to his feet. The garage door was slightly ajar.

'Four hours,' Marnal said. 'All it took them to find us was four hours.'

Rachel couldn't understand why it was so bright outside. It was like someone had put on a searchlight, but the quality of light wasn't as it should be. She checked her watch. It was three in the morning – it should be as dark as it got.

'Moths to a flame,' Marnal whispered, grabbing Rachel's arm. He looked pale, worried.

Rachel led him out of the garage. The air was cool. It was always quiet at this time of night, but there was almost a negative amount of noise, as though it had been sucked from the air. Marnal looked around. The surroundings were all there, the air smelled right. There was no sign of the police, but the road remained coned off. If the residents hadn't been allowed back, that would explain the silence.

'What is it?' Rachel asked Marnal.

He pointed up.

Above them in the night's sky there was a second moon. It was larger than the first, and partially eclipsed it.

The desire of the moth for the star,
Of the night for the morrow,
The devotion to something afar
From the sphere of our sorrow.

'To —, One Word is Too Often Profaned'
Percy Bysshe Shelley

Chapter Nine
The Sphere of Our Sorrow

Fitz was woken by the sound of helicopters beneath him. It was twenty past six on Wednesday morning, EST.

Trix was still asleep, her head on his chest, pressed against him. A little too heavily for him to be entirely comfortable, but nothing would make him move her away. Fitz lay there, feeling how warm she was, how smooth. Her hair smelled of hotel shampoo. She looked so peaceful, unguarded, when she was asleep.

They'd not closed the curtains properly last night. Outside, there was a two-foot chink of the Manhattan skyline. Vertical strips of skyscrapers, smaller buildings that would dwarf anything in London nestling among them, and the river and the New Jersey shoreline beyond. It was getting light, they were forty-something storeys up, and that was high enough for helicopters to fly beneath them.

Trix shifted away a little, took some more of the sheets.

Fitz eased himself out of the bed and his bare feet planted themselves in deep carpet. He unhooked the complimentary dressing gown from the back of the bathroom door and put it on.

If this was life after the TARDIS, then it seemed like a good deal. Even if they were fugitives.

Even if he didn't know her real name.

He hadn't asked her about it. Not for the hour on the tube to Heathrow, not for the two hours at the airport, not for any of the seven-hour flight, not for the hour of the taxi ride to the hotel. Even he had not recognised her when she'd first emerged from the cloakroom at King's Cross. They'd slipped through security so easily it was faintly unnerving, her with a fake passport that she just happened to have with her, him with one that wouldn't be issued for a few years. They'd been fingerprinted and photographed at JFK, and Fitz had thought the game was up, but apparently they did that with everyone now.

He took a cigarette out of the packet, then saw the big No Smoking sign. You couldn't smoke in bars in New York now. He'd found that out last night.

Fitz tiptoed over to the TV, switched it on and quickly turned the volume down.

He'd been too slow. Trix was stirring.

'What are you doing?'

'I didn't mean to wake you. I was just seeing if there's anything about us.'

'It's New York. Foreign news here is what's happening in Newark.'

'That's Big Ben. London,' he said, looking at the screen. He listened.

'... and coming up: what's the connection between the Vore attack and... Hillary Clinton? You won't believe the answer, only here on Fox News.'

They went to a commercial break. Fitz pressed a control on the remote, and pressed a couple more until he found a news channel.

'... follows the sudden appearance of a second moon in the sky, in front of the moon... the original moon. Coastal areas in many parts of the world have been devastated.'

'... According to scientists, Stacey, the tides are caused by the moon's gravity. Having two moons in the sky clearly means there's more gravity around.'

'Thanks for that, Sir Isaac Newton,' Trix sighed, going over to the window. 'I don't see one moon, let alone two of them.'

'We can't leave him alone for five minutes.'

'You think this has something to do with the... What am I

saying? Of course it does.'

Fitz had just noticed that there were words, fractured sentences like headlines, running along the bottom of the screen. The one that caught his eye ended:

'... that UNIT have designated "the Vore" / Devastation immense / Mayor of London "eaten" reports.'

'Hang on, what's that?'

A woman was reading the actual headlines.

'... at the bottom of the hour: giant insects devastate Europe. I'm Sienna DeLorean.'

'I don't care what your name is, tell me about the monsters,' Fitz yelled at the television.

'... Europe has been attacked by what one eyewitness describes as, quote, a swarm of giant locusts that walk like men, unquote. Amid reports of millions of deaths, the White House has issued a statement saying it is monitoring the situation. Scientists say there may be a connection with Tuesday's unprecedented appearance of a second moon. In California, celebrity lawyer Wim McBrit today declared the latest allegations made against his client to be a physical as well as ethical impossibility. More of that in a moment. A car bomb went off in Baghdad Tuesday killing thirty. And, as you can see from these pictures, the residents of a town in Ohio are taking part in their annual Throw A Potato Day. I'm Sienna DeLorean, and I'll be back at the top of the hour.'

An advertisement break started.

Fitz found another news channel. There were certainly enough of them.

'... SWAT teams have been readied to tackle the giant locusts.'

'Swat. Like you would do with insects, I suppose,' Fitz observed.

'Special Weapons and Tactics.'

'Ah.'

'... Not locusts, Jeff. From the pictures, I would say they looked more like robber flies, but robber flies are usually a few inches long, not the size of a person.'

'... Now, we've had an email on that topic from a viewer called

Paul. He asks, "How can the trachae of these insects possibly function given the square-cube law?" I'm very glad you asked me that. The answer is simply…'

'All I want,' Fitz said quietly, 'is someone to tell me what the hell is going on.'

'We need to get back,' Trix told him.

'Binks? Binky?'

Mr Winfield blamed the police for the disappearance of Binks. They'd ushered everyone in the street out of their houses just as they were getting ready for bed, told them there was an armed criminal next door and offered to put them up in a school hall. Mr Winfield had given them his sister-in-law's address and told them that was where he and his wife would be staying. There hadn't been time to round up Binks. It was dark, and she'd have been off on some feline amorous adventure. Or she'd just have found somewhere to sleep. Mr Winfield thought that was more likely, as he'd never really bought in to the theory that as cats slept all day it meant they were nocturnal. They'd been allowed back a couple of hours ago, but there was no sign of Binks. It was twenty past six, and starting to get light. Truth be told, Mr Winfield was already getting used to the second moon. The scientists didn't know where it had come from. That was scientists for you in a nutshell, wasn't it?

'Binky?'

He was walking past his neighbour's house. Marnal, the old writer. The Winfields had moved in ten years ago, but hadn't exchanged a word with him. Not even a Christmas card. Well, he was old. And a miserable so-and-so. Mrs Winfield had found one of his books for 30p at Scope. They'd both given it a try, out of, well, loyalty. Unreadable, senseless, risible tat. All that stuff about black holes and people being stabbed dead one minute and alive and well the next, and giant space needles. Rubbish.

There was a hiss from Marnal's garage.

'Binks?' Mr Winfield called out, keeping his voice down.

The garage door was slightly ajar. He decided to go up to it.

The inside of the garage was bare, apart from some of the usual rusting paint cans and garden tools. Binks was standing in the middle of the garage, her back arched, howling at the monster in the corner.

Some insects could be beautiful. Butterflies were, no one argued with that, but even some mantises and beetles looked like pieces of jewellery. The monster was not beautiful. It had an almost hunchbacked appearance, with a bulbous body and tiny head. It wasn't quite symmetrical. The carapace was dull silver, with thick black bristles poking from the gaps. As it stood on its powerful hind legs it rose to about the height of a man. It had two sets of shorter fore limbs. All six legs were moulded into vicious spikes, and sharpened curves and hooks. All the limbs and both eyes were constantly twitching – jerky, distracting movements.

It took one step towards Mr Winfield, watching him carefully. It had compound eyes like a fly, and a long, translucent abdomen that it seemed to be using to balance itself, like Binks used her tail. Its innards were visible in the abdomen.

Its mouth was moving in a complicated four-way chewing movement that seemed almost mechanical to Mr Winfield. Juices dripped from its mouth, and the smell reminded him of rotten fruit. Did that mean it was a vegetarian?

He stared at the creature, unsure what to do next.

'Welcome to our planet,' he said, trying not to sound scared.

The creature took another step forwards, plucked Binks from the floor and bit her in half, crunching off her head and shoulders. After a moment, it took the rest of her in its maw and gulped it down.

Mr Winfield gasped and stumbled out of the garage, and ran next door trying to find his wife. She heard him coming, and opened the door before he was halfway up the drive.

There were monsters all around him. Standing on his lawn, perched on his roof and in the trees, walking down the street. They were winged, he noticed. Transparent, delicate wings, each the size and shape of a canoe.

Mrs Winfield was shouting for him to get inside.

A few of the monsters were moving to surround him. He turned but there were dozens of them in every direction. Hundreds now. The air was humming as though it was full of Lancaster bombers. He daren't look up.

The monster nearest him opened its mouth and rasped a stream of white powder over him. It stung his eyes, made him cough violently. It smelled of fly spray.

His wife was screaming.

Across Europe, most people were woken by the buzzing above them. It was a little past dawn, but it grew dark again. A strange, restless darkness. But few people really noticed. Many had seen the news about the new moon and assumed this was a storm cloud or weather front associated with it. The sky grew ever more black, the buzz ever more loud.

Across eastern Europe satellite signals had been erratic for a few minutes. Digital signals were choppy, images pixellated, sounds disjointed. Aircraft started falling from the sky as the cloud pressed down, clogging up jet engines and jamming ailerons. Radar screens became bursts of static – swarms of points of light circling around, descending. Despite this, air-traffic controllers could see that planes were dropping down ahead of the cloud. Some were doing it deliberately. Most had lost all control. Some of the aircraft had started to break up.

Telephones began ringing.

Emergency services and government hotlines were active, although many were affected by the loss of satellite signals. Prime ministers and presidents were woken. Army units were being deployed, emergency plans were being dusted off, key personnel were being located and ferried to secure locations.

None of these preparations made the slightest difference.

When the base of the cloud was around two hundred feet from the ground, it was possible to discern that it was a swarm of insects. It was difficult to judge its scale at first, until the monsters began swooping down wherever crowds were gathering, lifting up men and women and taking them away.

Half an hour later the next wave passed over the crowds, spraying them with white powder, like crop dusters. Those not caught by this watched those who were die quickly and painlessly.

Armed police in Frankfurt were the first to fire on the monsters. It usually took two shots to down one. Hit it and it fell, twitched and died. Easy. But there were far more insects than there were bullets, and they converged on anyone shooting as though they were answering a call to prayer. The surviving police were soon falling back, trying to get other survivors inside buildings.

The streets of Geneva were thick with bodies, slowing down – but not stopping – people trying to escape and the ambulances and police cars that were making for the worst-affected areas. The sky was so black with swarms of the insects that every vehicle had its lights on. This only seemed to attract the monsters, which were strong and used their fore limbs like tin-openers to take the roofs off cars.

Fifteen minutes into the attack on Lyons, and policemen kitted up in riot gear were finding that tear gas had some effect in dispersing the swarms. It was also incapacitating the people they were trying to save. Whatever the insects were spraying could penetrate gas masks. Once again, as everywhere else, the police fell back.

Hospitals braced themselves for a catastrophe, fearing that they were about to be overwhelmed. Health-service managers knew, even if they never admitted it, that one nuclear strike on a city would generate more casualties than any nation's health service could deal with. But there weren't that many bodies left behind after the monsters had passed over.

The reports coming in were putting the number of deaths in the tens of thousands in just the first few minutes. There were almost no injuries. Fewer, in fact, than in a typical morning rush-hour. Most were the result of people trying to get away: there were car accidents and casualties caused by stampedes. Anyone who survived tended to be uninjured. Hospitals were inundated with people looking for relatives, and many people needed treatment for shock. Anyone who didn't escape died.

In various bunkers, urgent messages determined a name for the monsters: the Vore. No one was quite sure who coined it first, but it quickly caught on. Military planners started wondering whether anyone would be left alive by nightfall. It would be an hour before the question was asked out loud. By then, it was obvious: praying for a miracle wasn't working.

The Vore swarm made another pass, rasping white gas over troops taking cover behind a wall and a dozen or so civvies who'd made a run for it, despite being told to stay down. Sergeant Cartwright, huddled close by in another position, behind a van in front of HMV, saw them die. Civilians – presumably – were screaming all around him. He crouched down, out of sight, a small part of his brain hoping that if he couldn't see the monsters they didn't really exist. He could hear shots – even after four years in the army he wasn't used to how much louder real ones were than gunfire on TV – and glass smashing. Over every other sound was the buzzing of insect wings.

Modern military doctrine was to aim for ten-to-one superiority; that was the way the Americans wanted it. There were hundreds, maybe thousands, of Vore for each soldier. British army training didn't cover their tactics, and hadn't since the First World War. Rows of enemies hurling themselves at armed positions. Conventional wisdom had it that you couldn't win a battle if the enemy had control of the skies. There were so many Vore up there Cartwright couldn't even see the sky any more.

The sergeant's five minutes of fighting the Vore had proved that shooting brought them down in great numbers. Anything more substantial, like a tossed grenade or mortar, just arced up and fell back to earth again before exploding. At first, Cartwright thought it was like firing into a flock of birds. He almost felt sorry for the insects as they rained down. Was there some insane leader, safe in the monster equivalent of a chateau fifty miles from the front line, ordering them out regardless of the cost in lives?

Then the truth dawned: the swarm wasn't getting any smaller. Now, shooting into it felt more like shooting at a hurricane or an avalanche. The insects kept coming, kept spraying the lethal white gas that affected everyone wearing a gas mask, let alone civilians whose idea of protective clothing was a raincoat. The air was black with them, like a storm cloud.

'Covering fire!' someone shouted.

A small group of soldiers obliged, and were targeted with the gas for their trouble.

Cartwright's radio crackled. 'Change of plan: covering fire, escort civilians to safety, then fall back.'

Where, exactly, was 'safety'? He had a quick look round for it. The Vore were rampaging down the high street, tearing the roofs off cars, and flying into shop windows and smashing them (it wasn't clear whether this was planned or whether they just didn't see the glass).

Twenty feet behind him two Vore were emerging from HMV dragging a couple of screaming teenage girls out by their hair. They leant in, ready to gas them.

Cartwright stood up and fired three rounds. The first and third shots hit the Vore square in their mid sections – the 'thorax' if he remembered the quick briefing he'd been given. The second grazed the forehead of one of the girls, who swayed and dropped to the pavement alongside the insects.

He swore and ran over to the girls.

The one he'd shot was on the ground, blood pouring from her head. She was groaning – long, low moans that were trying to be words.

'You shot her, you –' the other girl started, the rest of her words melting into a mass of obscenities. She'd be a good-looker normally, he thought. Probably a bit older than she'd seemed at first too.

He did his best to ignore what she was saying. 'Keep still,' he told the wounded girl, whose eyes were rolling. There was no sign of a response. 'Medic!' he shouted.

One hurried over from a nearby alleyway and knelt beside the girl.

'Thought you'd be busy,' Cartwright said.

'Twiddling my thumbs. This is my first injury.'

As the medic tended to the girl the sergeant took another look around.

'Where are the bodies?' he asked.

'What's her name?' the medic was asking the other girl.

'Janine.'

There were no bodies. Not of people. There were dozens of Vore, almost heaped up in some places.

'Probable compression,' the medic was saying into his radio. 'Request ambulance. Victim having convulsions.'

The girl's arms and legs were twitching.

'You got the one that did this?' the medic asked.

Sergeant Cartwright nodded, a dull sensation filling him.

'Good.'

'What are the creatures doing with the bodies?' Cartwright asked.

All flights to Europe had been grounded, but it was amazing what someone as resourceful as Trix could manage with £150 million in her bank account.

It was getting dark by the time they arrived in British airspace in a courier firm's plane, heading for a landing strip outside Bristol. Virtually the whole of the aircraft was given over to the hold, which was full of relief supplies. There was a small passenger compartment at the front, right by the cockpit. Eight seats, but Trix and Fitz were apparently the only two people in any rush to get back to Europe and they had the plane to themselves.

They'd been virtually out of touch with the rest of the world during the flight, with only scattered pieces of news from the pilots who were monitoring the radio and getting updates from air-traffic control. There was a single mass of giant insects that had looked like a cloud formation about the size of the British Isles on the satellite pictures, before the satellites went offline. Radar still had them, down on the western seaboard of Africa, travelling at hundreds of miles an hour.

If it was a military attack it wasn't very well researched. Mali and Liberia weren't Trix's idea of high-value targets. She was ashamed to admit she'd never even heard of Guinea-Bissau. She searched her laptop's database for the natural resources the insects might be after. Guinea-Bissau's were rice, coconuts, peanuts, fish and timber. Sierra Leone had diamonds and bauxite, but its chief export was palm kernels.

'They're following the light,' Fitz told her, and he was right. Evening in – she looked it up – Mansoa on Guinea-Bissau's west coast, night all points east.

'So next, they'll hop the Atlantic.' She had no idea where they'd make landfall. It looked like Brazil, but she made a mental note to ask the pilot about wind direction.

'We should be safe, then.'

'For a while.' It all seemed so abstract from 35,000 feet.

'What's the plan?' Fitz asked.

'We find the Doctor.'

Fitz didn't look happy.

'Come on,' Trix said. 'I'm hoping he's already at the centre of things. We'll probably arrive in time to see him saving the day without us, like he does every time.'

'Not every time,' Fitz said darkly.

Trix shifted in her seat. 'He didn't save Sam, I know, but –'

'Or Miranda.'

'You've known him longer than anyone.'

'I've known him longer than he knows himself.'

'Fitz, he'll sort this out. He won't have left,' Trix told him.

She glanced down at the laptop, which was showing the swarm over the Atlantic on course for the Caribbean, unstoppable and unstopped.

'He *can't* have...'

As night fell the second moon became visible again. Twenty-four hours after its first appearance tidal waves and abnormally high tides were the least of Earth's problems.

Publicly, the United Kingdom authorities were putting the number of British dead at seventy thousand, but they suspected the total would be between three and four times that. With whole families wiped out, and few corpses, it was hard to come to any meaningful estimate. The government was still functioning, every minister was accounted for.

There was chaos across Europe and North Africa. Millions dead from all walks of life, so nothing at all was working as it should. For the moment the survivors were all too shocked to be angry or scared. Almost everyone was staying in their homes. This wouldn't last. Economies had ground to a halt, and it wouldn't be long before people started to run out of food and ventured out.

As for the monsters, the swarm had long departed but small groups had remained behind. The army were containing them, keeping them away from the population. Attack one, though, and every Vore in the area came crashing down on the person who'd fired the shot. It was a good deterrent.

It was unclear what the monsters' aims were. So far, observatories had seen no Vore on the surface of the new moon, so there wasn't even a proven link between it and the monsters. Jodrell Bank wasn't picking up any radio activity from the planet. The creatures did not have any obvious high technology, not even tools or weapons, and certainly no vehicles or spacecraft. There had been no attempt at communication, let alone any demands.

At the end of the first day, all anyone could do was wait and see.

The courier plane was cleared for landing. Fitz had guessed this already from the manoeuvrings, but the captain had just buzzed the news over the intercom to confirm it.

'For once, we won't be held in a stack,' Trix told him.

Fitz glanced out of the window. Fields and towns, strings of lights along roads. Nothing like the maps ever looked. He turned back to Trix, who was packing her laptop away.

A flash of silver in the window opposite.

Fitz tried to get a better look, but whatever it was had gone. It must have been a trick of the light.

'What is it?' Trix asked.

The plane was buffeted a little and Fitz and Trix exchanged nervous, amused glances. Fitz had flown enough to know that this usually happened around landing. He tried to comfort himself with the thought it was probably the undercarriage deploying, or something to do with layers of air.

The plane banked unexpectedly.

Trix seemed unsure whether to unbuckle or sit tight. Fitz put his hand on her leg.

'Stay seated,' he warned.

She nodded. There was a scratching from the rear of the plane. It was impossible to tell whether it was coming from the inside or the outside.

Fitz looked out of the window. 'We're still pretty high up,' he said. How could a layman judge altitude? None of the clues a human being used to judge size and distance applied when you looked out of a plane's window. The horizon was in a different place, there was nothing to scale the ground against. They were a lot lower than they had been, but the houses seemed a long way away. No doubt the thick plastic windows were distorting things too.

The plane rocked like a car that had just hit the kerb.

Fitz turned to Trix and saw she was wide-eyed, staring out of his window. He turned back.

For the merest moment he saw a pair of insect eyes and a set of mandibles, then the face at the window was gone.

They'd both seen it.

Now a puttering sound: thump, thump, thump from just outside.

'They're all in Africa,' Trix said.

'No they aren't.'

Fitz moved to unbuckle his belt.

'We have to sit tight,' Trix said.

'I just told you that,' Fitz reminded her. He strained to see out of the window.

'Oh...'

'What is it?'

The wing was heavy with insects, each his height, hanging on with what was clearly quite some effort. It was like an Indian train, passengers on the roof and hanging from anything they could grab on to.

That wasn't all of it, though. The insects were taking turns to leap off the front of the wing, like they were performing a parachute jump. As they did, they were sucked into the engines and there was a thump. Fitz described the process to Trix, who didn't believe him, and moved him out of the way to get a look for himself.

'It's deliberate,' Trix said. 'They're killing themselves.'

'It's going to bring us down,' Fitz replied. Of course it was. He'd read about birds and bits of stone being sucked into the jets, crippling some important piece of the engine. 'Do you think the captain knows?'

The plane was tipping one way, then the other. They quickly got back into their own seats.

'I guess he does.'

'Can you fly the plane?' Fitz asked.

'If I have to. It takes years to qualify to pilot one of these. We've got two guys in the cockpit who've been trained to deal with all sorts of emergencies. There's nothing we can do that they're not already doing. If it crashes, we get out as soon as possible and get clear, OK?'

'Yeah, of course.'

The plane was now bobbing around like a boat on a stormy sea.

'So why isn't the swarm in Brazil, like we thought?' Fitz asked.

'It is. Weather radar won't pick up individuals. It looks like the monsters can work at night too.'

'So neither of the only two things we knew about them are true?'

The intercom pinged, and the captain told them: 'Assume crash positions, brace for impact.'

They were way ahead of him.

The plane was only a hundred feet or so up now. The captain had found an area clear of buildings. Fitz couldn't tell if this was the airfield or not. The plane was steady now, but the engines were straining and spluttering. The moment before they landed the monsters leapt off the wings, spiralling up and leaving the plane to its fate – and destabilising it one last time.

There was a roar of air.

Fitz twisted his head to see. A window had broken.

A judder as the plane hit the ground. Normal, but Fitz could already feel the undercarriage giving way. He realised he had taken Trix's hand in his own. It took a couple of seconds for the landing gear to wrench away. They heard it clattering off down the runway as the belly of the plane hit the tarmac, forcing the air out of their lungs.

The plane swerved, tried and failed to right itself, then scratched its way across the ground, which was hard. The wings were swinging up and down. Out of his window, Fitz saw the wing tip touch the ground and throw up sparks. This was a runway, Fitz realised, as they ploughed through a cluster of landing lights and on to soft grass.

The plane slid to a rest.

Fitz was very aware of how heavy his brain was and how much it had sloshed around in his skull.

'Up,' Trix said, already unbuckling her belt.

'Yeah.' He fumbled for his belt. 'Any landing you can walk away from...'

'We've not walked away from it, not yet.' She was standing, heading for the door.

'We should check for monsters,' Fitz said, unsteadily.

'No. We should get out of the big metal thing full of sparks and aviation fuel.'

'You're right,' he said groggily.

Trix was pulling handles to open the door and deploy the emergency slide.

'Ladies first,' Fitz told her.

It was two hundred feet of running before Trix looked back and realised Fitz wasn't with her.

They'd come down the emergency slide and started to run. The captain and co-pilot had been right behind them. They'd overtaken Fitz and come alongside Trix. The air had been humming the whole time, and she'd thought it was the blood rushing into her ears after the crash. It was only when she looked up that she saw squadrons of monsters passing overhead.

The plane was pretty well intact, but there were flames on the ground and she could smell fuel so there was a real risk of an explosion. Emergency vehicles were heading their way, blue lights flashing. Fire tenders, an ambulance, smaller vehicles Trix couldn't yet make out in the evening gloom.

She stopped and turned around.

There was a crowd of monsters between her and Fitz.

A dozen of the creatures, about twenty feet away from each of them.

Fitz had skidded to a halt.

'Go!' Fitz shouted. 'They're after *me*.'

So, these were the Vore. Almost as one the insects were looking from Fitz to Trix, as if they were unsure what to do. They were grey flecked with silver, their bodies ungainly and a little asymmetrical. The light was glinting off compound eyes the size of beach balls. Their joints clicked and clacked as they moved.

Trix stood perfectly still, tried to work out why she wasn't dead. They were following their instinct to attack the nearest human, but with two targets identical distances away they were having difficulty deciding between them. They were animals, Trix realised, not intelligent beings. Some sort of social insect, like a bee or an ant.

Fitz understood the situation too. He started to take a step towards the Vore.

'What are you doing?' she screamed at him.

'Saving your life. Trix, you have to run!' he shouted.

'Stay back from it!' she yelled at him.

If she took one step away, she solved the insects' dilemma for them and they'd pounce on Fitz. One step towards them and they would take her, but he would be safe... for the moment, at least. Her foot lifted from the ground.

'No!' Fitz shouted.

'What do we do?' Trix asked.

The drivers of the emergency vehicles had seen the monsters and they were staying back. No help was coming. There was an aeroplane primed to explode behind Fitz. Backing away wasn't going to be an option.

'I love you!' Fitz shouted.

'Fitz... not like this. We can make it.'

'One of us can. You.'

'There's another way. There's time to –'

'You know there isn't. Trix... tell me your real name.'

She told him.

Even from this distance, she could see him smile. 'It suits you.'

Fitz took a single step forwards.

One of the monsters decided: half-walking, half-hopping, it loomed up in front of Fitz. The others decided too, all following it.

'Cigarette?' Fitz asked, holding the packet towards the Vore for a moment. There was an edge of nervousness in his voice. He took one for himself.

'It's my last one, I promise.'

Fitz lit the cigarette, took a drag.

'I've always used humour as a defence mechanism,' Fitz told the monsters. 'Right now, I'd prefer body armour, but there you go.'

One of the creatures edged forwards, jaws mashing. It seemed curious about the ciggie. They'd churned up the grass as they'd come over.

Fitz took a puff.

'The thing is, the joke's on you. I beat you. The woman I love is going to get away. I saved her. For once in my life I'm the bloody hero. So I'm going out on top, yeah? I win.'

Fitz flicked the cigarette away.

The monster raised a claw. Another had shuffled into place behind him. A third was to his left, a fourth to his right. A fifth, a sixth, a seventh, an eighth, a ninth... Well, after the first few it didn't matter any more. All of them were facing him.

'Are you lot waiting for my last words? Yeah? OK, let's have a think.'

Fitz made a show of scratching his chin.

'Got it. Here they are. The last words of Fitzgerald Kreiner, space hero.' Fitz jabbed two fingers up at the nearest Vore, right in front of its face.

Then, as one, the creatures leant forward, opened their maws, expelled rasps of white vapour and Trix saw Fitz die. She didn't hear him fall, he didn't cry out or make any other sound. One moment he was alive, the next he wasn't.

He'd fought an enemy that couldn't comprehend his heroism.

He'd died saving her.

She had to get away, for it to mean anything. Trix turned and ran, faster than she'd ever run. Behind her one of the aeroplane's engines exploded, then another, then another, then the last one. The fireball obliterated the Vore, and threw Trix off her feet.

She barely noticed.

Fitz was dead.

It was in *these* times that the visions came of the great Black Eye. It began to be scryed in the visions of the people, watching balefully over them. Not in the past, or the future, but in overtime. Written over past, present, future, in dreams and in waking, an alternity drawn *across* their history of now forever. All they could do was dismiss, push the thoughts back. Their presumption was that this vision, of another kind of themselves, was a pure symbol, a *representation* of the actual. That such a vision, themselves erased with only five ghosts to wander lost, could become true, that under the Black Eye their primate shadows would rule the spaces between moments, was *literally* unthinkable.

The quest came to consume those that followed it. The *fascination*, in both the ancient and modern senses of the word. For a race concerned with observations and acquiring knowledge this, the all-seeing void, was the ultimate negation. Yet it empowered them, made them gods. Do nothing, they cautioned, do nothing and all will be well in heaven.

Extract from *The Monkey to Time* saga
(*circa* November 2001) by Marnal

Chapter Ten
Ask Not . . .

The Doctor laughed out loud.

It was like a magic trick, or Sherlock Holmes' deductions, or the GU equation. When you put it that way it was so simple, so self-explanatory, so beautiful, so obvious that what had seemed the most Gordian problem was instantly almost mundane, and its elegance was its own proof. How had he not asked that question before?

Now he stood up. He had to tell someone.

He sat down again. No. First write it down, to be on the safe side.

He scratched out six words, autographed it with a question mark, read the six words back to himself, and he laughed and laughed and laughed.

Twenty minutes ago, the Doctor had reached a dead end in his efforts to work out what had happened. So he'd come back to the control room to act out the scene so far, to see if that triggered any associations. Seconds before Gallifrey had been destroyed he'd done something clever with the TARDIS computer. So, to re-enact that, he'd hovered at station one, examined the library computer, toyed with a few of the buttons. The panel and controls had been smashed by the explosion, but he was still able to retrace his steps. It made no difference; he couldn't work out what he'd done. Cryptic clues, hints, answers not-quite spelling out other answers. It was like the hardest crossword puzzle in the universe.

So he'd sat down, cross-legged on the control-room floor, frustrated. The TARDIS was still days away from its destination.

He'd sulked for a little while, but didn't enjoy it. Instead, he reached over for the book bag and fished out one of Marnal's novels. A slip of plastic had fallen out. There was a paragraph of text, in a language that looked like Greek at first until the Doctor realised it was an equation, and solving it resulted in a short message. An extraordinary way of communicating that was half-writing, half-maths. It was only after he read it that it struck him that it ought to have been impossible for him to decipher it.

It said it was a 'matrix projection' about 'the destruction of the cicatrix' that went on to predict dire consequences for the Time Lords. The slip of plastic showed no sign of age, but the book it had been in was covered with dust and looked as though it hadn't been touched for a hundred years.

The slip was an artefact from his home planet. The Doctor knew that he and the TARDIS were from Gallifrey, but this was different, somehow, because it was something new. He didn't know what the slip of plastic was referring to, and wondered if he could find out from looking up information in the handful of Marnal's books that he had with him. It hadn't taken him much longer to work out that the plastic slip was being used as a bookmark.

He'd started to read the book eagerly, but the words were drier and dustier than it was. It was a description of the 'Matrix', the Time Lords' central computer. It was amplified and panatropic, whatever that meant. It had exitonic circuitry, but the term wasn't explained. They used it to monitor the whole of time and space... then did nothing but observe. The Doctor's eyes had slid off the page before he reached the end of the first paragraph, and his mind began to wander into stray thoughts. First, about how hard the floor was, next about how bare the room was, then about what he might do to redecorate.

Ten seconds later, ten seconds ago, he'd asked himself the right question, the one that had been eluding him. And he'd laughed.

Now the Doctor read back what he'd just written, with a real sense of triumph:

What did I gain in return?

Trix thought she felt Fitz's hand on her hip, his kiss on her forehead. But she hadn't. She'd woken alone. It wasn't quite light outside and the second moon was screwing up that way of telling the time, anyway. As she checked the bedside clock she couldn't work out how many hours it had been since he'd gone, with all that travelling through time zones. Her watch was still on New York time. Her nostrils and shirt still smelled of his cigarette smoke.

The owners of the little hotel at the top of the hill had been delighted to get her business, although they'd insisted on cash – more than happy to take dollars.

'America's not had it so bad, has it?' the receptionist asked her.

Trix had told her about Fitz, but the woman hadn't seemed to hear. Everyone here had a strange mix of pragmatism and optimism. They thought the second moon could well disappear as quickly as it had appeared, and felt life would get back to normal. If the world was going to end, it was going to end. Their role, as they saw it, was to negotiate some sort of acceptable life between these two extremes. We are where we are.

Trix had been worn out, and hadn't wanted to outstay her welcome at the airfield. The car had been waiting there, as arranged. A nice powerful BMW, one anonymous enough to avoid police attention. She'd driven through the dark, surprised at how few cars there were on the road and how normal everything else looked.

Now she was already booting up her laptop and fiddling around with phone leads. The landlines were down here, but her mobile still had a signal.

The main cloud of Vore had swept right round the world, and was somewhere on the Russian steppes at the moment. The global death toll was being put at 9,970,000. That made Trix think of shops pricing items at £9.99, to make it look as though they weren't charging a tenner. A trick that worked, of course. Ten million people had died yesterday, and the sheer scale of this was incomprehensible to her.

Trix sat back and absorbed the news. She'd spent a day coming up with worst-case scenarios. You could talk about 'millions' or even 'billions' of people, but it meant nothing. Then she thought about what a planet was, related it to what she knew about. She'd just spent fourteen hours in the air, going both ways over the Atlantic. She and Fitz had travelled across a tiny segment of the Earth to get from London to New York. It was a big planet. The planet was still here, though: all the buildings, the museums, the libraries, the statues, the graves. The plants and animals, the seas and continents. Even thinking like that, without putting faces to it, it was too much to take in at once. As with everyone else on the planet, Trix's brain hadn't caught up with everything that had happened.

She turned the TV on. Endless pictures of people mourning. No piles of dead bodies, but it was breakfast television. There were church services. The new pope hadn't made a public appearance yet, but the Vatican was insisting he was well and hadn't been taken when the swarm hit St Peter's Square. Great swathes of the world had been completely unaffected. For some parts that had been it was just the latest in a line of natural disasters, and life had barely changed. When the famine in Darfur and rebuilding after the Asian tsunami were presented as 'life goes on as normal', you knew the world was in trouble. Cut against this were snatched images of Vore just walking down streets. Some of them had been seen munching on plants or killing livestock. They didn't seem to eat people, but they did occasionally grab them and carry them off into the air and none of those people had been seen again. The United Nations had declared the very first global emergency. GM-TV was listing the celebrities believed to have been killed. *EastEnders* had lost more than *Coronation Street*. Dec was fine, but there was no sign of Ant. The latest thing was a spate of unexplained injuries – people finding bruises they couldn't account for. Trix checked, and was surprised to find a livid purple mark on her arm.

The pundits were still only 90 per cent certain that the Vore came from the second moon. There were good photos of it now. It was the colour of sandstone, with the occasional straight groove carved in its surface, and features like stacks and mounds that looked artificial. There were no visible cities or roadways. The Americans and the Russians were considering a nuclear response, but Trix could immediately see a problem – even if there was a way to get them to the moon all the nuclear bombs in the world would barely dent its surface, and the monsters didn't even live on the surface.

She felt numb, like she was watching her own life not living it.

From her car last night Trix had phoned a few family and friends, trying not to fear the worst if she couldn't get through. Anji and Greg were alive. When she'd told Anji that Fitz was dead it was the first time she'd said the words out loud, and she'd had to pull over to the hard shoulder for a cry. She'd imagined Fitz sitting in the passenger seat, making some lame remark about a shoulder to cry on. Anji couldn't think of anything to say, or any way to contact the Doctor, but gave Trix a few government and UN numbers to try. All of them had been engaged, but she'd try them again this morning.

Trix was crying again.

Another Vore skittered over the roof. There was a heavy storm under way, possibly the result of weather patterns disrupted by the second moon, possibly not. It had knocked out the electricity in the street. With so many dead there wasn't even anyone to turn on the automated message at the power company, let alone send anyone out to fix the problem.

'We shouldn't just be cowering in here,' Rachel whispered.

'You're perfectly welcome to try going back to your parents' house,' Marnal replied.

He'd spent the last hour writing his diary by candlelight, and he'd made it very clear he didn't need any help from her. They were in his library. They'd barricaded the house, moved wardrobes and other bits of furniture to block the doors and windows. From time to time a black shape would pass by a window. She assumed these were Vore, but they could have been anything.

'We should be doing something,' she insisted.

'What do you suggest?'

'You're a Time Lord. Don't you have advice or skills you could offer to the government? You can't leave investigating that new moon to NASA.'

Marnal laughed at that. 'The human race will be dead long before they've mustered the rockets they need to do that. You do realise that planets don't normally just appear like that?'

'Of course I do. Do you know why it happened?'

Marnal's full attention was back on his diary.

'You do, don't you? Are they in one of your books?'

'No,' he said, surprisingly quietly. 'Once again, you can thank the Doctor.'

'I don't understand.'

'You wouldn't.'

He wasn't going to explain any further. Rachel had sat in the same spot for hours. But it was cold, and she needed the bathroom. She stood, very carefully, in case she made a sound and attracted the monsters.

'What do you think is going to happen?'

Marnal finished writing a sentence before replying. 'We may survive.'

'We... the human race?' she asked, hopefully.

'You and I, personally, may survive. I hope to, and I will do what I can for you. After that, I don't know. The Terran biosphere may have collapsed.'

'The what?'

'Earth may no longer be able to sustain life.'

'Because the monsters will have killed everyone.'

'The people don't matter so much as the plants. If enough plant life is destroyed, it will affect the atmosphere.'

'Like the greenhouse effect?'

'Yes, but much more rapid.'

He returned to his diary.

'Who are you writing that for?'

Marnal shrugged. 'Possibly just for posterity.'

One of the Vore was moving outside, Rachel could hear it dragging something heavy. She tried to imagine what it could be, but couldn't think of anything but a dead body. She'd watched a couple of them devouring an Alsatian yesterday from an upstairs window.

Rachel decided to stay where she was, just for a little longer.

Many American surveillance satellites had been destroyed or disrupted. The scientists were saying it was because of the disruptions to gravity caused by the presence of the second moon, rather than direct enemy action. The Vore had apparently not noticed, or weren't worried about, the International Space Station.

The surveillance network had been designed to function even if a substantial number of satellites were put out of action. It needed a lot of retasking, but within a day the Pentagon had good coverage. They concentrated on the main Vore swarm, which was following the computer models for it, keeping to the light and sweeping across the world. Contingency plans were being drawn up for this by the British and Chinese. The swarm wasn't bothering the American cities, it was sticking to the plains – the red states – although this was presumably a coincidence. Planners didn't want to provoke the Vore on American soil for fear they'd target one of the big cities in retaliation.

There was no nuclear option. They'd thought about bombing the swarm over the Atlantic or Pacific, but there would be nuclear fallout and plans were shelved when someone wondered aloud if it might set off a tsunami. There was no delivery system capable of getting nuclear weapons to the second moon.

Enemy numbers were stable. Estimates had it that there was one Vore for every two people on Earth – this ratio was continually changing in the enemy's favour, but this wasn't because there were new monsters arriving. Six out of seven of the Vore were in the main swarm, 90 per cent of human casualties were caught in the swarm.

The situation, then, was settling into a predictable pattern. The Vore were in control, systematically taking the human race apart, but now it was possible to see how they would do it, and there was plenty of time to get people evacuated or into shelters. Some people even started talking about things being 'manageable'. None of them, when asked, was able to explain how the swarm could be stopped or even slowed down, but governments around the world were beginning to feel the worst was over.

Then an analyst saw something, right on the edge of one of the African satellite images. And, once she'd worked out what it was, she panicked.

The Doctor had read all the books he'd brought with him. He knew a little more about his home planet now, but what he knew was hardly comprehensive. If he'd grabbed an armful of random novels from a London library, would he have a full understanding of the history and culture of Earth? He'd have to try it some time as an exercise.

For now, he'd got something else to do. The back wall.

The Doctor had found a cutting torch in one of the store-rooms. He had gone to the back wall and was burning his way through it. He'd cut a line up from the floor to the ceiling, now he began cutting a horizontal line. Even though the wall was damaged it was slow work, but it gave him time to think about what he'd read. Gallifrey was a contradiction. A world of futuristic control rooms manned by dusty old men in ornate collars. Monks walking on stone floors underneath which sat a black hole. Although Marnal's narration revelled in the ritual, the repetition, the routine, the Doctor found himself unmoved. It was no way to live a life.

He moved the cutting beam down. Finally, he reached a long crack in the floor.

The rough oblong he'd cut in the wall hung there for a moment, until the Doctor pushed it over. Through the new doorway was... more corridor.

It was with a distinct sense of anticlimax that the Doctor stepped over the threshold into the uncharted regions of his TARDIS. Fifty yards down the corridor, and his mood hadn't improved.

'There's nothing here,' he complained.

But he'd heard scratching at the wall many times. So this couldn't be true. The Doctor knelt down and examined the floor. Nothing.

At the far end of the corridor, round the first corner, he heard a whirring noise, like servo motors. It was heading this way.

The Doctor stood, ready for the new arrival.

It was a robot. It moved smoothly, hovering a little off the ground. It was battleship grey, with what looked like a gun and some sort of sucker cup. It watched him with a single electronic eye.

'You are the Doctor,' it said in a metallic voice.

'Yes. Delighted to meet you,' he replied.

The machine considered its response.

'I must kill the Doctor,' it concluded.

The gun flared with light, and the Doctor dived out of the way. The beam shot past him and was absorbed harmlessly by the wall. He'd been half-expecting a response like that. The Doctor was on his feet, running back to the hole he'd cut.

'Kill the Doctor,' the robot repeated, rolling after him.

The Doctor ducked left, and an energy bolt whizzed past him.

As he raced back into the part of the TARDIS he knew, the Doctor had one thought: why on earth would anyone build a robot in the shape of a dog?

* * *

The trick was to move quickly, and to know where you were going. The Vore swarm was in the Low Countries at the moment, but would be over the English Channel within two hours.

Trix did what she could over the phone, calling the police - not saying who she was, of course - and gradually piecing together the Doctor's movements. He'd traced the truck to an address in north London, and a few hours later the police had mounted an armed siege there, one that had been called off when the second moon arrived. The police had been busy with other things since then.

That was the best she was going to do. Spending several hours in the hotel's dining room - the only place with mobile reception - got her out of her bedroom, and stopped her thinking about Fitz. In theory.

Trix went back up to her room. She'd left the shower on. For a moment, she thought Fitz was going to pull a Bobby Ewing, she was going to find him in the bathroom wondering why she looked so surprised. When she got into the bathroom, though, there was an odd red stain on the mirror. It looked like melted lipstick, or possibly crayon. There was also the faint whiff of fly spray. She packed her bag. It took far longer than she thought it would to find her car keys, twenty minutes, and they only showed themselves when she broke down crying with the frustration of it all. Then she cleaned herself up and went downstairs. The receptionist wondered if she'd be back tonight. Trix couldn't tell her. She'd been the only guest last night, so was confident she'd get a room if she needed one.

A couple of Vore flew overhead as she threw her bag on the back seat of the car. They were hundreds of feet up and didn't react to her. There were so many around, and their rules of engagement were apparently so arbitrary, that all you could do was hope you didn't catch their eye. They were ugly things, and ungainly, but when they were individuals the wary could survive contact with them. When the swarm descended the rules would change. Were these Vore scouts? What were they scouting for?

Nothing on television or the Net suggested there was any sense of purpose to the attacks. Wherever the Doctor was, once he'd saved any lives he could save, he'd try to determine what the Vores' purpose was before he did anything else.

She sat in the driver's seat of her BMW for a moment, trying hard not to cry. There would be time for that later. Or she'd be dead too.

The sky was dark and grey, but it wasn't raining here yet. Her hotel was at the top of a hill, off a side road. There was gunfire from the town below. Trix decided to follow it. She wanted to see whether there was any effective resistance. The car was handling in a funny way again. It had been the same since she'd got it – the suspension was off, or there was something wrong with a wheel bearing. It wasn't a big deal. She drove the car down the hill, with the radio turned down so she could hear what was going on outside.

A couple of big army trucks were parked in what was usually a market square. Soldiers were sitting around, rifles at their sides, taking the chance to swig some drink or read the paper. There was a big pile of dead insects by the war memorial.

The lads looked pleased to see Trix as she got out of the car, and she duly did her best to flash them smiles and look impressed. She asked a squaddie carrying a petrol can where she could find his commanding officer, and he pointed out the lieutenant in charge.

'My name's Beatrice Macmillan,' Trix told him.

'Are you all right, miss?'

Not a pleasantry, a genuine question. Trix wasn't sure what she was doing that made him ask this.

'You're secret service, aren't you?' he said. 'You can always tell.'

Go with the flow, Trix thought. 'Normally, of course, I wouldn't admit it. How have you got on here?'

'Got all the bugs, didn't lose anyone.'

Trix nodded. 'Good. Lieutenant, if I said "the Doctor", what would you say?'

He shrugged. 'I would guess you don't mean you need a medic.'

'What are your orders?'

'Shoot bugs, burn the bodies. The smell keeps them away.'

Trix was looking around. She couldn't see any human bodies. The townspeople had either fled or found good hiding places. This was the second morning after the Vores had arrived. Already, the survivors would have ways of coping, new patterns of behaviour.

'You're not saving any for scientific research?'

'There's no shortage of them. Word is they've got dozens of live specimens, and I'm sure they've got more dead ones than they know what to do with.'

'Any idea where?'

Normally, an army officer wouldn't say anything. Loose lips sink ships and all that, but Trix clearly wasn't a Vore spy.

'Who knows? Probably all sorts of places.'

'Have you got any sense of their tactics?'

The lieutenant laughed at this. 'They're eating crops and livestock. They seem to like pigs the most, then sheep.'

'They can travel in space,' Trix said aloud. 'Probably interstellar space or hyperspace. We can't do that.'

He frowned, and Trix realised she must have sounded like a *Star Trek* character to him. She'd have to watch that.

'No we can't, ma'am. But they don't carry weapons or tools, they don't have vehicles. They don't even have clothing. The lads and I were talking about this before, and the best we can manage is they've come an awfully long way to eat pork.'

'There's got to be a better reason than that,' Trix told him.

The lieutenant shrugged. 'We'll leave all that stuff to you lot. They go down easy enough – you just tell us where to turn up.'

Trix saluted him. 'As you were,' she said, heading back to the car.

The robot dog was pursuing the Doctor down the TARDIS corridors, firing a pencil-thin beam of energy every time it got a clear shot at him. It wasn't hard to outrun the machine, but it clearly had some sort of detector that allowed it to home in on him. It also seemed familiar with the layout of the TARDIS – the Doctor had realised that it was herding him back to the control room. Perhaps it was some sort of sheepdog.

The control room was cavernous, but one thing it didn't offer any more was effective cover. There were a handful of alcoves, like the one the kitchen had been in. Once he was in there the robot would have him.

So, halfway down the last corridor, the Doctor stopped, turned and waited for the robot.

It trundled round the corner, then stopped, anticipating a trap.

'Why are you trying to kill me?' the Doctor asked.

Its ears waggled before it answered: 'I am following direct instructions issued by the Four Hundred and Thirteenth President of the High Council of Time Lords, keeper of the legacy of Rassilon, defender of the laws of time, protector of Gallifrey.' The voice was clipped, a little prissy.

'Really? Why?'

'Answer one: affirmative. Answer two: because my programming is to obey the mistress.'

'No, I meant –' This was a very literal-minded robot, the Doctor thought. 'Why was the order given?'

'The mistress Romana instructed me to execute you to prevent the fall of Gallifrey. A transmat beam delivered me to the Edifice, your TARDIS. My orders were clear. Your future self was responsible for the attack. I was to assassinate any of your temporal iterations I encountered.'

The Doctor hesitated. 'I see.'

'I have been obstructed from carrying out these instructions for one hundred and fourteen years, nine months, three days and six point three hours. I will now, however reluctantly, carry out those instructions –'

However reluctantly?

'Wait!' the Doctor called, holding out his hand. 'Wait... wait. Sit. Stay. Did she order you not to talk to me first?'

The ears waggled again. 'Negative.'

'So we can have a little chat first?'

'Affirmative.'

'Do you have a name?'

'I am K9.'

The Doctor grinned. 'Of course you are. And, obviously, you know who I am.'

'You are the Doctor-master.'

Something of a surprise. 'Your master?'

'You are the Doctor. The K9 unit was given to you by my creator, Professor Marius, on relative date one-one-one-five-zero-zero-zero. Professor Marius was unable to take the K9 unit with him back to Earth due to transportation costs and Y5K compliance issues.'

'We had adventures together?' The Doctor was rather cheered by the thought.

'Affirmative.' Its tail wagged.

'Then you ended up on Gallifrey?'

'Affirmative. Subsequently, I was authorised for independent missions in situations classed as too dangerous for Time Lord intervention. My mission was to protect Gallifrey.'

'Gallifrey's gone, old chum.'

The dog's head drooped. 'This was my supposition, but there was insufficient data to come to a definitive conclusion.'

You can say that again, the Doctor thought.

'I have failed in my mission. TARDIS architecture was reconfigured by your companion, trapping me.'

'Remind me to buy Fitz a drink the next time I see him.'

'As you wish, master. Is our conversation over?'

'Yes,' said the Doctor, patting K9's head.

The robot dog wagged his tail, then looked up at him. 'Now I must now carry out my instructions.' The nose laser extended again. 'Logically, this is the last opportunity I will have to issue the following reminder: buy Fitz a drink the next time you see him.'

'Wait!'

K9 paused.

'I need the answer to a question,' the Doctor told him. 'I think you might be able to help. When I was on the Edifice, all those a hundred and whatever years ago, I deleted my memories. But I gained something in return. Do you know what?'

'Negative.' The head lifted. 'However, I am capable of detailed cerebral scans and have experience with Time Lord brain patterns.'

The sucker-like probe extended from K9's head. After a moment, the Doctor angled himself so that it was pointing at his forehead. A minute later, just as the Doctor's knees were beginning to hurt, the probe retracted and K9 slid back a couple of yards. His ears were grinding away. There were lights on a panel on his back, which were now flashing furiously. The gun had retracted, too.

'Well?' the Doctor asked, when that performance was over.

'Initial analysis complete. There is sufficient data to make a report.'

'Er... Do you still want to kill me?'

'Negative.'

'You liked what you saw in there?'

'Affirmative.' K9 paused for a moment. 'The Doctor-master never loses,' he added, before explaining what he'd found.

Rachel flushed the loo, glancing at the ceiling to see if it made any difference to the Vore outside. She couldn't tell. The storm was worse. The swarm was due back over London any minute but the weather might divert it... no one knew. It was dark in the middle of the day, and had been brighter under the full moons last night.

She made her way back to the library, but she could hear Marnal walking about upstairs. He didn't seem all that worried that the monsters would get into the house. For their part, they seemed more interested in the empty garage than the house or its occupants, and that suited Rachel fine.

There was a flicker, a tiny thumping noise and the power came back on. It had been about four hours since it had gone off, and the house was cold.

Marnal emerged from the library. 'About time,' he complained.

'You could have rustled up another fusion reactor,' she noted, before a surge of panic. 'If you're down here... they're inside!'

The first Vore was plodding down the stairs, unsure of its footing, unable to stretch its wings. There were others behind it, almost pushing it over to get down themselves. Rachel turned to run out of the front door. The realisation that this wasn't the best idea she'd had and seeing that, anyway, she and Marnal had blocked the door off with a wardrobe came at the same moment.

The first Vore was at the base of the stairs. There were five of them in all, so far as she could see. Their heads twitched spastically, disconcerting her, making it hard to work out what they were looking at, let alone thinking. The way their mouths mashed made it look as though they were permanently hungry.

She'd only seen them through the window before now. The most powerful impression when she was face to face with them was the smell, which reminded her of disinfectant.

The lead Vore pushed her out of the way, as though it was opening a door. It hopped over to stand in front of Marnal. Rachel twisted to get a better look.

The Vore was standing there. She wanted to impose human thoughts and emotions on it, but knew she probably wouldn't be able to recognise what was going through its mind. The creatures' heads were actually rather small, and were mostly taken up with the eyes and the jaw. There was barely room for a brain.

She screamed, but the Vore didn't even flinch.

Rachel had never seen Marnal so still, not since he'd changed bodies at any rate. She wasn't moving either, not a single muscle. She was trying hard not to breathe. All this thinking might be too much... What if they could read thoughts?

One of the Vore behind her pulled her to her feet, claws digging into her arms. The one in front of Marnal grabbed him. Then they lifted them both, taking them in a direction that wasn't up or down, front or back, left or right.

They were somewhere else, a tunnel. It was dark, the air was thin but hot. Rachel felt like she weighed two stone. The Vore lowered her on to a floor that was thick with fine sand.

'We're on the second moon, aren't we?' she asked Marnal.

He nodded.

'Did... did they kill us?'

He looked puzzled. 'No.'

'How did we get here?'

'They can move through the fifth dimension.'

'I'm not even sure what that means.'

'They can manipulate hyperspace corridors. They travel down them like a spider down a thread of silk.'

The Vore pushed them both onwards.

'They want us to go this way,' Marnal said.

The two of them walked slowly, herded by the monsters. The ground was rumbling. It sounded as though they were in a subway beneath a busy road. Five minutes of walking, and they entered a chamber. It was roughly spherical, the size of a small house. The ground was more uneven. Vore hung from the ceiling, like bats, or walked easily across the pitted walls.

Marnal was looking around. They'd come in through the only door.

'Is this... What is this?' Rachel asked.

An execution chamber? A larder?

She turned to Marnal, who was looking up at the ceiling. Suddenly, a Vore grabbed his head in two of its claws. Rachel screamed, thinking the creature was about to wrench Marnal's skull off. Instead, it twisted his head down and round, until his attention was on the centre of the room.

There was a swirling visual display, a hologram. Rachel could make no sense of it. It flickered so fast it was making her dizzy.

'Imagine it seen through an insect's eye,' Marnal said.

She tried but couldn't.

'It's the TARDIS,' Marnal said. 'They want the TARDIS.' He sounded almost relieved.

'We don't have it –' Rachel began.

Marnal was ignoring her. 'I can get you this,' he told the nearest Vore, speaking slowly.

'What are you doing?' she demanded.

Marnal stepped over to her, and leant in close. 'If we summon the Doctor here, we can take the TARDIS. Escape in it.'

'Why do they want it?'

'They have an instinct to spread, to feed. Think how far they could go with a TARDIS.'

'Is that why they came to Earth in the first place? They were chasing the TARDIS?'

'Not exactly, but close enough.'

'With a TARDIS, they could go everywhere, in every time period.'

Marnal nodded.

'So we shouldn't even risk them getting their claws on it!' Rachel shouted.

Marnal stepped back and looked around, but the Vore weren't reacting.

'They can't operate the TARDIS. I can. We can get a long way from here.' He stepped up to the nearest Vore. 'In return, you spare my life. Our lives.'

The Vore stood, impassive.

'I agree to the deal,' Marnal said, carefully.

'Incoming transmission, master,' K9 reported.

He'd been helping the Doctor fix up the console. The Doctor was over at one of the walls, accessing some of the supply cables.

'From the Ruling Mind?' the Doctor asked.

The TARDIS, finally, was in the Northern Constellations, so someone on Klist would have spotted them by now.

'Negative. It originated in the solar system. It is being received on the ninth psychic wavelength.'

The Doctor frowned, and not only because he didn't realise the TARDIS could pick up psychic wavelengths.

'A telepath?'

'A Time Lord, master.'

Marnal appeared in the control room, right beside the console. The Doctor tensed, then relaxed. It was some sort of hologram, you could tell by the light falling on him, which hadn't come from anywhere in the control room.

'Doctor,' Marnal began, 'this is an emergency. You have to help.'

'Changed your tune, haven't you?' the Doctor asked, not sure he should be trusting a word of what he was hearing.

The message continued without Marnal reacting. The Doctor couldn't decide whether this was because he couldn't hear, or because he was too arrogant to take any notice.

'You must come to the following coordinates.' Marnal read out a string of numbers. 'Hurry – there isn't much time. Humans are dying.'

Marnal snapped out of existence.

'We need to get to Earth.'

'Master, our work here –'

'Unimportant.'

'I calculate a point seven eight probability that this is a trap.'

'It is a trap, I've no doubt about that at all.'

'Then –'

'Did you see it, K9? On the edge of the image?'

K9's ears waggled. 'Image analysis reveals alien object.'

'A leg, wouldn't you say?'

There had been something right at the edge of the shot, a spindly black limb with tiny hooks all over its hard, segmented surface.

'Affirmative. Initial identification: the fore limb of species *asilidae*, cross-checking database.'

The Doctor was already at the console, programming in the numbers Marnal had given him.

'Warning, master. Alien species identified. It is the Vore. By Supreme Council order, date index 309456/4756.7RE/1213GRT/100447TL, no Time Lord is to engage the Vore, all time ships are to observe an exclusion zone no less than one parsec and one century, in all five directions from any Vore moon. Further warning: this is a potential Last Contact. No further information.'

The Doctor sighed. It had taken a long time to get here. He couldn't dawdle on the return journey.

'Master?' K9 asked, as the Doctor started working at the console.

'I need to divert all power to the engines, K9. Slightly more than I dare. There, now all I need to do is –'

'Master. It is imperative you do not pull that lever.'

The Doctor's hand was on it. He hesitated.

'You must keep yourself safe, master.'

The Doctor grasped the lever. 'If that's your only concern…'

'Please consider your actions more carefully, master.'

The Doctor did just that, for a moment. This wasn't a decision at all, was it? People were in danger. What was his alternative – to run away and hide?

'We have to get back,' the Doctor said, pulling the lever.

He apologised to the ship. The lights flickered and dimmed, but the column in the centre of the console started pumping at something like its normal rate.

If anyone was monitoring the progress of the TARDIS on Klist they would have seen it powering towards them, before arcing around in a five-dimensional U-turn, picking up speed and heading back the way it had come.

'Before it's too late.'

Q: Which modern English word is derived from the Greek words *algos*, 'pain', and *nostos*, 'a return home'?

From 'Increase Your Word Power' in the *Skywords* in-flight puzzle book, Early Summer 2005.
(Answer on page 275)

Chapter Eleven
The Vore Games

Trix parked the car. Sat back in her seat. Her hands were only shaking a little. Why wouldn't she be a little nervous?

There was a lot of Vore activity in this area. Here, in London, it was the worst she'd seen it. There were police and army patrols out. The radio was on the air as normal, the DJ on Capital Radio occasionally dropping in monster sightings with the traffic reports. An extended news on the hour gave updates and emergency information. The Vore had attacked human beings, not infrastructure, so the main difficulty was staff shortages. There just weren't enough people around to deal with problems. The electricity and water were on, the roads were being cleared of abandoned and crashed cars. People were being urged to go to work, but to keep non-essential journeys to a minimum. The latest theory was that the Vore never attacked individuals, only groups. They never wiped out everyone. The DJ discussed this for some time with his guest, Badly Drawn Boy. That was the point when Trix tuned in to Radio 4, where it was being reported that batteries, petrol and fly spray were being rationed. The home secretary went on air to tell an interviewer that if everyone carried ID cards, establishing who was alive or dead and informing the families would be so much easier. Knowing where this kind of mentality would lead, actually knowing it because she'd been to the future and seen it, she shouted at the radio. She imagined Fitz telling her to calm down, and she calmed down a little.

Driving through London had rarely been so painless. There was more litter around than usual, but no traffic. There was, of course, still a congestion charge. From time to time Trix would hear gunfire, and this usually meant a roadblock ahead. The last one had been manned by soldiers just back from Basra. She'd joked and flirted her way past them, once she'd proved she hadn't stolen the car. They were letting the Vore walk and fly around – fire on them, the soldiers told her, and the creatures swept in to retaliate.

The streets, then, were all but empty. It matched her mood. She felt numbed by it all. No… She had to be honest with herself. She felt numb that Fitz had gone. The countless millions of other dead… well, they were just statistics. Brutal, but true. It was impossible to process what had happened, and the lack of levelled buildings and piles of rubble made it harder to accept that anything had happened, now all the bodies had been cleared away. Were they in mass graves or in cold storage? A rather morbid thought, but practical, and it had only just occurred to her. All the bodies had to have been taken somewhere. Were the Vore taking them? She was going to have to start thinking like the Doctor. He would have asked questions like this.

She was thinking about him in the past tense. Trix had noticed it first about an hour ago, on the outskirts of the city.

This, now, was where the trail for the Doctor ran out: a street full of Victorian town houses in north London. There was nothing to distinguish it from any of the other streets around here. Trix stayed in the car for a moment to assess the situation. Plenty of monsters, but they were going about their incomprehensible business showing no sign of interest in her car. For the moment. They could turn on her instantly, relentlessly. They were nestling all around one of the houses, in a way she hadn't seen before. The numbers here suggested it was interesting to them. Was that because the Doctor was around? There was a detached outbuilding – a garage? – that was practically submerged in a mass of Vore, all crawling over each other.

Time to put her theory into action. Trix got out of the car, and opened up the boot. She'd picked up a dead Vore, one just lying on the side of a country lane, possibly even road kill. Now she pulled it out. It seemed far lighter than before. She dragged it to the front gate and propped it up. The Vore nestling on the garage exhibited what could have been mild curiosity, but nothing more. Most of them angled their heads and craned to get a look, but none of them took as much as a single hop towards her. Nervous, even so, about outstaying her welcome Trix took a box of firelighters she'd bought out of the glove compartment, stuffed about a third of them under the dead Vore and, after a couple of tries, set light to one with matches. Once she was sure the flames had caught she retreated to the car and waited.

The burning Vore gave off thick smoke with a green tinge to it. It took a minute or two, but then Trix could smell it even inside the car. It reeked of industrial solvents, as though she'd set fire to a pile of old rags soaked in glue and creosote. The smell was unpleasant for her, and made her choke, but it had an extraordinary effect on the Vore, who scattered like birds who'd heard a shotgun. Trix waited a minute, but the monsters settled elsewhere. She could see them on nearby roofs and trees. There was a ring of them, resolutely staying away as though there was a glass wall blocking them.

Trix got out of the car and stood right next to the fire. The lieutenant in the town near her hotel had said the smell of burning Vore kept other Vore away. So, she'd come up with this experiment. The smell of burning humans would keep her away, she was sure, but there was more to this. This was more like spraying Vore repellent around. Chemistry, not simply psychology. Which was why she was standing here now, letting the stink get into the fibres of her clothes. There were no Vore within fifty feet of her, but they could fly that distance in a matter of seconds. The fastest way to get dead now would be to start thinking she had made herself invincible. But this was a start.

As Trix waited by the fire she looked over at the house. The

Vore had abandoned the outbuilding, revealing that it was a garage as she'd suspected. The house itself – like most of the others in the country by now – had its windows and doors boarded up or barricaded. First, she made her way up the drive to the garage. It was all but empty. Walking around it, Trix found what looked like a hi-tech piece of brewing equipment in the middle of the space, a three-inch strand of what looked like intestine on the rough concrete floor, and nothing else of note. The garage did give her a strange feeling, though – just a slight sense of being unsettled, like time and space hadn't been put back together quite right in here.

'Miss?' a woman's voice called out.

Trix turned. A middle-aged woman, wearing jeans and a sweatshirt, stood in the doorway. She was shaking. Trix instinctively went over to her.

'Are you all right?' she asked. The older woman's eyes were rimmed with black, a combination of smudged make-up and lack of sleep.

'I've been in my house since they came,' she said.

Although she appeared calm, there was something distracted about her, signs of trauma. Trix wondered if she herself looked any different.

'My name is Trix,' she said.

'Jackie Winfield.' The woman held out her hand, and Trix shook it, a little awkwardly.

'Have you lost someone?'

'My husband,' she said quietly. 'Killed in front of me, the monsters just stood there and breathed white dust...'

'They killed my boyfriend the same way,' Trix told her, not wanting either of them to relive it.

'Oh. I'm sorry.' The woman looked it. 'The smoke keeps the monsters away?'

'I really hope so. Have you seen a man around here? Mid-forties, long hair, probably wearing a long velvet jacket?'

Mrs Winfield shook her head. 'There's been no one like that.'

'A police box?' Trix wondered, aware of a note of desperation in her voice.

Mrs Winfield looked confused. 'The police were here, the night the moon appeared.'

'The siege,' Trix remembered. 'That was definitely at this house?'

'From what I could tell, it was this garage. They evacuated us, so we didn't get to see.'

Too much of a coincidence, Trix decided.

'Would you like some coffee?' Mrs Winfield offered.

The Vore were getting impatient, at least that's what Rachel assumed from their increased activity. If it had been a group of humans, the shuffling and looking around would have indicated it was an agitated one.

'The Doctor's TARDIS was damaged,' Marnal said slowly. 'Until it's been repaired it will travel more slowly than normal. You can see from your display that it is heading back this way. It will be here shortly.'

The hologram, or whatever it was, was still as impenetrable to Rachel as a magic-eye picture. She had asked Marnal if he could understand their language. She couldn't even make out sounds that might be Voreish; the only noises they made came from the chomping of their mouths. Marnal told her he was confident they could understand what he was saying, as Time Lords had a gift for languages.

Running through what had happened, again and again, Rachel wasn't sure why she and Marnal were still alive. The Vore had just made them stand here, and tended to bump into them to separate her from Marnal if she tried talking. They didn't do it every time, only when she and Marnal were facing each other. With all the monsters' jostling and wriggling about, Rachel wasn't sure if the same platoon of Vore had been watching them all this time, or whether there was a continual changing of the guard. It was like being in a room with a ticking time bomb – she got the sense the Vore could lash out at any moment.

They had been here, she thought, for about two hours. She was used to the low gravity now, and was dimly aware that if she got back to Earth it would feel like she was carrying sandbags around. The air was thick and bleachy. It smelled, Rachel reflected, not unlike an old people's home.

The Vore were now hopping and skittering. For moments Rachel thought this was the point where she was going to die, but quickly realised the insects weren't even acknowledging them. They were crowding around the display.

'What's happening?' she asked Marnal.

'I think the TARDIS has just entered the solar system. Yes, there it is.'

The display started to flare and spark. Whatever was happening was very dramatic.

'They're manipulating the hyperspace corridors, trying to trap the TARDIS.'

'You said they could use those like spiders use silk. They're weaving a web.'

Marnal nodded. 'You can get carried away with analogies, but that one seems apposite.'

Rachel assumed this was a compliment from the tone of his voice.

The hologram looked more like a firework display now, bright reds and blues splashing out and scattering. She still had no idea what she was looking at, but it was large, violent, garish and entirely silent. Marnal was watching as though it was a boxing match, wincing and gasping in turn. Finally, the colours died down.

'They've got him, they're reeling him in,' he said, the excitement in his voice making it clear which side he was on.

Rachel wasn't feeling so happy. 'If they can catch the TARDIS like that, how are you planning to escape in it?'

'I know a few tricks the Doctor doesn't.' He didn't seem worried.

The display vanished, and the Vore started filing out of the chamber. It reminded Rachel of the end of a movie at a multiplex.

Marnal joined the queue of Vore. 'We should follow them,' he said, shuffling along.

'They're going to the TARDIS?'

'They must be.'

Rachel got into place behind Marnal.

'How long were you and Fitz together?'

The answer was almost embarrassing. Mrs Winfield had just said she'd been married for thirty years.

'A few days,' Trix said. 'We were friends before this. We've only really kissed and cuddled.'

Mrs Winfield sighed. 'Bad timing.'

'An occupational hazard,' Trix agreed. She was feeling a bit more settled. This was a normal kitchen, with a normal person serving her normal coffee, and she was having a chat about human beings.

Every so often a Vore would walk past, stand for a moment staring through the window, then walk off in its strange, lumbering-yet-twitchy way. It wasn't easy to get used to.

'Why did you love him?' Mrs Winfield asked.

Trix hugged her coffee mug while she thought about that. 'Well, it kind of snuck up on me. And him, I think. We were, er, workmates. He's honest. What you see is what you get with Fitz. No matter what was happening, he was... well, he was Fitz.'

'Trust.'

'I trusted him with my life, so often it seemed like the most natural thing in the world. He didn't play games, no hidden agendas or emotional baggage. Even after everything he's been through.'

'I've had a couple of friends, and their husbands or wives, well, they weren't the people they thought they were. Or they changed for the worse. That wasn't true with Des. It sounds like a criticism to say that someone... I can't even think of a nice way to put it. That someone stays the same. Sounds like they're stagnant. Of course Des and I changed over thirty years, but I could rely on him.'

Trix looked around the spotless, barricaded kitchen. 'Can you cope on your own?'

'I keep leaving food out for Binks, the cat, but she hasn't eaten anything. I think the monsters must have got her.'

'Cats sometimes turn up after months. Don't give up hope yet.'

Mrs Winfield nodded politely. 'Best to move on, I think.'

Trix had known this woman for ten minutes, and she couldn't yet work out whether she was in a healthy, pragmatic state or in almost psychotic denial of what was happening.

'You still speak about him as though he's alive,' Mrs Winfield noted quietly. 'He's gone.'

Trix started crying then, great uncontrolled sobs that started somewhere in her gut and choked their way up into her mouth, nose and eyes. She felt Mrs Winfield's arms around her, telling her it was all right. She imagined that if Fitz was here he'd be telling her not to cry. If he was here, she wouldn't need to. As she sobbed, she got angry with herself, embarrassed that she couldn't contain herself.

She sat up, took deep breaths. It was several minutes before she was cogent again.

'We're all going to need counselling, aren't we?' Mrs Winfield sighed. She'd been crying herself.

'Who lives next door?' Trix asked, determined to change the subject.

Mrs Winfield told her about the mysterious old author next door, the one who wrote stories. She even managed to fish out one of his old books, the Scope sticker still on it. Science fiction.

'I need to investigate Marnal's house,' Trix said.

'Why?'

'My friend, the Doctor, might be in there, or there could be a clue to where he went after that.'

'Trix, dear, he was probably eaten by the –'

'I know what might have happened. But… No. It's the Doctor.

234

He's somewhere else, he's fighting them.'

Mrs Winfield smiled indulgently. Trix was sure she would have done the same if their positions were reversed, and that Mrs Winfield would feel just as patronised.

The air ripped open and the TARDIS fell into it, steam swirling off every surface.

After a moment, the lamp on top stopped flashing and the door opened.

The Doctor stood in the doorway, looked around and then looked down.

'Very uneven terrain, K9. I think you'd better stay inside.' Now, that *did* ring a bell. 'Monitor the TARDIS repairs. Help the old girl, if she needs it.'

The Doctor stepped out, closed the door and carefully locked it. A great subterranean chamber complete with stalagmites and stalactites, arches and chimneys. The air was warm and damp, filled with a deeply unpleasant smell, or mix of smells. There weren't any monsters, not that he could see, but there was little light. A layman might mistake this for a natural landscape, but then people often looked at fields and hedgerows and thought the same. The living rock had been carved and worn down by something with a real sense of purpose. These weren't random channels; these were surface conduits and lateral connectives.

A termite mound or an anthill.

Yes, that was what this reminded him of. He'd seen a termite mound in Africa, once. A spire of mud as tall as a tree, and – like a tree – extending just as far underground. A community with more citizens than any human city, all living in eusocial harmony – with each other, at any rate. Humans thought the Earth was theirs, but they were recent tenants of a world dominated by grasses, bacteria, plankton and nematodes. The termites had been around a thousand times longer than humans and there were countless numbers of them – never mind population size, by sheer weight they outnumbered people in Africa.

The Doctor had already known from the glimpse of leg that he was dealing with an insect species. Insects the size of men, and social insects by the look of all this. He mustn't fall into the trap of thinking the Vore were exactly like termites, though. He racked his brain for scraps of information he could use. He needed to get some idea of the layout of the chamber… which, now he came to think of it, looked awfully familiar.

The Doctor tried to get a better sense of the place. Far, far away there was sound, like a rushing river. There would have to be water here somewhere, but this could equally well be traffic or…

Where exactly was he? The last time he'd checked the instruments the TARDIS had been pretty close to Earth, certainly within the moon's orbit. The gravity here felt natural, and it was substantial. He guessed it was about a sixth of Earth's. About the same as the moon's, but this wasn't the moon. At some point, while trying to evade the hyperspace corridors, he must have fallen into a space warp. Something had gone very wrong.

He turned on his heel, to head back to the TARDIS and take some more readings.

A monster blocked his way.

The Doctor looked it up and down. 'So you're a Vore? I've heard the expression "time flies", I've never actually met one before. Hello.'

Others were crowding around him. The group started moving and, as though he was caught in a stream, the Doctor had little choice but to go with the flow. Within moments he was jostled against Marnal and Rachel, then the three of them were pushed in the same direction, leading out of the chamber.

'Fancy meeting you here,' the Doctor said. 'So, you had a TARDIS of your own tucked away?'

'My TARDIS is here… now.'

A couple of the insects jostled them apart.

'Friends of yours?' the Doctor asked.

'We've reached an arrangement.'

The Doctor grinned knowingly. 'One where they give you the

TARDIS if you give them me? Are you sure you checked the small print?'

'What do you mean?'

'Well I can't help noticing that the TARDIS is back that way, and we're all being marched off in the other direction.'

'He talked to them, Doctor,' Rachel said.

'Did he, now?' the Doctor replied knowingly.

'We reached terms.'

'Had a chat?'

'That's right.'

'You are aware that most insects are deaf, aren't you, Marnal? BOO!'

Rachel jumped, but not one of the Vore so much as turned its head.

'A lucky guess,' Marnal said, subdued.

'No. I just noticed that the Vore aren't making sounds, but they're clearly communicating. I imagine they're doing it with gestures and...' The Doctor sniffed the air thoughtfully. 'Yes, chemical signals. Interesting.'

Rachel felt a little foolish about all the shouting she'd been doing. She turned on Marnal. 'You said they understood what you were saying.'

'We're still here, aren't we?' Marnal reminded her.

The Doctor gave a wicked smile. 'Oh, we're here all right.'

Whoever had barricaded the house wasn't very good at it. Trix had found a small ground-floor window they'd missed, and easily prised it open. Wriggling inside, she found herself in a little downstairs loo. She couldn't hear anyone else in the house, so she made her way round to the nearest door, cleared the fridge that was blocking it out of the way and let Mrs Winfield in. The house was very cold.

'Do you know your way around?' Trix asked.

'I've never been round here before, but all the houses on the street are the same. You know what I mean: unless they've had a conservatory or knocked rooms through.'

Trix could already see this by comparing Mrs Winfield's kitchen with the one she was in now. Next door it was a lot more modern, and light and airy. The kitchen here, apart from the fridge, probably hadn't changed all that much since the Fifties. The cooker looked as though it had been as lovingly maintained as a vintage car; the cupboards had been kept clean, but were stained and faded with use and age.

There was also the distinct smell of old people – not the more unpleasant stuff, just the smell of violets and foot powder, dust and polish. For her part, Trix still smelled of cremated monster.

Trix's working assumption was that there was no one home – human or alien – but she stayed on the alert. She edged into the large downstairs library, half-expecting an ambush. She had the urge to take someone on. The monsters, the owner of the house, anyone really. She wanted to smash some heads. Take it out on something that deserved it.

'This is a dining room in our house,' Mrs Winfield said, not even whispering.

Trix ignored her. 'He has a lot of books.'

'Like I say, he was an author. He'd need dictionaries and things, wouldn't he?'

Trix was looking over the shelves. It was gloomy in here, and would have been even if the small window hadn't been blocked. It was possible to make out the titles, though, and the authors' names. After a quick sampling of the other shelves Trix mentally moved the apostrophe.

'They're all by the guy who lived here,' Trix said.

'All of them?' Mrs Winfield was working through a pile of *Interzones*. 'There's some stuff that's a hundred years old, these are from the Eighties.'

Trix nodded, and pulled down the leather-bound volume that looked the most valuable of all the books. 'Are they all first editions?' she asked.

'I don't think they'd be that valuable. I doubt he'd want to sell them.'

Trix occasionally forgot that things could belong to other people.

A pile of books fell over, and the two women huddled up to face whatever had done it. But there was nothing there.

Trix picked out a couple of paperbacks. 'They're all science fiction?'

'I'm not a fan,' Mrs Winfield admitted.

Trix opened the first one, *Valley of the Lost*, and was surprised to see the word 'Tardis' there.

'It's an acronym,' she muttered under her breath.

'An acronym? Is that some science-fiction thing?'

'It doesn't matter.'

The rest of the book was a little more opaque. It was set on an alien planet, and there was some visiting delegation from a Three Minute City, whatever that was. It wasn't the ideal way to discover an exciting new author, but after a couple of skim-read paragraphs Trix wasn't exactly hooked.

There was absolutely no way that the TARDIS reference was a coincidence. She and Fitz and the Doctor had been led to Earth by someone who knew about the Doctor, knew about at least one of his companions, knew about the TARDIS. Here, there was someone writing about TARDISes and...

'Oh my,' Trix said. 'How long has Marnal been living here?'

'A very long time,' Mrs Winfield said. 'As long as anyone can remember.'

These were books about the Doctor's home planet. The one that not even the Doctor knew anything about, the one that had been destroyed leaving few traces. Written over a period of a hundred years, apparently by the same man. An immortal time-traveller.

One of the Doctor's own people.

She'd walked into a trap, Trix realised. Had the Doctor already sprung it?

It was like Gaudí had built an aqueduct.

The Vore had pushed the Doctor, Marnal and Rachel up to a

narrow bridge across a half-mile-wide cavern. It was as level as any human engineer using a laser and GPS could have made it, but its lines were organic, pitted and curved as though it had been built from the bottom up out of mud pies.

Now the Vore started herding them along the bridge. They hadn't come this way before. The Vore struggled to keep to the boundaries of the structure. One fell off, making Rachel yelp, but it extended its wings and swooped up and landed behind them.

'Where are they taking us?' Rachel asked, before she had to stop speaking. The smell in this place was terrible.

'Very few people know anything about the Vore,' Marnal said, still trying to excuse his earlier mistake. 'They've killed everyone and everything they've ever encountered. I am the only person who has ever seen them and survived.'

'I've seen them before,' the Doctor said casually.

Marnal shook his head. 'They track down everything that makes any contact with them.'

'They've attacked Earth, Doctor,' Rachel told him.

The Doctor looked over at Marnal, who confirmed what Rachel said: 'In a matter of weeks the human race will be extinct, along with every other life form on Earth.'

The Doctor smiled reassuringly at Rachel. 'We'll see about that. What's happened? Has one of their spaceships appeared over London?'

Rachel nodded weakly. 'Something like that. What do they want?'

'They don't want anything,' the Doctor said. 'They're animals.'

'Capable of warp engineering?' Marnal sneered. 'Or even just building a bridge like this?'

'Spiders can spin webs and set traps, bees and ants can build themselves whole cities. They do it on instinct. The Vore are simply able to construct more complicated items. They have no individual intelligence.'

The Doctor patted the nearest Vore on the head. It hissed at him.

'Or conversation. They exist to consume.'

Marnal laughed. 'Of course. Yes. They're feeding. They'll grind all life on Earth into chyme, then transport it here.'

'Chyme?' Rachel asked.

'Sniff the air,' Marnal suggested. 'What does that smell remind you of?'

'It's like someone's been sick. A lot.'

'You've been sick in the past, haven't you?' the Doctor asked, so gently that the question threw Rachel a little.

'Er... I've thrown up, yes.'

'What you were bringing up was chyme, give or take.'

'Why not just say they want to eat us?'

'They don't,' Marnal explained. 'They want to turn the human race into vomit. They'll line their food caves with it, then plant fungal spores that will use it as fertiliser. The Vore will feed on that fungus.'

'That's horrible.'

'Your race is always looking for a purpose that will unite it. It looks like you've found it.'

'I hate to bring this up,' the Doctor said to Marnal, before looking apologetic, 'if you'll pardon the expression, but we really should be getting out of here. We're heading away from my TARDIS, I know that. Are we heading towards yours?'

Marnal shook his head.

'The Vore brought us here, Doctor, in one of their warp corridors,' Rachel said, more helpfully.

The Doctor frowned at Marnal. 'You said your TARDIS was here.'

'You brought it here.'

The Doctor rolled his eyes. 'You meant *my* TARDIS? I see. How very witty of you.'

'You stole it, Doctor.'

'I took it back, yes.'

'I mean all those years ago.' Marnal turned to Rachel. 'Centuries ago, when he was in his first incarnation. He stole it, fled.'

'Fled Gallifrey?' the Doctor asked. 'Why would I do a thing like that?'

DOCTOR WHO

'I only found out later, from my son. There were all sorts of rumours, but the real reason was because you –'

'Your son?' Rachel interrupted. 'You have four daughters, all from your wives' previous marriages.'

'Not those parasites. My real son visited once, back in the Seventies. He couldn't stay long, but he told me... Oh, it doesn't matter. The Doctor stole the TARDIS. Everyone knows that. Who did he steal it from, though, eh? Me. That's my Type 40. I recognised it the moment I saw it. We went through a lot together. It was with me when I first encountered the Vore.'

They continued along the bridge – the monsters weren't giving them any choice. Rachel looked over at the Doctor, who was deep in thought.

'How high would you say this bridge was?' he asked.

'Seventy feet?' Rachel guessed. 'It's too dark to tell.'

'Hmmm,' said the Doctor, then pushed her over the edge.

Marnal turned and saw the Doctor leaping at him, grabbing for his jacket. Before he could even raise his arm the Doctor had pitched them both over the edge, into the darkness.

HMS *Illustrious* had left Portsmouth for the mid-Atlantic within a few hours of the first Vore attack, leading a five-ship task force that had – at that stage – orders that talked loosely of counter-attacks and last resorts. During the Cold War, these were the orders given in the event of a nuclear war, and they boiled down, essentially, to playing it by ear if the United Kingdom was wiped off the map and no one was left to send further orders. Launch a counter-attack against the assumed aggressor, then make your way to Canada or – if Canada had also ceased to exist – Australia.

It had transpired that the Vore threat was of a different nature. UNIT personnel were seconded to the ship and the task force was sent new orders: to head to the West African coast to look at a mountain. Most of the crew knew the area. Less than five years ago they'd been sent to stabilise Sierra Leone.

There were satellite images of a new mountain in Guinea-Bissau. It hadn't been there a week before. Communications around the world were more erratic than normal, and the lines to Bissau were never the most reliable. The country was low-lying country - its highest point, according to the reference books, failed to reach three hundred metres. The new mountain was nearly two kilometres high. It was generating heat and it even had its own magnetic field. The satellite pictures, though, were hard to interpret and the UK, the US and Europe had little in the way of human intelligence on the ground there.

That the mountain needed investigating was obvious. When *Illustrious* got within a hundred miles of the coast Harriers were sent out on a reconnaissance mission, entering Guinean airspace at 500 m.p.h. It wasn't hard to spot the mountain. The Harriers gave it a wide berth on the first pass, then swept around and returned to their ship on a course that gave them a closer view.

That fly past was completed without any enemy retaliation. The pictures were relayed back to *Illustrious*, then on to London.

British helicopters had landed in the capital city, Bissau, and diplomatic contact had been made with the National People's Assembly. The people here had experience of locusts, and feared that the Vore were breeding. If they were like their terrestrial counterparts, each Vore could lay nearly three hundred eggs. When the locals were asked how they fought ordinary locusts, they said they used hoes and brushes. Insecticide was rarely used, because it was ineffective rather than because it was expensive.

In London, experts in insects and insect behaviour had been brought into military planning meetings within hours of the first Vore attack. They warned that there would be millions of Vore in the mountain, and that the structure would extend deep underground.

The *Illustrious* waited for further orders.

• • •

Marnal crashed, softly, into a pile of grey mush, catching his leg on something harder. The Doctor landed right next to him. Rachel was already standing, dusting herself off.

'We should be dead,' she said.

'Low gravity,' the Doctor explained. 'We can fall six times further than we could on Earth. We knew it would be a soft landing.'

'The Vore will just fly down for us,' Rachel complained.

'No,' said the Doctor, pointing at the floor. 'We landed in the mushroom patch. We smell like food now.'

'They'll *eat* us?'

'Not here they won't. The Vore follow strict patterns. They don't have thoughts in the way we'd understand, just a set of internal instructions, ways to react to stimuli. They can't take the initiative or use their imagination.' The Doctor pointed over to a line of Vore trudging through the mush, carrying what looked like twice their weight of it, which they'd collected. 'They eat elsewhere, probably in specially designated refectories.'

There were other Vore dotted around, tending to the mushrooms.

Marnal drew his gun, set it to kill and shot one of the lone Vore. It fell down.

The Doctor looked horrified.

'What the hell are you doing?' Rachel shouted.

'Testing a theory. Observe.'

None of the other Vore reacted.

'They can't sense us,' Marnal concluded. 'We can move around undisturbed.'

'Do you smell that?' the Doctor asked.

Marnal sniffed the air. There was a new scent mingled with all the others.

'Tetramethrin?' the Doctor asked.

Marnal shrugged.

A Vore landed close to them. Marnal raised his gun again, but it started walking in the other direction, towards the one Marnal had shot. Without hesitation, it bent down, grabbed the dead insect's abdomen, lifted it easily and then flew off, vanishing into the dark.

The Doctor had watched the whole process, fascinated.

'We have to get out of here,' Marnal said.

'Well obviously we have to get out of here,' the Doctor replied testily.

He turned to see Marnal pointing the gun at him.

'Do you know, I think I recognise that gun,' the Doctor said. 'Just like I recognise this place.'

'Your memories are coming back?' Marnal asked.

'I hope not,' the Doctor said, before quickly adding, 'No, it's not that. More recent. So much has happened in the last couple of days.'

The Doctor snapped his fingers. 'Of course. It didn't look like you. You were older, a man with white hair and beakier.' The Doctor drew a nose in the air. 'That's what threw me. But it was you, wasn't it?'

Marnal backed away. 'What do you mean?'

'The Shoal. A Time Lord launched an unprovoked attack on these creatures. Barely escaped with his life. It was you. And was that my TARDIS you were in?'

Rachel frowned. 'Wouldn't an attack like that break the laws of time?'

The Doctor grinned. 'Yes. That's a very good point. A little hypocritical of you to paint yourself as an innocent party, let alone as the judge of my actions.'

'I learnt a lesson,' Marnal spat.

'Before or after the Matrix projection?' the Doctor asked.

'What do you know about that?'

The Doctor took the slip of plastic from his pocket and passed it to Marnal. 'It mentions the Vore. And a cicatrix, whatever that is.'

'I think it's a type of parrot,' Rachel guessed. 'They used to have one on *Playschool*.'

The Doctor and Marnal ignored her.

'So... what happened next?' the Doctor asked. 'You set off an explosion, you barely got away in time. So you headed back to Gallifrey?'

Marnal hesitated. 'I don't remember.'

'That's my line,' the Doctor noted. 'As Boethius said, though, the history book on the shelf is always repeating itself.'

Marnal took a squelchy step forward, pressed the gun to the side of the Doctor's head.

'Marnal!' Rachel screamed.

The Doctor turned so that the muzzle of the gun was pointing to the dead centre of his forehead.

'Before you kill me,' the Doctor said reasonably, 'would you mind telling me about the Matrix?'

Interlude
Marnal's Error

Marnal's TARDIS emerged from the Vortex and passed along an authorised flight path through the powerful transduction barriers that enveloped Gallifrey, keeping it safe. From there, it was seconds – relatively speaking – before the ship materialised in its berth. Marnal was still shaking.

He carefully deactivated the time engines, collected up his belongings and opened the door. His hearts hadn't settled down after his escape from the Shoal. The other two ships in his squadron wouldn't yet know that he had got clear. If they'd survived, they would be following their orders to head back home. They'd all take different routes and would arrive at different times. Marnal had broken with protocol and come straight here. He needed to make a report to the High Council about the alien threat. What he put in and left out of that would need some consideration, and he had to calm himself. Everything he believed in had been vindicated, but would they see it that way? His squadron had been using cloaking devices, and he'd bribed the duty officer at traffic control, so the facts would be whatever he said they were.

He stepped out of the deserted landing area, and walked through an ancient stone archway and into the corridor.

A powerfully built man with white hair and a clipped beard blocked his way. 'What the hell have you done?'

Marnal tried to step around him and to disguise his agitation. 'Out of my way, Ulysses.'

He was one of the Time Lords who had given himself a new name – the latest fad among the independent-minded. Ulysses had called himself after an adventurer from the same primitive planet as his wife Penelope.

Behind him were two of his companions. One was Penelope herself, wearing her strange Earthling clothes: an ankle-length skirt and prim white blouse. Her red hair hung wild to her waist. The other was Mister Saldaamir, an alien with blue skin, the last survivor of the Time Wars in the ancient past. The three of them surrounded Marnal. They were trying to intimidate him, but they were running more scared than he was. That was obvious in a dozen tiny ways, from posture to nervous glances between themselves.

Ulysses asked him again.

'You've got blood on your hands, Castellan,' Penelope said quietly.

Marnal glanced down, but she was speaking metaphorically.

'The High Council authorised a reconnaissance mission. Close observation,' Ulysses barked at him.

Marnal looked at Ulysses, and thought about his response carefully. He'd always enjoyed baiting this fool. 'In closed session, yes. I'm sure they'd be interested in how you know about that.'

'You transgressed their orders. You treated the mission like a military assault.'

'The demands of this uniform –' Marnal countered.

'It isn't a uniform if only you are wearing it,' Penelope told him sharply.

'My suspicions proved justified. There was a threat to Gallifrey. Didn't I do exactly what you and your fellow *explorers* only talk about doing? The creatures in the Shoal had access to advanced technology. They were on the verge of swarming across the universe. The High Council will read my reconnaissance report and take it at face value. They won't worry if I leave out some of the details.'

Penelope sneered at him. 'They will if we report you. You committed genocide.'

'Better a million aliens die than a single Time Lord.' He sneered at Penelope, letting her know that the sentiment was a calculated insult. 'And better a pre-emptive attack fought thirty thousand light years away than those things attacking the Capitol.'

'There was no threat of war.'

'You have no idea what I found there.'

'A temporal cicatrix,' Mister Saldaamir replied.

'A scar where space-time has tried and failed to heal itself,' Penelope added.

'An area characterised by anomalies in time and space,' Ulysses finished.

'You were watching me?' Marnal tried not to sound rattled.

Mister Saldaamir smiled, baring sharp teeth. 'No. We were watching the cicatrix. They are extraordinarily rare, and rather useful for the project we're working on.'

'The creatures there were in control of the phenomenon. I think they built it.'

Ulysses laughed. 'They are attracted to it like moths to a flame. They've learnt to ride the hyperspace corridors formed naturally by the scar, but they didn't create it. The scar formed over the damage caused by the brief appearance of a naked singularity there centuries ago. Nothing at all to do with the insects.'

'They were plotting with other aliens to destroy Gallifrey. I saw their plans.'

Someone else had joined them. The young woman with the long blonde hair he'd just seen in the Shoal. 'No. You saw me send experimental data back here. I am the Lady Larna.'

Marnal looked the woman up and down. 'What's going on here, Ulysses? If she's a Time Lady, why don't I recognise her?'

'You wouldn't, yet,' Larna said.

'You're from the relative future?'

Larna nodded.

'That doesn't narrow it down as much as it might. But it does explain the advanced technology. You're from after the attacks, then, Larna?'

She stayed very quiet. The other three were staring at her.

'Ah... so you've not told the rest of this little clique?'

'Tell us now,' Ulysses ordered.

Larna took a deep breath. 'For millions of years Gallifrey has existed in isolation. Soon – not imminently, not all at once – there will be a spate of attacks. Omega, the Sontarans, Tannis, Faction Paradox, Varnax, Catavolcus, the Timewyrm. You know some of those names, you will come to know the others. It is very important that Gallifrey survives all these attacks.'

'Of course it is,' Ulysses said.

'You don't understand. All things must pass. Gallifrey will fall. But it must fall at precisely the right time. The enemy is unknown to us. It will be until Last Contact is made. If it's destroyed before that, by any of those other enemies, then the consequences...' Her voice trailed off. 'That is as much as I know.'

Marnal looked pleased with himself. 'The president and members of the Supreme Council know the prophecy. They have been told that a Time Lord now living will be central to all these events. That he will find the lost scrolls of Rassilon and lead Gallifrey from darkness.'

'I hadn't even heard rumours of this,' Ulysses admitted, rubbing his chin. 'This happens in our lifetimes?'

'Our children's, at the very latest. The council have been keeping it from even their senior colleagues. They fear the consequences if it is widely known.'

Ulysses and his companions looked at each other nervously. They all knew there would be disunity. Chaos. With each individual Time Lord wielding the power they did, such social upheaval was truly dangerous.

'There would be panic. Overreaction. Many would seek to kill or contain this Time Lord.'

'Others would seek to be him,' Mister Saldaamir said thoughtfully.

'It'll all end up in the public domain if the High Council investigate what's happened today. Still keen to report me to them?'

'They sent you because of the prophecy?'

'They are worried, Ulysses. Most of all by the idea that I am right, that the time for observation is over and we have to get out into the universe.'

'You're not the only person who believes that.'

Penelope had been listening to all this. 'We have prophets of doom on my planet too, plenty of them. The only thing they have in common is that they've all been proved wrong in the end.'

'The Supreme Council take it seriously,' Marnal said. 'They'll do anything to protect the status quo here. I killed a few aliens. So what? You've violated every law of time.'

Penelope looked worried. 'We will all suffer because of this,' she told her husband.

'No,' he replied, stabbing a finger at Marnal. 'He started a war, he's killed sentient beings. We've done nothing of the sort.'

Mister Saldaamir shook his head. 'The council know what we're doing. They always have. They won't be able to turn a blind eye to our activities any longer.'

Marnal realised that he gained some satisfaction from seeing them arguing. There was still more poison to drip in their ears. 'They won't touch anyone who doesn't have it coming to them, I'm sure. So why would any of you have anything to be scared of? Perhaps you're right and we should get everything out into the open.'

'He's trying to manipulate us,' Penelope said. 'Trying to scare us. He's the one who's done something wrong.'

Marnal looked at her. 'I'm sure they'll be very understanding about your son. How is little –?'

Ulysses turned around, punched Marnal square in the jaw and sent him slamming into the stone wall. Marnal hit his head and collapsed. He tried to get up but couldn't muster control of his legs.

'What are you doing?' Mister Saldaamir asked.

'He can't jeopardise our project. We know he's already covered his own tracks. There's no trail.'

'Are you suggesting we murder him?'

Ulysses spent just a moment too long considering the question. 'No, no, no. We go to his TARDIS. We use its telepathic circuits to erase his memory. I take him somewhere he can't do any harm and dump him, then come back here and hide his ship.'

'Where are you going to take him?' Mister Saldaamir asked.

'England, 1883,' Penelope said quickly. 'Earth,' she clarified for Larna's and Mister Saldaamir's benefit.

'That's where you're from,' Ulysses noted.

'Well yes, dear, once upon a time. I thought mother could look after him.'

'Is exile to your mother-in-law's the sort of punishment you had in mind?' Mister Saldaamir asked.

Ulysses grimaced. 'It's perfect.'

Chapter Twelve
Reloaded

'What?' Marnal said, keeping the gun pressed to the Doctor's forehead.

Rachel was trying to remember. She didn't want to see the Doctor shot, and wanted either to stop the execution or buy enough time to get away from it. 'The Matrix was something on Gallifrey, wasn't it?' There had been too much to absorb in Marnal's books, but she remembered that snippet.

'It was the repository of all accumulated Time Lord knowledge,' Marnal said.

Rachel smiled. 'That's right, it was the main computer.'

'So much more than that,' Marnal said quietly. 'When Time Lords died their memories were uploaded into the circuits of the Matrix.'

'And if all the Time Lords are dead,' the Doctor said, 'then logically all their memories would be in the Matrix.'

'The Matrix was destroyed with Gallifrey,' Marnal said. 'Yet another consequence of your –'

'No,' the Doctor stated firmly.

'Then where?'

'As I said to G.K. Chetterton, "Gilbert, the best place to hide a leaf is on a tree." It follows that the best place to hide a lot of memories would be...'

Marnal pulled the gun away. 'You're lying.'

The Doctor shook his head. Marnal was clearly concerned by the sudden movement. His whole attitude to the Doctor had changed in an instant, become full of concern.

'I don't understand,' Rachel said.

The Doctor clutched his lapels and looked insufferably smug.

'So please explain,' Rachel added.

'You spent all that time concentrating on what isn't in there. Not once did you wonder what was there *instead*. I had memories.' He paused to chuckle. 'Oh boy, did I have memories.' The Doctor paused, a little theatrically. 'My brain contains the entire contents of the Matrix.'

'It's impossible,' Marnal said, but his gun was down and he was swaying uncertainly.

'No, it was simple. Before Gallifrey was destroyed I edited out my own memories using the TARDIS's telepathic circuits, and downloaded every Matrix file into the space I'd cleared.'

'One brain couldn't contain all that information. How many Time Lord minds would be stored there?' Marnal asked.

'One hundred and fifty-three thousand eight hundred and forty-one of them,' the Doctor replied instantly.

'You've counted?'

'The maths is simple enough. You just have to remember to subtract five at the end.'

'All those minds can't be talking to you. You'd go mad.' Rachel said, although she'd always had her suspicions.

'No. They're supercompressed and stored away. I can't access them. If I tried... Well, it wouldn't be pleasant. I suspect it would kill me.'

'Are they alive in there?' Rachel asked.

The Doctor shrugged. 'They're dormant. They sleep in my mind. Beyond that... well, we get into metaphysics, and I try to avoid all that.'

Marnal was staring right at the Doctor's forehead. 'How are you planning to wake them up?'

'I only worked out they're in there a few hours ago. A cerebral scan made by an instrument that once accessed the Matrix, so knew what to look for, confirmed it.'

'You must have a plan.'

'I'm sure I did, but I must have accidentally deleted it with the memories. All I was left with was a very strong built-in aversion to opening the floodgates. If I probe what is in there too hard or, heaven forfend, get my memories back, the Matrix databanks will be overwritten and all the information will be lost forever.' The Doctor grinned. 'Of course, if you have any ideas how to get them out... ?'

'The Matrix was corrupted by Faction Paradox,' Rachel said.

Marnal and the Doctor turned to look at her.

'It was – we saw it happen when we watched that recording of Gallifrey being destroyed. What you have is infected by –'

'When I pulled the lever the future version of Faction Paradox was erased from the time line. It never existed to corrupt the Matrix. There was a tiny window of opportunity – less than a minute – after that, but before the energy beam destroyed Gallifrey.'

Marnal raised the gun, a little half-heartedly. 'You're bluffing.'

The Doctor bent over and pressed his temple against the muzzle. 'If you're sure of that, then go for it. I won't mind.'

Marnal snatched the gun away and the Doctor had to pull himself up to avoid falling over.

'So where are your memories now?' Rachel asked.

'Gone,' the Doctor admitted. 'Gone where, I don't know,' he added thoughtfully.

'Do you want all those other memories in there?' Rachel asked.

'Clearly I must have thought I could find a way to get them out. I've checked, and the TARDIS circuits aren't compatible so I can't just download everything into the old girl. But that's got to be the basic idea: find or build a computer that can hold the files and run the programs. I didn't save Gallifrey, but I did save all the Time Lords. That's got to be better than nothing. Home is where the hearts are, that's what I say.'

'We must dedicate ourselves to the task of building New Gallifrey,' Marnal said. 'Nothing else matters.'

'Millions are dying back on Earth,' Rachel said, shocking the Doctor. 'If you can do anything to help them, you have to do it.'

'Why didn't you say...?' the Doctor asked, pale. 'Marnal didn't say anything about deaths on that scale.'

'Humans don't matter,' Marnal stated, and the way he was fussing around the Doctor you'd have thought he was pregnant. 'We have to get you to a place of safety, and you have to stay there. Your TARDIS will be your sanctuary. We will marshal our resources, summon what allies we can. Together we will construct a city for the saved.'

'No,' said the Doctor. 'We go back to Earth.'

'The code of the Time Lords states –'

'Phooey to the code of the Time Lords,' the Doctor said angrily. 'In fact, I'm sure we're quorate, so let's vote on changing Time Lord foreign policy right here and now. I warn you, I do have a block vote.'

Marnal raised his gun.

The Doctor held out his hands, inviting Marnal to shoot. 'Remember?' he asked, impatiently.

Marnal scowled and lowered the gun. 'We only need your brain,' he said darkly.

'Well, it's coming with me, back to Earth,' the Doctor insisted. 'I have the feeling I'm going to need it.'

As Marnal, the Doctor and Rachel made their way across the terrain they were beginning to get a sense of it, even in the darkness. Marnal knew this would make a fascinating entry for his diary, and found himself trying to commit as much as he could to memory.

The food cave was the size of a city. It was a natural bowl in the rock – Marnal thought it had originally been an impact crater and had been covered over by Vore builders. The soil was thick, with the consistency in places of a peat bog. Rachel had added to the Vore's stockpile of chyme a couple of times at first, but now said she was used to the smell. The Doctor was alert, looking for the best exit.

There were pathways running down the sides of the crater. Off the path, individual Vore scurried like rats on a landfill. They must have been tending the mushroom garden, although it was impossible to make out exactly what they were doing.

Down in the valleys there were mile-long, perfectly straight lines of Vore everywhere. They trudged forwards, carrying pulped-up spheres of mushroom paste as big as they were. They moved in perfect unison, all of them swaying slightly, but exactly the same way. There was no sign of the beginning or end of the line, no sign of the Vore who must have chewed up the mushrooms to turn them into paste, or the ones set the Sisyphean task of rolling the paste into balls.

The whole place was quiet, the layer of fungus acting to absorb sound, the Vore going about their task with the silence and dedication of monks.

'No obvious physical differences to indicate a caste structure,' the Doctor said to himself. 'Perhaps a slightly higher intelligence means they can be generalists.'

The three of them were about halfway up a slope, heading towards a small tunnel opening that hadn't seen much Vore traffic. The creatures weren't reacting. The Doctor's supposition that they operated by smell, and so perceived the three of them as oddly mobile food, was almost certainly flawed, but was the best theory they currently had to go on.

The Doctor reached the opening first, and gave Rachel a hand up on to the small ledge that marked it.

'If I'm right...' the Doctor began. 'Yes! Look, the TARDIS.'

The tunnel was only a few feet long. At the other end was the cavern the TARDIS had landed in. The time ship was visible about four hundred yards away. The cavern buzzed and droned with Vore activity. The creatures crawled over every surface, even over each other. The air was thick with them. They were keeping a respectful distance from the TARDIS itself, and it was Marnal's fancy that those nearest it were facing it with the same deference that a primitive faced an altar or idol.

'I should have packed a dog whistle,' the Doctor muttered, incomprehensibly.

'They don't seem to notice us. Can we make a run for it?' Rachel asked.

'I think the Vore in there are guards. They'll be on the lookout for us. A four-hundred-yard dash over uneven rocky terrain, then hold them off long enough for me to unlock the door and the three of us to get through it?'

'I'll get us there,' Marnal assured them both.

'How?' the Doctor asked.

'I have a gun, remember?'

'It didn't do you much good last time,' the Doctor reminded him. 'There are probably ten billion Vore on this moon. Fire two shots a second, hit one every time, assume they don't breed and that you don't eat or sleep, and it'll be the fifty-ninth century before they're all dead.'

Marnal shook his head. 'We only need to get the ones between us and the TARDIS. They didn't react when I shot one before.'

'Those are clearly on guard duty. I'm sure they'll signal for reinforcements. Wait!'

Marnal had drawn the maser, set it to kill. He fired towards the TARDIS, scattering the Vore, creating a path.

The Doctor was running behind him, pulling Rachel along. She was screaming.

A Vore dived at them, Marnal shot it down. They'd covered a hundred yards.

Rapid fire, aimed in front, just clearing the way. There were two obvious flaws in the plan. The first was that firing ahead left every other direction unguarded. Vore were sweeping around, on the ground, in the air and charging at them from behind. The other problem was that it was obvious where the three of them were heading. Reinforcements poured down to block the way to the TARDIS. Two hundred yards run, two hundred to go.

Very little time indeed to adjust the settings, but Marnal managed to lower the power and range, increase the spread. A wide-angle attack, close range, hitting everything within an arc of about fifteen degrees with Serious Indifference. This got them leaving, and even ones that hadn't been hit seemed to get in the mood. Most were moving out of the way. One hundred yards to go.

By now, only one Vore remained in front of them. It stood with its back to them blocking the TARDIS door, but there was no indication it knew this was what it was doing.

Marnal raised his gun.

The Vore twisted around and sliced down with its claw, taking the muzzle of the gun and the tips of Marnal's fingers off.

The Vore lashed out again and Marnal yelled. He looked down to see its claw puncturing his chest, then being pulled out smeared in blood. He sank to his knees, surprised but not yet in pain. His chest felt warm. The Vore that had killed him simply scuttled off, clearly concluding its work was done. The Doctor was opening up the TARDIS and pushing Rachel inside.

The Doctor came back, pulled Marnal up and half-dragged him inside the TARDIS. He ran to the console and shut the doors, then rushed back to Marnal's side. Rachel was already there.

'You were right,' Marnal coughed wetly.

The Doctor eased him down. Rachel was examining him, making him comfortable.

'There's no need to do that,' the Doctor said quietly.

'I have to try.' But her body language made it clear she knew it was hopeless.

'Get the medical kit,' the Doctor suggested. 'First door on the left, down the corridor, second door on the right, down the corridor, third door on the left, down the corridor, fourth door on the right, top shelf of a white cupboard. You can't miss it.'

Rachel ran to get it.

'I'm dead, Doctor.'

'Yes.'

'I meant it. You must restore Gallifrey. That has to be your mission.'

'I will do everything within my power.'

Marnal managed a smile. 'Then it is as good as done. I know now you really did lose your memories. You saved as much of Gallifrey as you possibly could, more than anyone else would have. I once dreamt that all Time Lords would be like you, that we would explore the universe once more, help those who needed it, destroy those who would destroy. You do good... but perhaps it is as well that you are one of a kind.'

He was fading.

The Doctor leant in. 'You were my childhood hero,' he whispered.

Marnal's eyes widened, then closed.

Rachel returned to see that Marnal had already gone. She put the medical kit down and knelt beside him, holding his hand. She had seen once before what happened next.

Marnal's skin glowed, faintly at first. His features bleached out and then there was no face, just the light, and within a minute even that had faded. Nothing remained of him, not even the clothes.

Rachel was surprised to feel more upset than she had the first time.

'The first Time Lord for two million years whose memories won't be stored in the Matrix,' the Doctor noted matter-of-factly. 'His secrets die with him. Now, come on, we need to get going.'

A small robot dog was gliding towards Rachel with what looked like a gun sticking out of its nose.

'Intruder, master,' it said.

'Don't worry about Rachel, K9. How are the repairs going?'

'Proceeding ahead of schedule. List follows: the main –'

'Can we take off?' the Doctor asked, cutting him off.

'Affirmative.'

The Doctor moved around the console, dialling, twisting, pushing, pulling and slapping controls. The central column began rising and falling.

'I thought the Vore could –'

The TARDIS rocked violently, as though someone was grabbing it.

'They can. In fact, I'm banking on that.' He tapped a control and the TARDIS dived to one side. Although Rachel couldn't work out quite which side it was. 'It'll keep them busy. Feint with the left, strike with the right. The Vore are attracted to flaws in the space-time continuum. They exploit the flaws, use them to pull their whole planets through space. They don't get any choice, they're moths to a flame.'

'Master...' K9 warned as the TARDIS lurched again.

'I know, I know. I need you to do something, K9. When I give the signal, I want you to deactivate the ship's defensive systems.'

'Deactivate, master?'

'You heard. Rachel, could you come over here a minute? Every three or four seconds, press that black button, would you?'

Rachel looked down at it.

'Oh come on, it's not that difficult,' the Doctor complained.

'I'll do it,' Rachel muttered.

She tapped the button, and the TARDIS seemed to go into free fall for a few seconds. She turned to ask if it was meant to do that, but the Doctor was leaving the console room.

'Wait! Where are you going?'

The Doctor grinned. 'Infinity and beyond, as it happens. That's another three seconds, you've missed your cue.'

Rachel pressed the button again. This time, the TARDIS spun on its axis.

The Doctor entered the power room and strode up to the control panel on the back wall. The iron sphere sat in the middle of the room, as normal, completely inert. The floor shook as the ship completed another random evasive manoeuvre. He checked his pocket watch. It told him three different times, all at once.

He pulled the switch that opened the eye.

I know you, the presence trapped there told him.

'Bully for you.'

Why this is hell, nor are you out of it.

The Doctor shook his head, almost pityingly, at the misquote.

Your precious Earth has been devastated. A threat on a scale that not even you can deal with. Do you appreciate the irony, Doctor? You summoned the Vore to Earth. The atomic explosion damaged the eye, your hesitation in pulling the lever that would seal it off, your desire to know your past, allowed the creation of a cicatrix. A small one, but it was enough to attract the moths to the flame.

'Yes, I know. I was there,' said the Doctor, without looking over his shoulder. He opened the eyeboard, and got it to display the ship's current coordinates and to set up a communications link with the main console.

A lever that you didn't pull because you doubted yourself.

'Yes, dramatic irony, poetic justice, hoist by my own petard, history repeating. How very clever of you.'

In times gone by, Doctor, you would have called on the Time Lords to help sort out a threat of such magnitude, but now you are truly alone in the universe.

The Doctor checked his watch again.

He looked round for the first time. Fully open, the eye filled the room with a blue swirling light so bright that it roared. He couldn't conceive of the power involved, the energies being released. Had there really been Time Lords who looked into this and saw a mere source of energy to be harnessed? Were they as gods, or just lacking any imagination whatsoever? Assuming they couldn't be both. The TARDIS shook.

Your companion is dead.

The Doctor was jolted from his thoughts.

'Which one?'

The male. He died saving the female. Is that hesitation, Doctor? Do you finally realise the extent of my victory over you?

The Doctor took a deep breath. 'Oh, don't worry, I recognise a victory when I see one. You might want to budge up a bit.'

A cicatrix was forming, a scar on space and time itself. The Doctor winced, as though it was a paper-cut to his own eye.

He sent his signal to the control room.

With no force fields or other defences operating, there was nothing to stop the Vore from stepping right into the TARDIS and taking the cicatrix. A hyperspace corridor wide enough for a small moon to pass through it duly opened up, right in the centre of the power room. Time and space expanded to accommodate it, but not without screaming in protest.

The Doctor, to one side of this, suddenly felt very small indeed. This close the edge of the wormhole was a vertical horizon, perfectly straight.

Then the Vore moon passed through the corridor like a bullet through a rifle barrel, straight into the eye, the Vore heading for the cicatrix out of sheer instinct. Making a beeline. The moon was either dwarfed or shrank physically as it dropped into the swirling energy. It shifted a little as it tried to jump free, but despite its size it couldn't amass the force needed to escape, couldn't even disrupt the hurricane flow of its surroundings.

No! No! NO!!!!

The Doctor shrugged. 'That's your opinion, and you're entitled to it.'

He pulled down the lever, sealing off the eye. The room snapped back to its normal, cavernous dimensions.

The TARDIS shot up almost throwing the Doctor from his feet. Three seconds later it swooped down, just as dizzyingly.

'You can stop pressing that button now, Rachel,' the Doctor shouted at the intercom.

From the Earth, this is how it appeared.

Trix and Mrs Winfield were still in Marnal's house. They were in the library, looking out of the small window up into the night sky. The two moons were both beginning to wane. The second moon's light was redder than Earth's own moon, the colour of sandstone.

'I'm getting used to it,' Mrs Winfield said. 'I'm not sure I'll ever get used to them, though.'

Then the second moon exploded, in a flash of blue light that bathed the whole hemisphere facing it. Then there was nothing left.

Trix and Mrs Winfield ran outside and stared up into the sky, looking at nothing. Trix felt a sense of elation throughout her whole body, the sort of emotion that only comes when you realise that every other human being watching will be feeling the same way. For one priceless moment in the whole history of man, all the people of the Earth were truly united. Trix was rooted to the spot, staring up, tears in her eyes. One moon, pristine. Perhaps there was something in astrology after all. Now that the second moon wasn't in the third house of Mars, or whatever, it felt like the world was right.

That's where the Doctor had been, and he'd won, Trix realised. Sacrifices had not been made in vain. Humanity had won, and the war without end had ended.

And then, throughout the world, the Vore retaliated.

One leapt out of the sky and down at Trix, maw mashing, four arms outstretched, ready to grab her.

Trix rolled out of the way but the thing was on her, punching down, sharp claws embedding themselves in the soft lawn, ripping their way out and stabbing at her again.

Mrs Winfield was running inside. On the threshold she hesitated.

'Bolt the door!' Trix shouted, as half a dozen Vore alighted on the patio.

The door slammed shut. The Vore immediately started pummelling at it, and the wood began to splinter.

Trix's hand found a rusty garden trowel. She dug it into her Vore's left eye, scraping it down.

The Vore didn't even register pain. It lashed out, batting her away, then hopped over to her, stretching its wings for just a second or two to carry it along. Its comrades had all but broken down the back door, but Trix couldn't worry about Mrs Winfield for the moment.

The monster's mouth was working away in two different directions. It was watching her, like it was deciding what to do. It took a while, but then it followed its decision through so quickly she could barely see it. Others were landing now. All around, Trix could hear screaming and dogs barking. The Vore weren't rasping that white dust over everyone, they were just slicing and battering away.

Instinctively, Trix brought her elbow down on the Vore's forearm. There wasn't a self-defence teacher in the country who'd say it was a bad move. She nearly broke a bone on the hard carapace.

The creature pulled her round, then let go to get a better attack in. Its claw sliced towards Trix, who realised that this was where she died.

A hand caught the Vore's claw.

The creature hissed, tried to push down. But the hand stayed firm. The Vore shifted its ground but couldn't get any leverage.

Hand and claw were locked in place. The Vore tilted, and cocked its head to get a good look at the man in its way. Its compound eyes twitched, adjusted.

It stared into the man's eyes.

More than that, it understood what it was looking at.

Then, for the first time, the Vore took a step back. All around it all the other Vore were doing the same. They were massing for a last attack, Trix thought. Strength in numbers.

Now, though, the hand released its grip. The Vore took another step back. A moment later, as if frightened by a loud noise, every Vore was airborne, spiralling away.

'I'm back,' the Doctor said.

He helped his companion up and nodded an acknowledgement to a startled Mrs Winfield.

'How the hell did you do that?'

'They're running. It's what you're meant to do when you see a monster – a fact you seem to have forgotten.'

'It was you that destroyed the moon? Wait... but didn't you just come from inside Marnal's house?' Trix had seen movement from the corner of her eye.

'Never mind that. Have you seen Fitz?'

It took a moment for her to find the words.

'He's dead,' she told him.

'But have you seen him?'

Trix looked up, finding it hard to imagine the Doctor could be so cruel to her.

The Doctor took her hand.

'I saw him die,' she said. 'The Vore just struck him down, hissed poison over him. He was doing it to save me,' she sobbed. 'But I know you...'

Trix paused, not wanting to say it.

'You can... bring him back. Whether you should or not, I don't know. But you can. He was your friend.'

She looked him in the eye.

'And I have faith you'll do what's right. No, not faith. Something better: knowledge. Certain knowledge. You never lose, not in the end, not like this. Please –'

The Doctor put his finger to her lips.

'I brought the dead back to life on my very first day in the job,' the Doctor told her.

Behind him stood Fitz.

Darkness cannot drive out darkness; only light can do that. Hate cannot drive out hate; only love can do that.

Martin Luther King Jr

Chapter Thirteen
It's the End...

Trix and Fitz were hugging and kissing. The Doctor moved away, giving them their space, and found himself next to Mrs Winfield whom he'd run past on the way out of the house to save Trix. It was a pleasant summer's night in England.

'Mister... sir...' It was a small woman, probably in her late fifties.

'Doctor,' he corrected her.

'My husband died too. They got him before he could get inside the house, that first day.'

'He's right here, Jackie.'

'You know my name?'

'Des loves you. He's been with you all this time.'

'I felt like he was standing next to me.'

Trix was looking over at the Doctor. 'What's he doing?' she asked Fitz. 'He's acting like some medium at the end of a pier. He'll be asking the crowd if they know anyone called "John" next, and telling whoever puts her hand up that John's saying she should get on with her life.'

Fitz was biting his lip. 'No. Watch. Because just when you think you know how bloody brilliant he is, and you think you've seen him do everything...'

The Doctor took Mrs Winfield's hand in his, reached out.

'I can feel...'

The Doctor nodded.

'Do you remember the first time we held hands, Des?' she asked.

'I remember,' her husband replied. 'I was so nervous.'

The Doctor took Mr Winfield's hand in his hand, and led him back from the dead. A middle-aged man in cords and a raincoat stepped forward, and stood before his wife. The two of them were crying.

Trix wiped away a tear herself.

'I tried calling out to you,' he said. 'Touching you, blocking your way, writing you a note. I even texted your mobile but you didn't have it on.'

'The battery had gone. I never know how to recharge it. You do all that.'

('I wrote to you in lipstick on the bathroom mirror,' said Fitz. 'You never saw the notes I left you. I shouted until I was hoarse, I grabbed your arm. I tried to hug you. I sat next to you in the car, you couldn't see or hear me.')

'Then I thought, well, perhaps I *was* a ghost. So I followed you around. I didn't know what else to do.'

('That's what I did,' Fitz told Trix.)

Mr Winfield hugged the Doctor. 'How do I thank you?'

The Doctor shrugged, a little embarrassed. 'It was nothing. Now, find yourself somewhere safe. This isn't over yet.'

They nodded, still dazed, but with the presence of mind to do what he suggested. They hurried next door, still holding hands. The Doctor, Fitz and Trix went back inside Marnal's house, where Rachel was waiting for them.

'"It was nothing"?' Trix echoed.

'I don't like to blow my own trumpet.'

'As opposed to the Last Trumpet?' Fitz suggested.

'Oh, I get that. That's good.'

'Thanks.'

'You are going to explain,' Trix told him.

'Of course, he's going to explain,' Fitz said. 'It's got something to do with parallel universes, I reckon. Usually when stuff around here makes no sense it's –'

'Beehives,' the Doctor said smugly. Not that he wasn't within his rights to look a bit self-satisfied.

Trix rolled her eyes. 'And that would be the explanation? Well, I suppose at least it's light on technobabble.'

'Dead bees, specifically. When a bee dies it needs to be cleared out of the hive. There are bees whose only job is to tidy up. A dead bee secretes oleic acid. You can probably work out the rest.'

Trix smiled sweetly. 'Humour me.'

'The acid is the chemical signal that tells a bee that another bee is dead. So far, so good. If you daub a live bee with oleic acid, though, the other bees assume it's dead, and carry it out of the hive. Even if it's struggling. It's not that the bee smells dead – to the other bees, it is dead. They treat it exactly as if it's dead, their brains block out any evidence that contradicts that. The Vore must have evolved along the same lines – they have to know when to clean their nests – but they've refined the technique into a weapon they can use on others. They daub some equivalent of oleic acid on a person and that makes everyone else think that person's dead. Smells like fly spray. Our brains are easily tricked, especially if all the senses are being deceived. If reality doesn't seem to match up with what our eyes and ears tell us, our brain ignores enough reality until it does... or we go mad, of course. Meanwhile, the Vore's enemies are completely demoralised and thrown into complete chaos, leaving the Vore free to concentrate their efforts on achieving their aims, not on fighting their enemy.'

Trix was shaking her head. 'I saw Fitz die.'

Fitz waved at her. 'Alive,' he pointed out.

'It's all right, I know you're not dead, but I... I saw it.'

The Doctor smiled. 'Your eyes have played tricks on you before now. You've been fooled by optical illusions. You've been scared watching a horror video – that's just pixels on a TV screen. All around the world, millions of dead people who couldn't see each other, who couldn't understand why no one could see them. All trying to attract attention, none able to break down the doors of perception.'

Trix shivered. 'How much more reality is my brain blocking out for me?'

'Well, only you can answer that one,' the Doctor grinned. 'The Vore are adept at warping space, and it seems they can warp perceptions just as easily.'

'So how did you know?'

'They clearly had to tailor their chemicals to one life form, and that was humanity. I suspect they abducted humans early on to work out exactly which formula they had to use. I'm a Time Lord, and I wasn't affected. So, when I arrived at Marnal's house I just saw Fitz and Mr Winfield standing there and asked why they looked so miserable.'

'What's a Time Lord?' Trix asked.

'Long story, albeit one with a sudden ending,' the Doctor said. 'I'll explain later. Now we have to contact the authorities. The United Nations. Get the message out, bring everyone we can back.'

'No one really died?' Fitz said. 'You're going to bring millions of people back from the dead? God, you're cool.'

'No,' said the Doctor sadly. 'It's too late for some of them.'

'But…'

'The Vore simply killed some people,' he paused. 'And many religions bury their dead quickly. Or cremate them.'

Trix recoiled, thinking of a bee dragged from its hive kicking and fighting.

'There will have been accidents. Suicides… both among the dead and the living, if you get my meaning. Many will have died in the panic, all around the world.'

'It can't be many.'

'It will be tens of thousands,' the Doctor said. 'We're not done yet.'

The Doctor used Trix's mobile to call the United Nations, working his way through various switchboards and layers of admin. He left Marnal's house and made his way down the street as he talked. The signal was better outside. Every time he was put on hold he would knock on a door, see who was home – living and dead –

and where he could he would reunite them. Number Four got their children back, crying and a little sick from eating nothing but biscuits for the last few days. Mothers and fathers, husbands and wives, brothers and sisters, young and old... The Doctor alone could see them and have them return to the land of the living. The dead had almost all followed their friends or families around. Now that the living knew where to look the signs were everywhere – the notes left, the furniture moved, the emails and messages on answering machines.

It was half an hour before the Doctor had explained to the right UN person on the other end of the phone how his technique worked. An hour later, it was the main news on every TV and radio channel. Shortly after that some preachers, mediums and shamans showed up on the news channels saying they had always claimed this was possible. As Rachel noted, if only people like that could predict things before they happened instead of afterwards, the world would be a better place.

The total death toll would never be known.

And the Vore weren't beaten yet.

It was going to take some time to explain the situation to the authorities and to give them advice. The British government was sending a car for the Doctor, who suggested that – instead of sitting around – Fitz, Trix and Rachel should load the contents of Marnal's library into the TARDIS. The three of them grumbled, but started work. Luckily for them, when the TARDIS returned from the Vore moon it had landed right in the middle of the library. The Doctor would have helped, he said, but he kept getting priority phone calls.

They were about halfway done with their task when the Doctor got off the phone once again.

'The Vore have built a fortress – that was the word the analyst used. Every Vore in the world seems to be heading there,' the Doctor announced. 'It's a termite mound, but one the size of a mountain. There are waves of Vore flying in that direction.'

'Where?' Trix asked

'Somewhere called Guinea-Bissau,' the Doctor answered. 'I hate to admit it, but –'

'West African coast,' Fitz said. 'Its chief exports are rice, coconuts, peanuts, fish and timber. Its population is about 1.4 million, half of whom are animists, almost all the rest being Muslim. The national motto is Unidade, Luta, Progresso. It was called Portuguese Guinea in my day.'

The Doctor looked impressed.

'He cribbed it off my laptop on the flight over from New York,' Trix told him.

'Seven hours,' Fitz said. 'You get a lot of time to read.'

'We're going out there, joining HMS *Illustrious* and liasing with the UN. My reputation precedes me apparently.' The Doctor smiled at the thought. 'If anyone finds the visualiser that Marnal built, that might come in handy.'

'It's in the garage, I think,' Rachel said.

She went looking for it. Trix vanished into the TARDIS with another armful of books.

'Doctor,' said Fitz, once the two of them were alone. 'I know about Gallifrey. My memory came back a while ago.'

'I think I must have wiped your memories too. To keep my secret.'

'If that was you, it wasn't a brilliant job. The last couple of years, some times I've remembered, some times I haven't.'

'I was in a hurry and had other things on my mind.'

'I… wasn't sure what you knew. I didn't want to burden you with…'

'With the knowledge I had destroyed a planet?'

'Yeah. I didn't really know how to handle it. Not really the sort of thing you already know how to deal with.'

'No,' the Doctor said quietly.

'You remember what happened, now?'

'I don't remember it. I've only seen it. I don't think it's quite hit me yet.'

'You did the right thing,' Fitz said, 'from what I understand of it.'

'I killed a lot of people.'

'Saved a lot, and a lot more since.'

The Doctor rubbed his lip. 'The one doesn't excuse the other. I destroyed Gallifrey. I'm not off the hook for that, and even if I save the Earth from the Vore that won't redeem me.'

'What will?'

'That, my dear Fitz, is the right question.'

'Are you going to take it easy now. Keep yourself out of harm's way?'

'Not really my style.'

'What about *them*?' Fitz asked.

'Let's sort out the Vore first.'

'And... er... that little robot dog thing? Is he coming with us?'

'I'm sending K9 off on a little errand to Espero, to see if he's any good as a bloodhound.'

The Doctor paused, looked distracted.

'Are you OK?'

'It's odd. I've been having the most unpleasant sensation. I can't remember Gallifrey, but it hurts when I try to think about it. Wanting something to be the way it never was, and never can be again.'

'You've never felt nostalgic before?'

The Doctor shrugged. 'It's a pretty meaningless concept when you're a time-traveller.'

'The pain of returning.'

'Pardon?'

'It's the literal meaning of nostalgia. From the Greek.'

'I have to say, since you died, your general knowledge has radically improved.'

'Everything changes, a Time Lord even more so. Everything and everyone is changing, all the time. There's sticking to your guns but if you stay as you are, and you don't grow or take risks... you still change. But it means you seize up, end up just repeating yourself. Become your own museum or descend into self-parody.

What's happened·has happened. It can't be undone. Even if some weird timestormy parallel paradoxy universy thing came along, and outer space went all wobbly and Gallifrey came back, just as it was... well, you'd still be the man who did what you did. All you can do now is go forwards.'

The Doctor nodded. 'And you? What about you and Trix?'

'We're going forwards together.'

'Good for you.'

The doorbell rang.

The Doctor stood. 'That will be General... er... Lethbridge-Stewart, I think he said it was. Fitz, could you round up the others?'

A little over a day later they'd reached the *Illustrious*.

Rachel and Trix needed to freshen up after enduring hour after uncomfortable hour in a succession of transport planes and helicopters. The Doctor and Fitz stood on the deck. Around them Harriers were being readied. The deck was long and ended in what looked like a ski jump. It was a warm evening. The sea and sky were both a deep, rich blue.

They were a mile off the coast – a thick, flat sand-and-green line. The Doctor had acquired an impressive navy-issue pair of binoculars. Fitz could make out the Vore mountain without them. It was quite a way inland, more of a column than most mountains, and leant to one side. All the better, the Doctor said, to catch the sun.

'It's not quite as tall as Kilimanjaro. Apparently it is still growing, though,' he added.

'How many monsters will be in there?'

'Lots,' the Doctor said, after running out of fingers.

He handed Fitz the binoculars.

Like all tall mountains, the top was obscured by clouds. Uniquely, these consisted of giant insects as well as water vapour. Every so often, a new mass of Vore flew in. There was something like a stack at a major airport as the arrivals waited their turn to land.

'We can't negotiate, we can't come to terms. There's nothing in the Vore hive to negotiate with. They can't compromise, any more than a plague of locusts can. They have a right to exist, but *not here*. Not at this cost.'

'Couldn't we just bomb it?' Fitz asked.

'There's a reason why terrorist warlords and Western military commanders alike build their shelters under mountains. Conventional rockets and missiles would just bounce off. A nuclear weapon... Well, that would kill a lot of people too, in the short and long term, and would bury a lot of Vore underground. If they really are laying eggs, like all the insect experts seem to think, I'm not sure that's as definite a conclusion as I'd like.'

'I think cockroaches are meant to be able to survive a nuclear war, anyway, aren't they?'

'Oh yes. I've been to planets where that's happened. Never had the cockroaches start the war before now, though.'

A pair of RAF planes roared overhead. Fitz swung the binoculars round and watched them go, saw the other ships of the small Royal Navy task force a little further out to sea, nearly blinded himself looking into the sun by mistake.

'The planes are keeping their distance. Sensible.'

'Yes,' concluded the Doctor. 'We'll have to get closer.'

'How close?'

The Doctor raised an eyebrow.

It is the next morning, and they are standing above the clouds on the flattened top of the Vore mountain in the Tombali region of Guinea-Bisseau. It is dry, and sand lifted up by the hot *harmattan* wind obscures the view to the east. To the west is the sea, dotted with the ships of the Royal Navy task force. It is the first time Rachel or Trix has been to Africa, and they both regret dressing for a British summer.

The air is thin here, at the summit. All around the plateau are dotted great vents, fifty yards wide, chimney shafts that go straight down as far as the eye can see. Ammoniac air wafts up from depths of the mountain, thick with heat and carbon dioxide and sulphur.

'This is how they keep the temperature and oxygen content of the hive constant,' the Doctor explains, staring right down into the pit. 'Cold, fresh air will be sucked in at the base of the mountain, the waste gases get expelled here.'

'So what now?' Trix asks.

The Doctor looks at his three companions. 'You tell me.'

Rachel takes a deep breath. 'We all die. The Vore find us here, murder us like they murdered Marnal. They go back and wait, feeding on the people they've already killed. They breed, safe in this mountain, able to ignore anything we throw at them, from a squad of troops to a nuclear bomb dropped straight down one of these holes. Then – probably sooner than we think possible – they fly out of these holes, kill all the people, kill all the animals, kill all the plants, kill all the other insects, until it's just them and their mushrooms left. The whole world becomes a hive, they find a way to pilot it around like they did that moon, and the cycle starts again.'

Fitz has a lopsided grin. 'You really haven't been paying attention, have you, love? They're monsters, he's the Doctor. There's only one way this is going to end. Look – this is a whopping great *ventilation shaft*. It's a way in. The Doctor leaps down it, coat tails and hair flapping, lands, finds out what the Vore are planning, discovers their weakness, he confronts them, and then he kicks their arse. An hour from now, we'll all be watching from a safe distance as this mountain explodes, taking every Vore with it.'

'"Leaps down"? Falls down, more like. No one could survive that.'

'The Doctor could.'

'I can't even imagine how he hopes to beat them.'

'That, Rachel, is your problem, not his,' Trix tells her.

'Nothing ever ends,' Fitz says. 'Especially not him.'

'He'll die.'

'If he does, he'll do it saving the Earth and then he'll come back, all-new and better than ever.'

'With a bit of fashion sense this time,' Trix suggests.

The Doctor has been listening to them. He can also hear the monsters down there, millions of them at home in the darkness. The Vore are massing. Soon, unless stopped, they will emerge and bring the darkness out with them. There are countless more like them all across the universe – those that have destroyed more than they have created. They must be fought. A man cannot fight them all, though, not without becoming the worst monster of the lot. One day, the Doctor knows as he gazes down, he will fall.

He tugs at the lapels of his frock coat, perhaps for the last time. 'I have a plan, but I can't beat them alone.'

Fitz smiles, takes Trix's hand. 'You won't have to.'

'Shall we?' the Doctor asks.

And he leaps...

Fitz's Song
Contains Spoilers

I've travelled to the past, sweetheart,
And I've been to the future, too.
Once, a few hundred years from now,
I thought I'd ask after you.

An obvious formality
Because our love was oh so true.
Together for eternity.
That shows how little I knew.

I saw your file in black and white
Describing everything you'll do.
And read you won't wait for me.
I would have waited for you.

We used to talk of destiny.
And in the future you still do.
The sting in the tail is that I'm
Not the man you'll say it to.

When I say that you are history,
Well, it is literally true.
They only seem like choices, love.
I've seen just what you'll do.

You'll sometimes be spontaneous
Would you like to know what you'll do?
I know how long you've got with him
Can't take that away from you.

You'll leave me, but no hard feelings.
Because I've had my sneak preview.
You've moved on in your life, so I
Won't spoil its twist ending for you.

The Gallifrey Chronicles
The Album

1. 'The Wheel Rolls On', Archie Bronson Outfit
2. 'Brain Stew' (Godzilla Remix), Green Day
3. 'One Armed Scissor', At the Drive-In
4. 'Elderly Woman Behind the Counter in a Small Town', Pearl Jam
5. 'Horse Tears', Goldfrapp
6. 'The Becoming', Nine Inch Nails
7. 'The Story of Our Life So Far', Salako
8. 'This Mess We're In', PJ Harvey
9. 'Aenema', Tool
10. 'Pets', Porno for Pyros
11. 'Last Cigarette', Dramarama
12. 'Non Zero Possibility', At the Drive-In
13. 'Eraser', Nine Inch Nails
14. 'Escape from the Prison Planet', Clutch
15. 'Hello Spaceboy', David Bowie

About the Author

LANCE PARKIN has written a number of books and other things, including the first-ever original Eighth Doctor novel, *The Dying Days* (which is available for free on the BBCi site, and for rather more than that on eBay), and the BBC novels *The Infinity Doctors*, *Father Time* and *Trading Futures*. His most recent works are the science-fiction novel *Warlords of Utopia*, and (with Mark Jones) *Dark Matter*, a guide to the author Philip Pullman.